PRESBYTERIAN PRINCESS
Nancy Jean Carrigan

Editors – Dick Carrigan
and Caroline Carrigan

Presbyterian Princess

© 2018 Richard Carrigan & Caroline Carrigan

ISBN: 978-1-887229-50-0

Published by First Flight Books
A division of Bruce Bendinger Creative Communications, Inc.
2144 N. Hudson • Chicago, IL 60614
773-871-1179 • FX 773-281-4643
www.firstflightbooks.com

FIRST FLIGHT BOOKS

First Flight Books is a specialized publisher dedicated
to helping authors optimize their offerings.
Lorelei Davis Bendinger– President, Producer, & Publisher
Bruce Bendinger– Executive Editor & Copy Chief
Gregory S. Paus – Director of Design
Patrick Aylward – Composition & Typography

DEDICATION

Dedicated to Brooke Anne Carrigan (born 2001), the fifth generation of strong women involved in the *Princess*, including Carrie Hurrie (née Begler, 1871), Edith Bohn (née Hurrie, 1897), Nancy Carrigan (née Bohn, 1933, Anna in *Princess*), Caroline Carrigan (born 1958, Meg in the *Princess*), and Brooke herself (born 2001).

FOREWORD

Anna Marie Mackenzie is not your ordinary *Preacher's Kid* (PK). Just ask her grandmother. "She'll need a strong hand, that one. She's too clever for her own good and pig-headed besides." In that regard, Nancy Carrigan was fond of the anonymous quote:

A shoemaker's child gets his shoes fixed for nothing, a dentist's child gets her teeth fixed for nothing. A minister's child gets to be good for nothing.

Anna's real problem is that she's an observing sort of girl and too literal by far. She thinks that when her minister father "is called up to Chicago", it is to play ball in a park with little bear cubs. In fact, Rev. John Mackenzie is to become pastor of a large Presbyterian church on the north side of the city.

But as she grows, her literal take on religion and wry observation of how it is practiced makes her the perfect storyteller for this tale of one woman's journey from a child of the Great Depression, raised in a manse, which is more castle than a house, to her abdication as a 'Presbyterian Princess' when she marries a scientist who is far from the clerical outlook on life.

Her search for "goodness" is often serious, but more often a series of comic turns and sins of omission. Her quest for rationality in a spiritual life is resonant with many people at this time of polarization of spiritual practice.

Nancy Carrigan, author of this autobiographical novel, began work on this book on the back of church bulletins as soon as she could write. Daughter of a prominent Chicago pastor, granddaughter, sister, and niece of a clerical clan, she is well equipped to tell the story of a PK or *Preacher's Kid*.

Presbyterian Princess is Ms. Carrigan's third novel. Her other books, *The Siren Star* and *Minotaur in a Mushroom Maze*, both co-authored with her husband Dick Carrigan, were serialized in *Analog Magazine*. *The Siren Stars* was published by Pyramid and translated into French and Russian. She was a member of the Poets' Club of Chicago and won many prizes for her work including two in the Writer's Digest competition. She was a guest of the Chinese at the 19th World Congress of Poets in Tai'an City. Her poems have been published in Chinese as well as English.

Beyond her poetry and writing, Carrigan had an active life as a Chicago area artist. In order to research dance "from the inside out" for a series of paintings and sculpture on the subject, she took lessons in many forms of dance for over ten years. One of the dance pieces she designed for a Chicago company was featured in *National Geographic*.

CONTENTS

Predestination   1

Now Be a Good Girl   7

Butterfingers and Fly Balls   19

Called Up to Chicago   27

A Different Kind of Church   37

The Castle Ghost   47

Are You Saved?   53

It's War!   57

Behind the Black Door   61

Mary, Martha, and Mom   73

Family Album   87

The White Carnation   91

Pets in a Goldfish Bowl   97

Our Own G.I. Joe   107

Putting on Airs and Other Sins   113

Back to Champaign   127

Decisions, Decisions!   133

But Does He Like Dogs?   141

The End of the Beginning   149

Life Among the Stars of Stage, Screen and Baseball   155

Here Comes the Bride   169

There Went the Bride   179

Art Gallery   187

Not a Real Episcopalian   197

Does God Have a Funny Bone?   207

It's Doctor Herrington Now, Thank You   215

Juggling Acts   221

Who's the Student Now?   229

Shall We Overcome?   235

Sprechen Sie Deutsch?   243

What Did You Do in the War?   251

Lost in Translation   255

Auf Wiedersehen   261

Saving Raymond   269

Afterwords 1970   277

With These Words…   279

Art & Poetry   285

The Other   291

The Kansas church where The Presbyterian Princess's grandfather was sent when he came to America as a missionary.

PREDESTINATION
A Prologue February 1933

If heritage means anything in the future life of a newborn, then Anna Leigh Mackenzie was predestined to be a good girl. She was a pedigreed Presbyterian who could claim, in addition to her father, a grandfather and three uncles who were members of the Presbyterian clergy. Thus, the child was delivered to this earth burdened with high expectations.

Her arrival on a Saturday morning in February of 1933 pleased the Reverend John Mackenzie, D.D. no end. His congregation, like so many others, was suffering the effects of a depression in full swing. Bread lines were longer every day and it seemed that the sun had forgotten how to shine.

Anna's protesting cry at the insult of being thrust into such an inhospitable place was the first hint of a spirited new presence in the church family. So Reverend Mack, as his parishioners called him, checked that his wife Emma was resting comfortably after her brief labor and that the child had all her necessary fingers, toes, and so on, then rushed off to the church office to add the happy news to the announcements in that Sunday's church bulletin. It was one of the last times Anna would ever be prompt, but her arrival at least had been auspicious.

The next morning, in the venerable red brick church on the northeast corner of Wesley and Main in Champaign, Illinois, the congregation greeted the news with properly restrained smiles. The child's maiden Aunt Marie and her coterie of friends laid down their plaited-straw, *Courtesy-of-Davidson's-Funeral-Parlor* fans and applauded tastefully.

After the service, these same ladies gathered in the church vestibule in a small, twittering flock. Bright feathers of the fashionable birds decorating their winter felt hats fluttered as their owners gleaned crumbs of fact and rumor about the birth. As fragments of autobiographical birthing stories mixed with Aunt Marie's second-hand information about the actual event, Anna grew from her seven-pound, six-ounce birth weight to a lusty nine-pounds, ten-ounces. That was, coincidentally, the exact weight of Mrs. Smythe's son Harold at his birth forty years before.

> "…*and you know what a fine boy Harold turned out to be," Mary Smythe added proudly. The birds on the hats of the Bird Ladies nodded wisely in consent.*

Weeks, then months passed, and it appeared that the prophecy of Anna's goodness was correct. Her engaging smile and occasional merry giggle won over the gruffest of parishioners. If she was feeling shy, she would grasp a proffered finger and hold on as she hid her face coyly in her father's shoulder. Her victims soon succumbed to a coquettish glance from her wide sapphire eyes.

As naptime and Sunday worship coincided, Anna slept quietly on her mother's lap during the service. When the last blessing was said, and the congregation moved to the church parlor, Anna woke in time to flirt outrageously with the Bird Ladies at the coffee hour after.

"Such a good girl," they would coo, offering bits of cookie to their little darling. And her mother would answer, "Not a bit of trouble."

There were two people, however, who had their doubts. The first of these was Anna's six-year-old brother Joey.

He wanted a brother and had even selected Andy for his sibling's name. The girls he knew were trouble, always getting in a guy's way with their giggling. They got mad if you wouldn't let them be cowboys in Cowboys and Indians. But if you let them be an Indian and captured them, they'd get madder, especially if you tied them to a tree. There is just no pleasing girls. His pals Jim and Bill never giggled, except sometimes when girls were around. Without girls they could play Cowboys and Indians for hours without a squabble.

"Dear God," he had prayed. "Please let it be a boy."

The second doubter was the child's maternal grandmother.

Josephine Lowrie, farm-bred and bad-luck hardened in the Illinois heartland, once had a fine chestnut mare out on the farm. A glance from Schatzie's beautiful eyes could convince the toughest farmhand of her sweetness until the fool found himself neatly bucked off into the dirt. Jo Lowrie soon saw something of Schatzie in Anna. Those big blue eyes of hers had that same stubborn determination not to succumb to rein and saddle.

Grandma Lowrie's love of the little girl was fierce and true, but that didn't blind this savvy old lady to the child's faults.

"She'll need a firm hand, that one," she predicted. "She's too quick for her own good."

Unlike Joey however, she kept her views to herself as she usually did. Her habit of silent acceptance of fate began on the day that her mother had come running into the barn where Jo was doing the evening milking.

"He's been bit! Papa's got bit by a rattler. Ride Schatzie into the town and get the doctor!"

But by the time Doc Saxon got to the field where the injured man was lying in the shade of the hay wagon, Axel Mueller was dead. Half-orphaned at seventeen, Josephine was forced to find a job in town to earn cash to support her mother and three younger brothers.

A staunchly Presbyterian family, owners of Lowrie Plumbing and Well Company in the hamlet of Mazon, Illinois, five miles from the homestead solved her problem. Their only son, Andrew Lowrie, heard about Jo from a well digger who had installed the pump and windmill on the Mueller farm.

"She's a pretty lassie, is Jo and a good cook. Learned thrift from old Mueller 'fore that snake took him off. She's a Catholic like all those Bavarians over to the river, but you ain't going to marry her, so that'll be no problem."

The fellow was partly right. Jo was a pretty lassie. Young Andrew fell in love and married Josephine in less than a year, and the girl became mistress instead of maid in the Lowrie household. She adopted her husband's religion and told no one about the rosary she kept in the dresser drawer, just in case.

So she kept her counsel about her little granddaughter. It was two years, but Grandma Lowrie was proven correct on a late summer day of Anna's second year of life.

The weather had been unusually hot and the church, built long before air-conditioning, was only slightly cooled by a cross-breeze from the open panels at the top of the tall, stained- glass windows on either side of the sanctuary. Even the most devout of the faithful were thinking as much of iced lemonade as of salvation.

Emma Mackenzie and her mother were exhausted. The two women had risen early so as to prepare as much of the Sunday dinner as possible in the cool of early morning. Perhaps they drifted off for a bit, or each thought that the other was watching Anna. In any case, neither saw the child slide carefully down from her mother's lap to sit on the cool tiles of the floor under the family pew.

Anna looked around her.

She found herself in a forest of legs. Limbs of all shapes and sizes stretched as far as she could see. Even more intriguing was that the legs rose from a garden of feet. There were feet in polished wing-tip shoes, feet slipped from the confines of brown and white spectator pumps, toes of all shapes revealed by open-toed sandals, men's feet encased in light-blue or tan stockings with pretty patterns running up the sides resting on the cool floor next to their discarded tan or white oxfords.

Anna crawled under the pew to the one behind. Heaven! She found a set of toes with painted pink toenails peeping out the front of pink shoes that matched the pink of the straw handbag next to them. She loved pink! Best of all, when she poked the pink toes, they wiggled. Above her, Mrs. Reinhold's face appeared, holding on to her pink bonnet, her puzzled, brown spaniels' eyes staring down at the child in surprise. Anna waved bye-bye to Mrs. Reinhold and headed under the pew to the one behind.

There she found another delight. When she touched the sole of Dr. Hansen's shoeless foot, he jerked it away so fast the hymnal on his lap fell to the floor. It would have hit her if she had not already gone on to inspect an interesting pair of feet under the next pew. One foot wore a silky stocking that went all the way up under the lady's dress. The other, a man's, was wearing one of those light blue stockings with the pretty designs up the side. What intrigued her was that the two feet were trying to wrap themselves around each other like they were playing tag. She patted them affectionately and continued on her way.

Then she glanced behind her and saw, three pews back, the startled faces of Mommy and Grandma hanging upside-down between their legs. This struck her as the funniest sight of her short life and she started to giggle.

The infectious sound followed her as she crawled through the foot-forest until she reached the last pew. There, stopped at last by the back wall, she collapsed in a heap, helpless with laughter. Fortunately, her great friend, Professor Ganzert, was there. He scooped her up in his arms and took her out into the church anteroom, and from there for a long walk in the church garden. They were found after the service, dozing contentedly on the circular bench surrounding the great trunk of an ancient elm tree.

Rev. Mackenzie, meanwhile, gamely changed the focus of his sermon from *Saved by Grace* to *…and a little child shall lead them,* which many parishioners declared to be one of his best of the year.

However, the episode was the first crack in the pedestal the Bird Ladies had built for the little girl. She had tasted the thrill of exploration, had literally peeked at the underside of humanity, and Anna Leigh Mackenzie would never be the same again.

But she did not yet know that 'being a good girl' was not an option for a Presbyterian Princess. It was a non-negotiable commandment.

First Presbyterian Church
Champaign, IL

NOW BE A GOOD GIRL
Early summer, 1937

Mommy says it. Grandma says it. Sometimes even Daddy says it. "Now Anna, be a good girl." They know what it means, I guess, but I am not sure. Last night at dinner when I wouldn't eat my liver and onions, I got sent off to my room so I'd learn to behave. But I was behaving! I heard Auntie Marie say I was behaving like a spoiled child. Mommy said I was behaving like a baby. So, I was already behaving. I didn't know what I was supposed to learn in my room. So, when I got upstairs I found T. Bear waiting in my rocking chair. We had a long talk about being good, but T. Bear didn't seem to know any more about that than I did.

"They change the rules too much," he said when I told him about last Sunday.

I had been quiet and sat and drew pictures on the paper Mommy gave me while Daddy was talking in church. That was good. But the paper got filled up, so I drew a picture in that book they sing from. That was bad. Daddy said my picture was real good for a four-year-old but I put it in the wrong place. But it wasn't in the wrong place. That old book needed some pictures.

There wasn't anything in it but lots of lines with spots on them. That's not fun like the picture I put in. It had that hat Auntie Marie wears all the time…the one with the yellow bird in a nest on top. Now that's fun.

Then there was that Easter egg. It was big and round with a white flower on top. Inside, there was soft chocolate that tasted like warm ice cream. I found it in a shoe box on the floor in my brother Joey's room. I thought he put it there because he didn't want it. So I ate it. It was good, but Joey got really mad at me and told Mommy. She said if I did that again I'd have to go to the dentist. I went there once and I'm not going again, no matter what.

Yesterday, Mommy and I went to Doctor Hansen's office. He stuck a needle in my arm. It hurt, so I cried and said he was a bad man. But Mommy said he was a good man 'cause that needle had stuff in it to keep me well. But how do I know that? I wasn't sick to begin with.

It's all a puzzle.

But today was fun. Mommy and Grandma took me to the ladies' tea party downstairs under the church. They have this room there for parties and stuff.

Auntie Marie came with her friends. I call them the Bird Ladies because they all have hats that look like birds are sitting on their heads. It makes me laugh. But Auntie Marie says I shouldn't laugh at somebody's hat. I thought that that's why they wore them. A funny man in the circus had one just like Mrs. Hackberry's, and everyone laughed at him and it was okay.

Anyway, Miss Albert set me on a couple of telephone books on a wobbly chair by a table. Auntie Marie brought me a pretty little cake with a red flower on top and a cup of warm water with a piece of lemon and some sugar in it and told me to be a good girl. Then the *Bird Ladies* went off to get tea and cakes of their own.

They didn't look at me much after those first kisses that leave red marks all over my cheeks. So I thought I'd listen to them real good because they're big people. They know about things. Soon they were talking about a lady I know 'cause she stays with me when Grandma goes to visit Uncle Henry in Saint Paul.

What do you think about Ella Hobart's niece?

Gladys? She's a piece of work, that one – flirting with the boys the way she does, tossing that blond hair of hers at them and skirts above her knees.

Did you know she wears lipstick, and her just turned fifteen?

I saw her and that boy from Saint Sebastian's. They were walking in the park and he had his arm over her shoulders like he owned her. He's Catholic, you know. That will never do. She's trouble, she is.

Sssh! Here comes Ella now.

I didn't understand. I really liked Miss Hobart. She looked like those pretty girls in the pictures in the magazines Mommy and Grandma read all the time.

We laughed all the time when she came to take care of me.

Sometimes a boy came with her. He was lots of fun. We played hide-and-seek. He tickled Miss Hobart when he found her. Then they hugged and kissed while I played with T. Bear. I think she liked that 'cause her cheeks got all pink when they did. The boy always left before Mommy and Grandma came home. So why was Miss Hobart bad? I thought she was fun.

Then those ladies went off somewhere. Mrs. Heffernan came over with another cake and gave me a kiss on the cheek. "Are you being a good girl?" she asked. I don't know why she laughed when I said I didn't know.

Pretty soon Auntie Marie's friends came back. This time they were talking about Billy Hillman. I hate Billy Hillman. He pulls my hair whenever he gets near. He always pushes me over when we go roller skating in the park. Then he laughed when I skinned my knee and that's not fair because he was bigger than me. He did that to anybody he could, even other boys who are smaller than he was. So you could see why I was surprised when I heard the Bird Ladies talk about Billy Hillman like he was nice.

Such a joy to his mother!

Poor child has such a hard time since that awful Mr. Hillman ran off with his hussy from Chicago. What was he thinking, leaving a young boy and his mother to shift for themselves?

I understand that Alice did quite well with the divorce settlement though. She doesn't seem too hard up.

It's not the money — it's having to raise the boy herself. It's so nice for her that Billy doesn't give her a bit of trouble.

Yes, he's a good boy, he is.

It was lucky Grandma came and got me to go home so we could listen to some bear cubs play in a park in Chicago. I wondered if Mr. Hillman would be there. Maybe he took his hussy to the park so it could run and play with the little bears.

I'd have told those ladies the truth about Billy Hillman if we hadn't left. But that would have been "contradissing" my elders and I'm not allowed to do that.

On our way home, I asked Grandma what a "Cat-'o-lick" was and why being one would never do.

"Who told you that?" she said. So, I told her what some of the Bird Ladies had said at tea. "They were talking about some boy from Saint Sebastian's and Miss Hobart." Grandma told me, "They are very small-minded women, some of them. I was raised a Catholic and I think I do very nicely, thank you."

"But what about the cats? Do they lick you a lot?" I asked.

Then Grandma explained that being Cat-'o-lick was belonging to a kind of church like being a Presbyterian was and didn't have anything to do with cats. She showed me a pretty necklace of black beads with a cross on it.

"My priest gave this to me at my confirmation," she said.

"What does being confirmed mean?" I asked her. "Does everybody get a necklace for their cat to play with when it happens?"

But Grandma didn't have time to explain.

"Never mind," she said. "We've got to hurry. The game will start in a few minutes."

Sitting in Grandma's room and listening to the bear cubs playing base-ball is my favorite thing to do. A man talks about these little bears with men's names running all over a park. I'd like to see that.

After the game was over, we went down and helped Mommy get sup-per. It was liver and onions. When we said grace, I prayed that the liver and onions would turn into fried chicken, but it was still liver and onions when I opened my eyes. Daddy had prayed for some children in a place called Armenia or Marnenia or somewhere who didn't have any food. I guess God didn't listen before, because Daddy has been praying about them for a long time.

So as soon as he said, "Amen", I got an idea. I got down from my chair and started for the closet where there's boxes and wrapping paper.

"Just where are you going, young lady? I didn't hear you being excused from the table," Mommy said.

"I'm going to get a box to put my liver and onions in, so I can send it to those children in Marnenia. That way they won't be hungry, and I won't have to eat it."

Daddy started to cough and covered his mouth. Mommy said, "Come back here and eat your dinner or there's no gingerbread for you tonight."

"But I'm just helping God."

I don't know why God had to take my gingerbread away when I was just helping him do his job.

After supper, Daddy read from the Bible. That's a book where you learn what good is. But sometimes I can't understand it.

Like that story about Jesus getting born. Some king or somebody had a whole bunch of little boys killed because he was afraid of the Baby Jesus. And in another place, God smote another whole bunch of little boys with a stick called The Plague, so they got dead because their mothers and daddies belonged to some bad king. It's all pretty hard to understand because in Sunday school we sing a song about God loving all the little children of the world. So why does He let the Marnenian children starve? And why did He smite those little boys, or didn't stop that first king from killing the others? Maybe He just wasn't watching, but He should be, I think.

T. Bear was right. They change the goodness rules too much.

That's why I got into real trouble a few weeks later when the cherries on the tree by our back fence got ripe.

We wait all year for the cherries to get ripe because my Mommy and Grandma and Auntie Marie make the best cherry pies and jam and things in the whole world. My job since I was three is to pull the pits out of the cherries so they can cook them. Grandma gives me one of her big wire hairpins, and Daddy takes pliers and bends the loop at the end of it over.

Then I put the loop inside of the cherry and pull the pit right out. It's fun for a while, but sometimes I go into the kitchen and get some lemonade and one of Auntie Marie's sugar cookies.

So I had been sitting on the back-porch stairs, pitting cherries when I decided it was time for a cookie. Mommy and Auntie Marie and Grandma were talking as they made pie pastry and put jam jars and Mason jars in really hot water so they'd be all clean for the jam and pie filling.

Auntie Marie was saying, "We're lucky to have enough food to eat. There's so much suffering with this depression. The camp down near the rail yard gets more crowded every day. Men are having less and less luck finding work. Entire families are living down there now with more coming every day."

"I know," Mommy sounded sad. "So many fathers out of work… the women do what they can, doing laundry, working long hours cleaning houses and offices, then back to the shanties in the rail yard. I even had a young girl not more than twelve ask if she could paint our back fence. So much need. I feel sorry for them all."

Grandma sniffed.

"I don't feel sorry for some like that pair of bums sitting on the park bench across the way yesterday. They were laughing and talking about what a good scam they had as they rehearsed their bogus speech to beg food they could sell to pay for their whiskey. 'Gotta have a good sob story,' one said, and showed the kind of face he puts on when he goes begging. His kind will be bums, depression or no."

Just as I went back out to the back porch to pit more cherries, the back gate squeaked and a man peeked into the yard. Then he came in and shut the gate behind him. He looked awful thin, but his hair was combed and he was clean.

"Are you a bum?" I asked him.

He looked like I'd said something mean to him.

"I ain't no bum, little girl. I'm a fella who wants to work for some grub. Could you ask your Momma if she'd like me to finish picking them cherries off the top of her tree there?"

"Just a minute," I said. "I'll ask her."

I went into the kitchen. Grandma was rolling out piecrusts. Auntie Marie was pouring sugar and lemon juice over the cherries I'd pitted to get them ready for the jam kettle.

Mommy looked up from where she was measuring flour for more piecrust.

"Mommy," I told her, "there's a man out in the back. He says he's not a bum 'cause he wants to pick our cherries for some grub."

Mommy told me to stay indoors and help Grandma with the pies. Then she went out to the porch and talked to the man for a while. I heard her say, "You let me know when you've got that bucket full, and I'll bring your dinner out to the picnic table."

Then she came inside and took out some paper plates from the cupboard and began to fill them with stuff. She was talking all the time about the man outside.

"He's only fourteen and he's got to provide for his sister and his mother. His father left last year to go to California where he'd heard some jobs were. They haven't heard a word from him since. That child has quit school to help support his mother and sister. It's awful. I think of what Joey would have to do in that boy's place and my heart breaks."

Then she went back to the icebox and added two more fried chicken legs to the already full plate. Grandma put some of her German potato salad with the nice bacon-y smell and some green jelly salad with little pieces of pineapple on another plate. Aunt Marie cut a piece of cherry pie and put it on a littler plate. Then we all carried the food outside to the picnic table.

The man had set the pail of cherries on the back steps and I started pitting again.

He watched me as he ate. I guess he was hungry 'cause he talked with his mouth full. "You're one lucky kid to get grub like this every day."

"Not every day," I told him. "Sometimes it's liver and onions."

"How old are you?"

I sat up as tall as I could and said, "Four going on five."

"Hey! My kid sister's 'bout your size. She's going on seven and she's not much bigger than you. That's 'cause we ain't had much to eat for a while, and she don't even have no bread."

"Is that why you tied some of Mommy's bread and chicken legs in your bandana?"

"Yeah. But don't tell your Ma I took some away for my kid sister Junie. She's a good woman, your Ma. Everybody down to the rail yard knows that."

"Why? Have they met her?"

"Well, here's how it is. They come up your alley and see the sign on your back fence that says so."

"I never saw a sign there. What does it say?"

"It tells 'em that a good cook with a big heart lives here. But I gotta be getting on. Tell your Ma I thank her. Bye."

I told him, "Bye." Then after he went away, I opened the gate and looked at the back fence for the sign. The only thing I could see was funny squiggle in white paint against the green paint of the fence. It was almost hidden by the bright blue morning glories Grandma planted on the fence every year. If you looked up close at the strange squiggles, you might think it was a plate of food inside a drawing of a heart.

I thought that being a good cook and having a sign on your fence sounded like more fun than sending liver and onions to little children in Marnenia. Maybe Auntie Marie might help me bake some sugar cookies I could give that man at the rail yard for his sister. I'll bet that girl would like them even better than Mommy's homemade bread and fried chicken.

But I got to be good girl even sooner than that because the next day another man came to the back gate while I was sitting on the back porch putting Hollyhock blossom skirts on my clothespin dolls.

This man was older than the other fellow, but he had the saddest, loneliest face I ever saw. His clothes sort of smelled, and lots of the teeth that should have been in his mouth weren't.

"Good afternoon, little lady," he said in a sort of whiny voice that whistled where his teeth weren't. "Would you be so kind as to ask your good mother if she could spare a crust of bread for a starving man?"

I went inside to find Mommy. She and Grandma were busy setting the table for a dinner party that night. They were polishing those silver things they put candles in and talking. But I knew what to do. I thought, "I won't bother them. I'll get the food all by myself."

The paper plates were on the bottom shelf of the cupboard, so I got out two.

Then I opened the icebox and got out some of Grandma's pastries filled with chicken salad. I cut some jelly from a thing that looked like a Christmas wreath with fruit salad inside. Then I got another plate and put a piece of Mommy's devil's food cake I found on the kitchen table on it. Real careful so's not to spill, I took it all out to the sad-looking man.

The man got real happy when he saw the plates. He called me his "little angel of mercy." He didn't even stop to eat the food there. He just grabbed it all up and went right out the gate to tell everyone down to the rail yard about me.

Daddy's right, you know, when he says it's nicer to give things to people than the other way 'round. I felt so good I even ate a little piece of the cake myself.

So why did Mommy and Grandma send me up to my room until they said I could come downstairs again? I had to sit there on my window seat and watch fat Mr. Robertson coming up the sidewalk to the front door. I wanted to go down and shout at him, "You don't need chocolate cake. Some people's sisters don't even got no bread."

I asked T. Bear, who was watching with me, if I should do that. He told me not to.

Finally, Grandma came up to my room and said I could come down the hall to hers. She had some fresh rolls and milk and applesauce for supper. It tasted so good. I thought about that boy's sister and wondered if we could send some to her. After the food was gone, I climbed on Grandma's lap. We sat real quiet while she rocked me in her rocking chair like she does when I'm feeling bad.

"Why wasn't it good to give that man some food?" I asked. "You gave that other man some."

"Well," she said after a few rocks of her chair, "usually it's good to share what we have, but…" she rocked a few more times. "It all depends."

"On what?"

"On…on…circumstances."

"What are circums dances? Are they like ballet class?"

"Nooo," she said, making the word real long. "They're just something you learn growing up. Now about a game of "Fish" before bedtime?"

"Could we read a Pooh story instead…the one about Pooh eating too much and getting stuck in Rabbit's front door?"

"We'll see. Now finish your milk. That's a good girl."

So Grandma read me the story about Pooh getting stuck in Rabbit's hole. Then I went to sleep and had a funny dream. I lived in a hole like Rabbit's. Winnie the Pooh came to the door and asked me for hunny. He was real skinny and hungry-looking, but I told him no.

"You haven't learned your circums dances," I said.

BUTTERFINGERS AND FLY BALLS
August 1938

The day I heard about going to Chicago was the kind of day I liked best. It was just before school opened. The rain was tapping on Grandma's window, but not too hard so we could keep the top part open for the breeze. The pear tree by the house was full of ripe fruit. Its branches almost reached to the window. The porch roof is right under Grandma's window. Joey and his friends, Bill and Jack, were sitting out there in the rain. They picked the ripe pears and ate them. Then they held their hands out to the rain to wash off the sticky pear juice. Grandma and I put down our crochet work and ate two fat yellow pears they passed in to us. When we were done, we had to wash sticky pear juice off our hands. I wanted to go out on the porch with the boys, but Grandma made me go wash in the bathroom sink.

In Grandma's room I have a nice green rocking chair just the size I am, and Grandma had a nice wood one just the size she is. We both sat doing our handwork. Grandma was crocheting a pink blanket for my new cousin Grace in Saint Paul who'd just got born. I was weaving a yarn chain on a spool with four nails in it. Here's how that works. You stick one end of the yarn down in the center of the spool. Then you take the rest of the yarn and wrap it around the nails and hook every other loop over the nails. As you work, you pull the chain through the hole in the bottom of the spool. My chain was getting longer and longer, almost to the length for Grandma to take it and stitch it into a little hat that would match Grace's new blanket.

That day I was glad it wasn't raining in Chicago so the Cubs could play outside in their park. Grandma said the Cubs weren't baby bears, like I thought. They're big men. I still didn't understand why they were called Cubs. Anyway, they were playing in the park because it was nice and sunny there. There is a man on the radio who tells you all about their games. He gets real excited, and even yells sometimes and says things that made Grandma mad, but we have fun anyway.

It's a beautiful day here at Cubs Park. The game is tied…top of the ninth and the great Mel Ott is at bat for the Giants. Southpaw Larry French rubs the ball, nods to Mancuso behind the plate…aaaand here's the pitch. Ott pops it up straight to Bartels at short…an easy out and HE DROPS IT!!!! Bartels muffs an easy out. Highball scores and Ott is safe at first.

Wrigley Field circa 1938
The New York Yankees swept the World Series against the Cubs
in four games.

20

I knew this was bad because Grandma started rocking faster and faster, like she does when she's mad. I heard her say something under her breath. It sounded like, "Damnbutterfingers. Send him down to Peoria."

I tried to rock faster, too, but I missed a stitch and almost ruined my chain. "What's a damnbutterfingers?" I asked as I tried to fix it.

"It's a ballplayer who's so clumsy he couldn't catch cold if he was standing in the snow in his BVDs," Grandma said as she took the spool and untangled the yarn.

"What are BVDs?"

"They're underpants."

"Oh," I said. "Where's Peoria?"

"That's where you go 'til you get rid of butterfingers so you'll be good enough to get sent back up to play in Chicago again."

"Do you have to be good to play in Chicago?"

"Sure do. The Cubs were the champs in '08 and won the playoffs three times after that. You see, ballplayers first start in the minors like Peoria. Then when they get good enough, they get called up to the big teams like the Chicago Cubs. But if they get so they drop fly balls and lose games, they get sent down to the minors again."

"Are there mines in Peoria?"

Grandma shushed me so she could hear what was happening in Chicago.

…And so the Cubs go three up and three down, and the Giants win. This is your announcer, Quinn Ryan, hoping you'll be with us tomorrow when we wind up this series with the Giants here in Chicago, and wishing you so long and better luck than the Cubbies had today.

Grandma didn't talk for a while, just crocheted and crocheted.

I sat and wondered about this new rule for being good. You had to learn to catch fly balls.

A fat horsefly buzzed in through a hole in Grandma's window screen. I thought I'd better try catching it before I tried to catch a ball of flies. How do they get flies into balls anyway? I couldn't even get that one to sit down. I thought maybe I'd ask Joey, but he and his buddies Bill and Jack had just come in from school. I was afraid they'd just call me "Peskyanna" like always and go build model airplanes or something.

Peskyanna means they think I'm a pest and they try to get rid of me. Once, they took the ladder Mr. Bidwell had left out in the church garden when he was working out there. Billy climbed up high enough to reach the sill of those pretty colored windows with Bible stories on them. Joey called me to come see a robin's nest in the tree by the window and when I did, he took me up the ladder and handed me up to Billy, and he put me on the windowsill and took the ladder away. Mr. Bidwell came later and got me down. He said it was a miracle I didn't fall off and get hurt. But it wasn't. The mother robin watched me and told me not to move.

"Just sit still," she said, so I did until Mr. Bidwell came because Joey told him where I was.

I talk to birds a lot, but not out loud. Big people don't understand birds, but they would if they listened hard enough.

Those boys got in real trouble that day even though I didn't fall off.

Anyway, now I measured out my chain and took it to Grandma to see how much more I had to do. Grandma's head was nodding and she'd put down her handiwork. That meant she was going to take a nap before dinner. So I got up on her lap and took one, too, until Mommy woke us up.

Mother! Anna! Get your hands and faces washed. Dinner's ready.

We ate outside on the picnic table that had dried from the rain while we slept. Daddy cooked nice big hamburgers on the grill and some corn a farmer had just sold him off the back of his truck. While we were eating, Daddy said to Mommy, "I've gotten sent down to Peoria for a committee meeting. I'll leave the first thing next Monday. It's just some minor thing. I should be back late Monday evening."

Now that was so mean, and I told Daddy so.

"They shouldn't send you down to the mines in Peoria! You're not a damnbutterfingers."

I guess I said something bad 'cause Mommy asked me where I heard that. I told her Grandma said it. Mommy asked Grandma, and Grandma said she was sorry, it was the Cubs again. She promised not to do it again in front of me because 'little pitchers have big ears'. I didn't know what she meant 'cause none of our pitchers had any ears at all. Sometimes big people don't make sense when they talk.

But pretty soon Daddy got back from Peoria okay and the summer went away. Mommy aired the jackets and sweaters so they hardly smelled of mothballs any more. Daddy and Joey raked up all the pears the squirrels messed up by eating the seeds out of them. Mommy and I planted new tulip bulbs by the front porch. The leaves on the grass and sidewalks turned bright red and yellow. Daddy and Mr. Bidwell raked them into big piles that scrunched when we jumped in them and scattered the leaves all over again.

Now I am five and getting ready to go to kindergarten. I'll have Mrs. Wilson for a teacher, just like Joey did when he went to kindergarten. He said she was really nice. A week before school started, Mommy and I were sitting in the porch swing looking at school dresses in the Sears catalog. One dress I liked had a pretty pleated skirt, and a little blue vest and white blouse. Mommy said she liked it, too, and maybe I could have it to wear to school.

But then she said, "Maybe you'd like to wait and see what the little girls in Chicago wear to kindergarten before we buy too many school clothes. You see, Anna Banana, Daddy's just gotten called up there. What do you think of that?"

"Daddy's gotten called up to Chicago? I'll go tell Grandma. She'll really be excited," I said and jumped down from the swing.

"Wait a minute. Grandma already knows."

"What did she say? Will we go to see him play and learn to catch fly balls?"

"Play? Fly balls?"

Mommy didn't seem to understand, so I explained. "Play in the park with the Cubs. Isn't that why Daddy was called up to Chicago?"

I didn't understand why she thought that was funny, but she said, "No dear, there's a church in Chicago that needs a pastor. The one they had got sick and had to leave. So some people from the church came down here to Champaign to hear Daddy preach. They liked him so much that they wrote and asked if he would come up there and be their new pastor.

"He told them he would like that, so we will be moving to Chicago in October. When we get there you'll go to a nice new school in Chicago."

"But what about Janie and Mary and Isabel? We were all going to school together. Will they come too? And Grandma and Auntie Marie and…"

"I'm sorry, dear. But Janie and Mary and Isabel will stay here. Their daddies have jobs at the University, so they won't be moving. But they can come to visit when we get all settled in our new home. Then you can introduce them to your new Chicago friends."

"I don't want new Chicago friends. I want Janie and Mary and Isabel," I said. "I don't know anybody in Chicago, except maybe that man who tells Grandma and me about the Cubs games."

Mommy put her arm around my shoulder and said, "Have you forgotten that Uncle Robert and Aunt Lillian and Cousin Robbie live in Chicago?"

I sat up.

"Will they be close by? Do they still have that funny dog with the squished-up face?"

"They sure do. Their apartment is three blocks away from the church. We'll be almost neighbors. Robbie, Jr. already goes to the same school you and Joey will go to. And Bulldog Dan is doing fine. Uncle Robert says you can come over and take him for a walk any time you want to.

"Grandma will have a big room right next to yours just like always. Uncle Robert found Auntie Marie a good job with some people who live in a beautiful big house on the shore of Lake Michigan. Auntie Marie will be their housekeeper and cook."

I said, "That'll be nice", because I thought I should.

But I really wanted to stay and go to school with my friends. I had a friend named Betty who lived down the street but moved away to a place called Texas last year and I've never seen her again. What if Chicago is like Texas, and if you go there you never see your friends again?

It will be nice having Uncle Robert and Aunt Lil living nearby, but they aren't friends like Janie and Mary are. And Robbie sure won't take the place of Isabel. He's the same age as Joey – six whole years older than me. The boys will be in grade five and I'll probably never see either of them. And even if I do, they won't play with me.

I went up to Grandma's room to ask her what she thought and why we had to move. She said that sometimes things happen you don't want to happen, but you have to do them anyway. I still don't want to go to Chicago. I think it's a dumb idea.

CALLED UP TO CHICAGO
October 1938

I sure was right about that Chicago thing. Everything here is all messed up. Grandma and Mommy are wrapping up all the plates and glasses and stuff in paper and putting them into these big fat boxes. There are other tall, fat boxes in our bedrooms that Mommy and Daddy hang our clothes in like they were closets. Now we have to keep wearing the ones that are left.

I'm pretending that naughty fairies live in those boxes and they keep hiding things.

Mommy and Grandma can't find the stuff because they keep saying things like, "Where did we put that glass bowl?" and "Where's the blue hat I wear with this dress?"

Last week the Bird Ladies had Mommy and Grandma and me and Auntie Marie over to the church parlor for a tea party. When they talked about us leaving, they got all weepy. I hate it when ladies get all weepy. It means something bad has happened, like somebody died or something. Maybe Chicago is like Texas, and they think they'll never see us again. But Mommy says, "No, our moving to Chicago is going to be nice." If that's so, I wish they'd stop sniffling.

Then on Sunday, there was another party after church. Everyone who wanted to come and say goodbye did. They gave Mommy and Daddy some silver pots to serve tea in. They all said nice things about Daddy and Mommy, and the Bird Ladies got weepy again. I'm beginning to wonder if Mommy is wrong and this Chicago thing really is like moving to Texas. I think Grandma maybe thought so, too. She has gone to Saint Paul to visit Uncle Henry and Aunt Millie and Cousin Grace. She told me she'd be back when everything in Chicago got settled down a bit.

Finally, it was time for us to go. Daddy put our suitcases with the clothes that didn't go on the big truck that came yesterday into our car. Mrs. Reinhold brought over hot coffeecake and scrambled eggs and ham for our breakfast, which was really nice. Billy and Jack stopped on their way to school to say goodbye to Joey. They went out on the back porch and slapped each other on the back and stuff. When Joey came back in, though, he looked a little like he was almost weepy or something. But boys don't cry. Maybe he just had something in his eye.

I felt sort of weepy myself at the thought of leaving my friends and nice people like Professor Ganzert and his family. I missed Janie and Mary and Isabel already, and we hadn't even gotten into the car yet.

Daddy said, "All aboard," just like the man on the trains down at the station by the rail yard. Then we got into the car and left our home for Chicago.

We drove and drove and drove. Joey watched for license plates on cars going by that had different names than our Illinois ones. Then he wrote the states down in a notebook.

I talked to T. Bear about Chicago because he wasn't quite sure about it.

It will be real nice. Daddy says so. There's a big, big lake there. It's bigger than Fishtrap Lake in Wisconsin where we went last summer to go fishing. This lake's more like an ocean, I think.

He says we'll have lots and lots of room, so I think that means I can have dogs and ponies like I always ask Santa for. And the Cubs live there, so we can go to the park and catch flies and lightning bugs and stuff with them.

But I was just saying that to make him feel better. I still didn't think Chicago was a good idea. It was a real scary one.

We stopped for dinner at a place called "Miss Jolly's Truck Stop", and they did 'cause there were lots and lots of trucks there. Daddy said that's because Miss Jolly makes the best food from Champaign to Chicago. The truckers tell each other about that so they all stop at her restaurant.

Miss Jolly really was almost as good a cook as Mommy and Grandma.

I had meatloaf and fluffy mashed potatoes with a hole in them to hold the gravy. There were fat green peas and green tomato relish. Miss Jolly came to our table herself and said, "Hi Reverend! How about some of my lemon meringue pie for dessert? It's on me."

She was all nice and clean, and I couldn't see any pie on her anywhere. But Daddy laughed and said, "Miss Jolly, I wouldn't miss that for the world."

So she brought us some pie, and I was glad she did.

After we all got back in the car, Mommy and Daddy talked real quietly. Joey got out a magazine he likes that shows you how to build things like radios and telescopes and stuff. But T. Bear and I were sleepy so we took a nap.

When we woke up, there wasn't a cow or a horse or a barn anywhere. Instead there were lots and lots of buildings that were so tall you couldn't see the tops of them. I didn't like the way they hid the sunshine so the street looked gloomy. There weren't any real trees, but some buildings had little Christmas trees in pots by their front doors. The trees didn't have any lights on them, but they were all trimmed so that there wasn't a branch stuck out wrong anywhere. Lots of people were walking up and down the street. A train was going past on tracks that were way over our heads. I was sure that it would fall on top of us, but Daddy told me that it was called the elevated train – the "L" for short, and it wouldn't fall off because it had been up there a long time.

Then he said, "Look up ahead. There's Lake Michigan."

Joey and I looked over Daddy's shoulder and saw, way ahead, lots of water making big, white-capped waves. When we got almost to the shore, Daddy turned a corner and we drove right along the lake. T. Bear and I were on the side where the lake was. We watched the giant waves hitting a row of big rocks that stopped the water from coming any further into the street.

The white water on top of the waves flew high up in the air. Then it fell down on a path that went along the row of rocks. On Joey's side of the car there was a second road where the cars were going in the other direction. There were buildings all along that street. Some looked like fancy houses in a picture book. Others were taller and not so pretty. These had more of those little trees in pots by their front doors and men dressed up like the guards in that poem about *Changing the Guard in Buckingham Palace*. They were there to open the door for people. That was strange.

Don't people in Chicago know how to open their own doors?

"Are we almost there?" I asked because T. Bear was wondering.

"Pretty soon. See that big pink building there on the lakefront? That's one of the most famous hotels in Chicago. Lots of famous people stay there, even the Giants and the Tigers when they come to play the Cubs."

I looked out at the park by the hotel, but there weren't any giants or tigers anywhere.

Maybe they were taking a nap or something. At the next corner there was a second pink building.

Daddy said, "Almost there now," and turned across a big street with wind howling down it like it wanted to blow us right back to Champaign. At the next corner he stopped the car in front of a gloomy building made of grey stone blocks. It looked sort of like the castle in my *Snow White* story book, except that it didn't have those towers that look like upside-down ice cream cones on its roof.

Daddy opened the back door of the car and said, "Come on out. We're here!" Joey climbed over me and T. Bear and stood looking up at the gray building.

"It's all right," I told T. Bear as I climbed out onto the sidewalk. "The house must be behind that grey castle thing."

It had to be because we were standing on a corner with no houses on it at all. Kitty-corner from the grey castle was a taller building covered with bricks. It had colored lights running up the side. The letters spelled L-A-K-E-S-I-D-E H-O-T-E-L. On another corner was a shop with a sign on it that Joey said spelled MANNY'S DELI. I didn't know either of those words.

Right across the street was a pretty building that might be a house, but it looked way too big. It did have a sort of garden in the middle. But the flowers were not in real dirt because there wasn't any. They were all in big round flowerpots. They looked stiff, like they didn't like being there. One pot had only water in it. It was broken and dribbled into a bigger pot underneath it.

Before I could ask about that, Daddy picked me up. "Where are we going?" I asked.

"To our new home," he said as he carried me up three wide stone steps that led to huge wooden doors that went into the grey castley-looking place.

Daddy pulled open one of three big doors in front of us and we all went into a room that had a second set of three big doors.

"But…?"

He laughed and said, "We're almost there," and he took a key from his pocket. Instead of opening one of the big doors, he unlocked a small door in a corner of the room. Behind that door was another little room. Inside that room was a funny door that folded up like an accordion.

Daddy pulled this door open and we all went into a sort of box. I felt like the White Rabbit in *Alice in Wonderland*. Things were getting curiouser and curiouser.

"Hey!" yelled Joey. "It's an elevator just like the one in Dr. Grant's building."

"That's right," Daddy said. "How about you press number four up there and take us home."

Now I didn't like that one bit. If we were going to live near a dentist's office, I was leaving right away to go live with Uncle Robert and Robbie and Aunt Lillian. And I would've, too, except the elevator thing was going up so I had to stay. Mommy held my hand while we waited for the elevator to stop.

When it did, Daddy opened a folding door on the other side of the elevator thing. We went into another little room like the first one. Then Daddy got out another key and unlocked that room. T. Bear was getting nervous, but it made Joey laugh.

"Hey, Dad," he said. "Is this a joke? What's going on?"

"No joke, son. We're home!" Daddy answered and let us in to the biggest, darkest room I had ever seen in any house. I looked all around for a door with "Dentist" written on it in gold paint, but I didn't see any, so I guessed it was okay. I held T. Bear tight so he wouldn't be afraid, and went in.

A big voice boomed out, "It's about time you got here!"

And there were Uncle Robert and Aunt Lillian and Robbie and Bulldog Dan. They had a picnic spread out on a quilt on the floor in front of the biggest fireplace in the world. Some big logs there made a pretty glow as they burned. Little lights made to look like candles were stuck into candle holders on the wall. It was sort of cozy, except that our voices echoed in the bigness of the empty rooms.

Bulldog Dan got up and waddled over to say hello. That got everyone laughing and saying, "Hello, what took you so long?" and, "That food looks good enough to eat." and "How's the weather been?"

Uncle Robert gave me a big bear hug and patted me on my head. "Well, will you look at that," he said, holding up a quarter for everyone to see. "Why does Anna keep money in her ear?" And I laughed, 'cause he always finds money in my ear when he sees me. Then he asked me, "Well, little princess, what do you think of your castle?"

"Is that what it is? It's not as good as that one in the movie about Joey." and all the grownups laughed.

Joey laughed too, but you could see he felt a little jealous, so Uncle Robert put his arm around him and then held up the baseball cards Joey always carries in his pants pocket.

"Say, young man. You better be more careful of these. Somebody might steal 'em off of you in the big city." And we all laughed some more 'cause he always does something like that all the time to Joey, too. We kids like Uncle Robert. Magic things always happen when he's around. Once I asked him how he did all that stuff, but he just winked his eye at me and said, "Ask me no questions, and I'll tell you no lies."

While the grown-ups got our supper ready, Joey and Robbie went around the apartment to look it over. They let me come with them because they knew I would anyway.

We found the dining room and the kitchen and a nice big room beside the kitchen with the biggest icebox I'd ever seen. Robbie and Joey went off somewhere. They just disappeared, so I went back into what Mommy said was our new dining room. There was a funny lump in the rug in the carpet there. When I stepped on it, Robbie and Joey came running in from the kitchen and called, "Hey, Dad. Somebody's ringing a bell somewhere."

I was still jumping on the lump for fun. It would just pop right back up again. Jump!

Jump! Jump!

Dad came in from the front hall and saw me jumping on the bump. "It's okay, boys," he laughed. "It's Anna ringing the maid's bell."

He explained that the lump was hiding a bell that you could step on under the table and bring your maid running to see what you wanted. But we didn't have a maid and never had, so I guessed it was really just sort of a toy.

Aunt Lillian called us to get our hands washed and come to dinner. We all sat on the pretty quilt she put over the ugly brown carpet in what Mommy said was our new living room. So we sat on the floor in front of the biggest fireplace I'd ever seen and ate our first supper in Chicago.

It was pretty exciting, but finally Aunt Lillian said to Mommy, "Did you bring their nightclothes? Those two look pretty worn out," meaning Joey and me.

Mommy went and gave her a little suitcase Daddy had brought up from the car. Aunt Lillian asked Mommy if the cots in the apartment were okay, and did Mommy find the linens for them.

Mommy hugged her and said they were fine, and thanks for having everything ready for us.

Uncle Robert said, "Now let's get these kids to bed." and shooed us over to the elevator. Robbie Two put a leash on Bulldog Dan who got up from his nap and yawned the biggest dog yawn ever. Then he walked over in that waddly way he has and crowded into the elevator thing with us. Uncle Robert held me up and let me press "One". We ended up where we had come in.

Outside it was dark except for some street lights. I held tight to Uncle Robert's hand. We walked through a rain that blew in our faces and got to where Uncle Robert, Aunt Lillian and Cousin Robbie lived. Their building had an elevator, too, but it was smaller than ours and was down the hall from where they lived.

Their house was smaller than ours. I'll bet the whole place would fit that room where we had our picnic in front of the fireplace. Robbie had his own bedroom, though, and Joey slept with him. Uncle Robert and Aunt Lil had a nice bed that pulled right down from the wall. I had a puffy mattress on the floor next to them. Bulldog Dan thought it was his. He crawled up beside me and we went to sleep. I mean Bulldog Dan did. That dog snores real loud, so I mostly stayed awake. Was I really going to be a princess in that big, dark place Uncle Robert called the castle?

Maybe it was. It was lots bigger than our old house. But the walls were the color spinach gets when you don't cook it right away. The floors were all covered with a carpet that looked like furry stale chocolate. Maybe this castle had a bad fairy who didn't get invited to some party, so she picked out those colors to get even.

When I finally fell asleep, I dreamt there was this old witch dressed in a soiled brown cape and hat who kept telling me she'd made me a special pie, but it was filled with some icky green pudding. The witch got really, really mad when I wouldn't eat it.

I was really, really glad when Aunt Lil touched my arm and said it was time to get up.

*The Presbyterian Princess outside the
Edgewater Church holding T. Bear.*

A DIFFERENT KIND OF CHURCH
October 1938

Joey and I slept a long time. Robbie had already gone to school when we woke up.

Aunt Lillian was in her tiny kitchen making her special French toast with lemon sauce and whipped cream on top. After we were finished eating, Uncle Robert said, "Time to go" and clipped Bulldog Dan's leash onto his collar. Dan has a real strange collar of thick leather with silvery metal things sticking out all around it. Uncle Robert says it is like that because bulldogs are a fighting breed. Bulldog Dan, a fighter? Well, maybe, if you can get him to wake up enough he might nudge your hand real hard to make you scratch him behind his ears.

Aunt Lillian bundled us all up to go out into the rain. Uncle Robert picked up our small suitcase. Then Joey, Uncle Robert, the dog and I crowded into the little elevator down at the end of the hallway that went to their apartment.

Uncle Robert and Bulldog Dan walked Joey and me back to the grey building. Even with our winter coats on, the wind was the coldest I ever knew. It carried raindrops that stung like little needles on our faces and turned our cheeks bright red. After three blocks, I was glad to go into one of those three big doors into the castle.

Inside Uncle Robert went to a gold-colored box with little holes in it next to the elevator room door. He pressed a button and Daddy's voice said, "Is that you, Rob?" It was just like he was on the telephone.

Uncle Robert answered into the box. "Sure is. I have a couple of kids with me."

The door to the elevator room started buzzing, and Uncle Robert went over and opened it and he didn't even need a key. The elevator was there, and we got in and went up to our new house.

Mommy and Daddy were waiting in the big dark room. Today, though, there were some of those lights made to look like candles in holders on the walls, so it wasn't so gloomy. We all hugged and asked each other how they had slept. Then Uncle Robert and Bulldog Dan went home. As the elevator carried them away, Daddy clapped his hands together.

"Now," he said, "let's all go see our new bedrooms. The moving men set up the beds this morning."

He turned away from the room with the fireplace and took us instead to a long, long hall on the other side of that first gloomy room. One side of this hall was just blank. The other side had four doors in it. We stopped at the first door. Inside was a big room with tall windows that went all the way to the floor. There were the same green walls and icky brown carpet as all the rest of the house. It didn't seem to bother Daddy. He sounded real happy and proud when he said, "Here's where Mother and I will sleep."

Two big beds were there covered with pretty flower-garden quilts Mommy and Grandma had made. Two bureaus stood on one wall facing a pair of big beds with a table between them.

I recognized the bronze reading lamp with the double lights that always stood on that table and almost felt like home. But if it was our lamp, why did it all seem so small?

Then Daddy showed us a big bathroom next to their room with little squares of black and white on the floor next to their room. We could walk right through it into another room.

Joey's bed was in this second bedroom. The sturdy set of bunk beds that had been in his room in Champaign had been unpacked and set up as twin beds. Joey bounced on the new mattress and then opened a large box the movers had set in the middle of the room. To his delight, he found the two things he had worried about when he had seen them packed away in the box. His bright, brass trumpet arrived nested in its case. And the model airplanes Bill and Jack and he had so carefully made in Champaign weren't broken at all. We left him to unpack and see if everything had gotten here okay and went back out into the hall to the next room.

"Here's your bedroom, Anna."

There was my dear spool bed, the one that looks as if the headboard and footboard were made from old spools of thread. It even had my white bedspread with those little fuzzy knobs on it.

T. Bear, who had been quiet all day, clapped his paws when he saw all his stuffed animal friends piled on top of the familiar white bedspread. I hugged Tygeretto. He is a tiger with a growly button inside. He told me the animals were all there and glad to get out of the big truck.

I whispered that I was glad to get out of the car, too. I promised to take everybody out soon so they could get some air after lunch. He purred, and I felt a little better about things.

Then Daddy went through another big black and white bathroom like the first one. I followed him into the next room. And there was Grandma's bed! My green rocking chair was right next to her wooden one. Her African violets were on the little table where they always were.

"She'll be back next week," Daddy told me, and suddenly the day was a little brighter.

Then Joey came in and went over to one of the strange windows I had noticed in my room. Each room had two of them. They weren't regular windows. They were more like tall glass doors that almost reached the ceiling.

"What's out there?" Joey asked, pointing out past the rain running down the small glass panes.

"A surprise!"

Daddy unlocked a handle in the middle of the window and pushed the two sides out, and there was a long porch that looked like the top of a roof.

We stepped over a sill into the cold and wet.

"This is our new front yard," Daddy said, waving his hand like a magician.

Joey and I just stared. It wasn't a yard with flowers and grass and pear and cherry trees.

It was just a long narrow porch. *Our front yard…?* A stone wall with little holes like little windows in it all the way down the other side.

A storm had blown some dry leaves all the way up there. They looked lonely, spinning round like a leaf whirlpool in a corner of our *front yard*. I peeked through one of the holes in the wall. Way down below, I could see the heads of people walking bent over from the wind and cars going past on the street. It made me feel kind of scared, like I felt on that window sill in the church garden. Mommy said an angel saved me that day. But it was really that mother robin telling me to sit still. There were no trees for robins here.

Our front yard…?

And I thought we'd have a real yard with room enough for a pony. If there wasn't a place for a robin, I sure wasn't going to get a pony.

But Daddy acted like Joey did when he'd gotten his new bicycle.

"Just wait until you see it with a barbeque and flower boxes and all. It will be beautiful."

Joey and I looked at each other. *Front yard…? Beautiful…?* Our eyes said as we went back inside and Daddy closed the window door to keep out the cold wind.

Now, Daddy knows most of the time what his parishioners are thinking even before they do. That's why he's so good at helping people in trouble. But sometimes he doesn't notice other things like that Joey and I didn't think our *new front yard* was very nice. At least he didn't ask us what we thought about our *new front yard* today. It saved us from telling a fib.

Joey started unpacking more models, but Daddy said it was time for lunch and that Mommy was heating up bowls of Aunt Lil's homemade tomato soup and those buttery, hot scones her Grandma Mclean taught her to make that have lots of butter in them for our lunch. And all of a sudden Daddy and Joey and I were all hungry.

Daddy said, "Let's eat!" and marched out to the hall with me right close so's not to get left behind. But when I looked behind us, I saw the outline of a door that looked like the other four, but it was closed and dark at that end of the hall, and Daddy was walking so fast and I was afraid of getting lost. Then we were in that first big old dark room where the elevator stopped.

Daddy went past that room and into the place where we had our picnic on the floor yesterday, with the giant fireplace and nice sunny windows. Daddy called it our new living room, but it was way bigger than our living room in Champaign. It seemed that we would never find where we would eat as Daddy went on into another room he called the dining room with a mirror on the wall that looked like the one in *Snow White* with gold all around it. From there, we went through a room with lots of places to put glasses and stuff, which Daddy said was a "Butler's Pantry". Its doors swung back and forth when Joey pushed them. Now we could smell the buttery smell that could only mean that Mommy had heated up Auntie Lil's Scottish scones and was waiting for us at the end of this house that never seemed to stop. At last, we found Mommy in the biggest kitchen there is. On the kitchen table were plates of sandwiches made with Aunt Lil's famous roast beef, and potato salad and a jar of Grandma Jo's fat homemade dill pickles.

It was all magic and wonderful, but how would I ever find my room again? There were so many rooms to remember, I felt like the White Rabbit in *Alice in Wonderland*.

When we were finished, Daddy said, "I've got to go to a meeting of the deacons now, but I'll be through in a couple of hours. Then we can go down and see some more of the building."

It was almost four o'clock when he got back. Joey was reading the latest Hardy Boys book he had borrowed from Cousin Robbie.

I was busy getting my toy animals in order on my pretty new bed the movers had set up for me in my bedroom. This was the third of the four bedrooms leading off from the long hall. But when Daddy had time to do something we went, because if we didn't he might not have time for a while.

So, we followed him back to the dark room by the elevator. In the wall next to the elevator, there were two doors stuck together we hadn't noticed in the dark the night before. When Daddy pushed them open, we saw a large landing leading to wide stairs going down to the next floor. At the bottom, we walked over to a door with glass on top you could sort of see through. There was a thumping noise behind the door and girl's voices cheering. Daddy took us inside. I'll bet the room was bigger than our whole house upstairs. There were two torn fishnets hanging from rings on the wall on each end of the room. Someone had painted circles and lines of the wood floor under the nets.

On one side was half a wall. It had benches on it that went up like steps.

Some girls were sitting on the benches. A bunch of boys were throwing a big brown ball at the broken fishnets. Everyone got excited when the ball fell through the torn part. I don't know why they didn't just mend the nets.

"Why do we have a gym under our house?" Joey asked.

"Our new church is a little different from the one in Champaign," Daddy explained. "It was built for what people call a community center. That's a place where people from the whole neighborhood can come and do things like play basketball and badminton and volleyball. Those boys are practicing basketball today because our church team is going to play United Methodist next Friday."

"But where does that Jim person and all those other fellows pray?" I asked.

Daddy laughed. "Sometimes they pray right here when they shoot a basket. But there's a place of worship downstairs."

"But where's the church?" I asked again.

"I'll show you tomorrow," he promised. "The sanctuary's rather plain now, but when times get better, we'll build a beautiful church at the other end of the block. There is a picture of what that building will look like in my new office downstairs. You can see that later. For now, though, we have to wait until we can get enough money to finish paying for this building.

"Come on. I'll show you some of the other rooms."

So, we walked up and down halls that echoed so that it sounded as though there were lots of us walking by. Daddy showed us a room with a ping pong table and one with frames for making quilts for the Ladies Sewing Circle. One room had cribs and toys in it for little babies to stay while their Mommies and Daddies went to church. A special room was decorated like a log cabin with a fireplace for roasting marshmallows. Daddy said it was for the Boy Scouts. I didn't see one for Girl Scouts. My friend Isabel's sister is a Girl Scout, and I'll bet she'd like one.

Finally, Daddy looked at his watch and said, "I didn't realize how late it is. Mother will be wondering where we are. Lucky we're here by the stairs to the kitchen."

And suddenly, in front of us was one of those stairs that seem to pop up everywhere in this odd place.

There was no light there except what came from the hall, so it was very dark at the top. I thought I saw two big round silvery monsters waiting to snatch us up there and I wouldn't go, but Daddy picked me up and carried me. Joey said I was scaredy-cat. But the way he laughed when Daddy turned on a light and the monsters turned into garbage pails, I thought he saw the monsters, too.

Daddy got out a key and opened a door, and there we were in the hall to our kitchen. "This is the entrance for the maids. Never go out this door without a key to get back in or you'll get locked out," he warned us. He didn't have to worry about me. I wouldn't go there anyway. It was too spooky.

I was beginning to wonder if the castle was a church at all. But the next day, Daddy had time to solve the mystery.

It was Saturday, and there was lots of hustle and bustle downstairs when we got off of the elevator on the second floor. In one room, the choir was practicing. In their room, the Boy Scouts were sorting canned goods to put into bags for the poor. In another room, a man was tearing open little letters with money in them. He put the money in a pile. Each time he did, he'd write something in a book. Some ladies were holding a meeting in the quilt room. They were deciding who would serve coffee and sweet rolls at the coffee hour the next day. In another room, more ladies were talking about a game called rummage, or maybe it was rummy. They didn't play cards in church at Champaign.

But on one side of the hallway, there were some nice wood doors that were different from the others. Daddy opened one of these and inside was half a big room that stuck out over another bigger room. When he turned on the lights, you could see rows of chairs all facing a stage on the lower floor with a place for a choir, and a pulpit and chair for Daddy.

"This is the balcony of the church," he said. "Let's go downstairs and see the church itself."

"Finally!" I thought. "So far this place had been like *Alice in Wonderland* except for the White Rabbit."

When we got to the bottom floor, we found more of the pretty wooden doors. We went inside, and we were under the half room. The great big fancy lights hanging down from the ceiling on heavy chains were on. But where were the windows that made pretty colors on the floor? And where was the sunshine? The only light was from those electric lights up there. And the pews were strange. They weren't all in one piece like at home. They were more like chairs all stuck together. Their seats were pushed up against the backs. Daddy had to show me how to put the seat down so I could sit on it when church was going on. The seats were more cushiony. Joey said that they looked like the seats in the "Rialto" in Champaign.

"That's because these seats were donated to the church by a local movie theater that was getting new ones," Daddy told us.

"So, this is where we all will be worshiping tomorrow. What do you think?" he asked.

"I think it is swell," said Joey.

Why didn't he notice that something was missing? "Where is the bell tower?" I asked.

I could not believe Daddy's answer. "This church doesn't have a bell."

No bell? No tower with the cross on top that reached to the sky?

Was there no room where the bell rope waited on Sunday morning for me and Daddy to come to pull it until the great bell rang calling, "Come to church! Come to church!"?

Would he never hold me in his strong arms while I rode the rope up and down to heaven until the rope stopped moving and the bell got quiet again?

I started to cry.

"I want to go back," I sobbed. "I want to go back home."

Edgewater Presbyterian Church
Chicago, IL

THE CASTLE GHOST
October 1940

Two years ago today, we moved to Chicago, so Uncle Robert and Aunt Lillian and Robbie and Bulldog Dan are coming over for dinner just like they did then.

I'm sort of used to our apartment now that I'm seven-going-on-eight. I'm not so scared of the dark rooms and long halls as I was that first night. But Grandma and I are reading *Alice in Wonderland*, and sometimes, I still wonder if living in our house isn't sort of like falling up instead of down.

Our apartment is full of funny places, like a butler's pantry and a maid's room, and a big room that is just for coming into the apartment called a reception hall that we never had before. Daddy doesn't just have an office like the little one on the second floor of our old house. He has a big room on the corner of the apartment, with another room all lined with pretty wood they call walnut. The shelves are filled with books like the public library behind our old house in Champaign. He even has a little room all filled with drawers and stuff for his clothes, and a whole bathroom just for him. It's like a little apartment all by itself down its own hall and when the hall door is closed, we know not to go in because he's got guests or is writing a sermon, or dressing for some fancy thing.

The kitchen is so far away from my bedroom, I can't hear Mommy and Grandma talking while they're doing dishes or smell bread baking anymore like I could before we moved. There's a long porch that's all along one side of our bedrooms called a balcony, but it is way above the street so that people look funny from up there, and it's too scary to look down anyway. There's no pear tree or any hollyhocks for dressing clothespin dolls in. And you always have to take your key with you because you'll get locked out if you don't 'cause you have to open the elevator door with a key. My friends have to press a button on a box downstairs to tell Mommy or Daddy they're there and stuff, so they're a little scared of our house and don't come very much.

The living room is bigger than our whole downstairs was in Champaign. The best thing is it has a fireplace that Santa's whole sleigh could fit in. On cold nights like tonight, it's nice, and we sit around it and toast marshmallows on long forks or pop corn in a big wire basket. Then the rest of the rooms are dark and spooky. It's worse when the fog comes in from the lake and the foghorns go *Woooooo-ap, Woooooo-ap*.

Last night was a night like that. Mommy and Daddy asked this guy over to dinner because he had just finished that school where you learn to become a preacher like Daddy. Daddy wanted to talk to him about coming to be his assistant, so they were having this party dinner to celebrate. The man's name was Reverend Maxwell, but Daddy called him Stuart because that's what his first name was.

Anyway, Reverend Maxwell was asking Daddy at dinner what he thought about ghosts. He said he wanted to know what to tell people who were scared of them and thought they were real, which is real funny 'cause even I know that they're not real and I'm only seven.

It turns out Rev. Maxwell's mother lived in what he called "The Old Country", but I thought that she was from Scotland like Grandma and Grandpa Mackenzie. Anyway, this lady thought ghosts were real and that you could make them tell you what was on 'The Other Side', but I don't know where that is. So Rev. Maxwell was worried about his Mom believing in ghosts and maybe doing silly things because she did.

Daddy said, "Why don't we go talk about that by the fire? It's getting kind of chilly. Looks as if the fog's coming in."

Rev. Maxwell said, "Okay." So they did.

Joey and I took the dirty dishes off the table. Mommy went out to the kitchen to get the coffee started and put slices of hot apple pie on some plates. Then we all went in to listen to a story Daddy told about a man called Mr. Reckinger who believed in ghosts. Here's how it went:

Bill Reckinger's a smart fellow. He is in to all sorts of business affairs and has become very well off. But two years ago, his son Paul succumbed to polio. You remember how bad it was then? The boy had the worse form of the disease, so there was nothing they could do to save him. Bill's wife and he were devastated by grief, and Maud Reckinger had a nervous breakdown and went into decline.

Then someone told Bill about Madame Sophia. She's a medium who claims that she can put grieving parents in touch with their deceased children, and Bill was desperate for anything that might help Maud.

Pretty soon, he was completely under the influence of Madame Sophia, who claimed that she could talk to Paul. She told Maud that her son was happy on the other side and had developed a way to read the future. In fact, Madame Sophia claimed she had learned to read the future of financial markets and wanted to help his family earn money they could give to the March of Dimes to cure polio.

Smart as he is, Bill fell for it. Now he's giving Madame Sophia money to invest for him. Every month she asks for more, but Bill never seems to notice he never gets anything back on his investment. I'm afraid that Bill will be bankrupt if I can't talk him out of believing in her. I can't understand why he's so gullible, but he wants so hard to believe that he still has a bond with his son and she's the only way to keep it.

It's so cruel to take advantage of grief that way.

I had heard Mommy and Daddy talk about this before, but Rev. Maxwell wanted to know what Madame Sophia did that made Mr. Reckinger believe her. Dad said Madame Sophia told him ghost stories, and not very scary ones either. In fact, Dad said he'd heard better ones around the fire at Boy Scout camp.

Anyway, Rev. Maxwell asked, "Like which ones?"

And Daddy said, "Oh you know – like the one about *The Little Girl in White.*"

"How does it go?" Reverend Maxwell asked.

I knew Daddy would tell it 'cause he loves to tell ghost stories. I climbed up on his lap so I could hear his big deep voice rumble in his chest. He drank up his coffee and began:

The Chicago version goes like this. During the terrible influenza epidemic of 1918, there was a little girl who lived not far from where we are now. She fell ill with the flu, and no matter what they did, was unable to fight off the disease. As she lay dying in her mother's arms, she cried and cried to see her father, whom she dearly loved, one last time.

The poor mother did not have the heart to tell the child that her father had taken ill, too, and was near death. She told her instead that he would come to her soon, but both father and child died that night.

The old building in which they lived still stands not a block away from here, and they say that in the fall of the year, the child is seen to wander the neighborhood dressed in her pure white shroud and asks each man she sees, "Father, father, please come to me. I need you."

A log on the fire dropped into the grate and we all jumped. Daddy is that good at telling stories.

Reverend Maxwell said, "My mother tells a story like that but hers takes place in a castle on the Scottish moors. She swears she knew people who had seen the little girl."

Dad said, "I think there's a story like it in every culture, and each one swears it's true. Then Mom came in with more coffee.

"Have you seen the fog out there? It's closing in so fast you can't see across the street."

We all went to the window. It looked like someone had hung a big, gray blanket over everything. You couldn't even read the Manny's Deli sign on the corner, and the fog horns sounded like ghosts. I was a little scared, what with the story and the fog and Grandma being in Saint Paul for a while with Cousin Grace's new brother so she wasn't there to read me to sleep.

But Mom said it was time for bed and she would read me a story from *My Book House* that Robbie had given me because he was too old for it now. So we went down the hall to my room. Mom read a story about a boy and a magic sword and a magician, but I fell asleep before she finished.

So I didn't know that Mom and Dad had told Rev. Maxwell that the fog was too bad to drive home in so they would let him have their bedroom and they went to sleep in Grandma's room next to mine.

Anyway, I had one of my dreams in the middle of the night with foghorns and a big white cat. The dream was like the one in a poem the teacher read to us this afternoon. Now the cat was pawing at my window and asking where its father was. I have lots of dreams like that, especially since we moved to this great big place. So, I got up and went to Mom and Dad's room like I always do. Then I went to Daddy's bed and pulled his nose to wake him up like I always do and whispered, "Daddy, Daddy, Wake up! I need you."

But it wasn't Daddy. It was Rev. Maxwell and boy, did he scream! I guess I screamed a little too and ran out of there so fast I nearly tripped on my favorite white flannel nighty.

Mommy and Daddy came out of Grandma's room and turned on the hall light. Daddy picked me up in his arms and told me everything was okay. Then Mom rocked me for a while in Grandma's rocking chair and Daddy carried me back to bed.

In the morning, when Daddy went to call Reverend Maxwell for breakfast, he didn't answer until he had moved Mom's heavy dresser he'd put in front of the bedroom door to keep out ghosts.

Silly man! I'm not a ghost. I'm just a little girl in a white nightgown.

But Daddy says that people believe what they want to and sometimes that makes them do silly things. I hope I don't get like that.

ARE YOU SAVED?
September 1941

One of my favorite ladies in the church was Miss Marigold McDaniel. She was small and perky as a bird and liked to laugh like she really thought things were funny, not because she should.

But Miss Marigold had a cousin who sometimes came to visit, and she never even smiled. Her name was Hazel May Guttmacher. Her hair was big and her voice was big. And when she stood next to Miss Marigold, they looked like Mutt and Jeff, those two men in the funny papers. She lived way far away in Tennessee where I guess everyone needed to be saved from something.

I knew this because at the church picnic in Hubbard Woods she tried to save me. That was a nice place in the country with big tall trees and daisies to make chains to wear round your neck. We had finished our acorn cups and served purple aster cookies on pretty green leaves.

I didn't know Miss Guttmacher was coming until her shadow got there first and made the party all dark. Molly got up and ran. But I was too late.

"What are you girls doing?" she asked in a voice that was dark like her shadow. "Molly and I are having a tea party for some fairies," I answered.

She stooped down and looked me straight in the eye.

"That is the work of heathens," she said, kicking away the acorn cups and flowers. "You must be saved."

"From what?" I asked.

She stooped down and grabbed both of my arms real tight and pulled me to my feet. "From the fires of hell. They are waiting to burn little girls who dine with fairies."

"But I never go near fires, because my cousin Robbie got burnt really bad at Boy Scout camp this summer getting too near the fire. His wiener fell off the cooking stick and dropped into the fire. Robbie tried to fish it out with his hands and they got all burnt. The camp doctor bandaged them up and Robbie couldn't play baseball any more all summer. So I know not to get near fire like that."

For some reason that made Miss Hazel really mad and she squeezed my arms so hard my eyes watered.

"Don't be impertinent," she said, giving me a shake. "Impertinent children go to hell."

"Mom!" I yelled and there Mom was, right behind me. Mom's not so big or as strong as Miss Hazel, but when the lady saw my mother she let go real quick.

"What are you doing to my daughter?" Mom asked, stopping after each word to make sure Miss Hazel understood.

"Instructing her about salvation. She doesn't seem to know the danger she is in of burning in the fires of hell if she continues to talk to fairies and be impertinent to her elders."

Miss Hazel was backing away from us as she talked.

"Well," Mom said in a real mad voice, "you surely will be down there to greet her if you continue to bully little girls with your nonsense. I forbid you to be near my daughter again.

"Come with me Anna. We'll toast our last marshmallow, then it will be time to go home."

Soon Joey and Dad and the rest of the men had got the picnic area all nice and neat, I helped pack up the food. Then everyone gathered around the fire, which glowed in a sort of sleepy way like the sun did as it went down behind the trees. We all stood around the campfire and held hands as we sang, *Now the Day is Over* and *God Be with You 'till We Meet Again*.

There weren't any fires of hell that I could see.

On the way home in the car, Mom put her arm around me and I started to fall asleep. But there was something I needed to know first.

"Mom, what does impertinent mean?"

"It means being sassy or rude."

"But all I did was tell her about Robbie's accident with the wiener so she would understand that I wouldn't go near a fire? Was I impertinent like she said?"

She gave me a hug.

"No, you weren't. She was."

Could an adult be impertinent? That was a brand-new idea.

I would ask Grandma about it when she was home from Minneapolis. But for then, everything was alright. I was saved after all.

IT'S WAR!
December 1941

Dad was right about last Sunday. That was the afternoon when Japanese pilots got into their airplanes and dropped bombs on some ships in a place called Pearl Harbor. The bombing killed lots of sailors when the ships sank. Pearl Harbor – that's such a pretty name for a place where something so bad happened.

I don't know much about what war is. I know my Uncle Charlie who lives up in Saint Paul was a soldier once in something they called "The Great War". That was a long time ago when Mom was young. There's a picture of him in a scrapbook I found in the cedar chest in Grandma's room. He looks like a grown-up Boy Scout in his uniform, sort of like he was proud, but felt a little funny being a soldier. He went to France to fight the Huns and he got shot, but he got better. There is also a real pretty necklace of round pink stones with pretty white ladies' faces carved on them in the chest. When I asked about it, Mom blushed and said they were from a sailor who got them for her in Italy when he was there in the Great War. That was before she met Dad.

I asked if she liked him, but she said it was just a wartime romance. I wonder what that means.

Anyway, last Sunday afternoon Mom was in her room taking an afternoon nap. I was reading *Little Women* with Grandma in her room. Joey was over at his friend John's building model airplanes. It was just like every Sunday afternoon. Then Dad came down the hall from the living room. He looked real sad like he does when somebody's died. He went into their bedroom. I heard his voice and then my Mom said, "Oh no!" real loud.

Grandma put down the book and went to her bedroom door. "Is something the matter, Emma?"

Dad said to come there, he had something to tell us. When we were all together, Dad said, "I have bad news. The Japanese have bombed the American fleet in Pearl Harbor, Hawaii. There's been terrible loss of ships and lives. This means war! We can't let it go unanswered."

Grandma nodded grimly.

"It's been brewing a long time. How many were lost?"

"They think many, many thousands. The ships were all in the harbor like a flock of sitting ducks. It was a surprise attack. The Japanese got most of them."

That night at evening vespers, there were so many people that Dad moved the service from the little chapel to the big church. Everybody was real sad, and when we sang *Now the Day is Over* like we always do and got to the part that says, "Guard the sailors tossing on the dark blue sea…" you heard some people crying. I did, too, 'cause it made me think of all those sailors who didn't get guarded and got killed.

Today, when Joey and I were walking home from school, the newsman on the corner was yelling, "EXTRA! EXTRA! Read all about it! U.S. declares war on Japan. Congress unanimous except one."

Joey was real excited. He and his best friend John had a whole bunch of model airplanes and knew all about what happened in Pearl Harbor and how we'd get big guns and big airplanes and pay the Japs back and stuff. But I don't even like firecrackers, so I think I won't like war very much.

The boys talk about the draft, something about how their number could come up and they would have to go fight, and how they might get to go, too, if the war lasted long enough. Mom and Grandma hate it when they say that and get real nervous, but I think boys think war would be fun.

But it isn't, because Mrs. Williams that goes to our church – her husband was on a ship called the *Arizona* in Pearl Harbor and he got killed and now Jeff Williams, who's in my Sunday school class, doesn't have a dad anymore. Mom and Dad take turns going to see how Mrs. Williams is getting along, but she's not getting along too good. I heard them talking about it and Mom said what a shame it was, and Dad said, "It's only the first." And Mom nodded her head and sighed. I wonder what they mean by that.

BEHIND THE BLACK DOOR
August 1, 1942

Years ago, when we first moved here to Chicago, I noticed a door away at the very end of the hall that runs all the way past our bedrooms. The light from the hall didn't reach there so it looked like it was all black. I could hear lots of funny noises that sounded like somebody was walking behind it, so it was pretty creepy. I didn't want to find out who was walking there, but when I did, it wasn't so bad after all.

Mom had called as she passed my bedroom, "Anna, please come here for a minute. I need your help with this laundry."

T. Bear and I were rocking in my wicker rocking chair. I was telling him a story about a pig that could fly. I wasn't finished so I didn't really want to go, but Mom used her 'right now' voice, so I went.

She was standing by the black door with a big basket of laundry in her hands.

"Please open the door and then put that piece of wood there on the floor into the opening so the door can't shut and lock us out."

I did that while she held the door open with her back.

We turned left into one of those long halls that seemed to be everywhere in this weird house. We were just walking past a door in the wall when it opened, and a tall lady came out. She was skinny and looked like the pictures in my *Mary Poppins* book, except that she wasn't stiff like Miss Poppins, but had a nice smile and when she talked, she had a kind of up-and-down voice like she was singing.

Good morning, Mrs. Mackenzie. May I help you with that laundry basket? No, thank you, Mrs. Olsen. But I'd like you to meet my daughter, Anna.

Taag, Miss Anna. Do you like it here? It's big and scary for a little girl, Ya?

That's why I'm bringing her to get acquainted with the laundry room. Then she'll know where things are and that it's really not so strange after all. Besides, she's my laundry helper, aren't you Anna? The laundry really piles up when you're moving in.

By the way, I do have a question for you about that steel box with the rods inside in the laundry room. Is it really a clothes dryer? How does it work?

Ya, it's a clothes dryer, sure enough. Sven calls it 'Fafnir' because it breathes fire like Sigurd's dragon. But it does get the clothes dry when the weather's wet outside. I'll yust take some cookies from the oven and be right there to introduce you to our dragon.

That would be awfully nice if you have the time. Come on, Anna. We'll sort the first load of white things while we wait.

Mrs. Olsen shook my hand and said, "Nice to meet you, Miss Anna. Sven and I miss our grandchildren. It will be nice to have a youngster around again."

Then she turned and went back inside the kitchen. Those cookies she was baking smelled really good. I hoped she'd bring some when she came back as it was just about time for "a little something," as Winnie the Pooh likes to say.

"Who was that?" I asked.

"That's Mrs. Olsen. She's the custodian's wife. Mr. Olsen takes care of the building and keeps it clean. Mrs. Olsen does the cooking when the church has big suppers and weddings and things."

"Why does she talk like that?"

"The Olsens are from Sweden. Wait 'til you taste some of her Swedish cookies. Are they good!"

"I didn't know other people lived up here. Do they have children I can play with?"

"Their children are grown up and live in California. They have two granddaughters close to your age and a grandson who is three. Mrs. Olsen and Mr. Olsen love them a lot and are often lonely for them. You'll find out. And yes, the Olsens do live here. Those two doors there are to their apartment. But they are very busy cooking and taking care of the building, so you mustn't bother them unless they ask."

And in a few minutes, I found out that Mom was right about the cookies because Mrs. Olsen came to the laundry room across the hall from her apartment with a big plate of them for us. Some were buttery and had pretty icing on them. Some were crispy with ginger in them, and others were chocolatey with an almond on top. I never tasted such good cookies, even when Grandma or Mom or Auntie Marie made them. We all had some, and then Mrs. Olsen explained Fafnir the dragon to us.

This contraption was a great big, long, tall metal box that looked like a freight car they pull behind a train.

Mrs. Olsen opened the doors on its side. There were lots of metal rods that went all the way across the insides from one end of the box to the other.

"You yust hang the clothes on these rods and turn on the heat. See, it works yust like your oven. The pilot light's down here, so be sure it's on when you turn up the gas. I'll be home all morning. Yust call if you need me."

While Mom and I finished sorting the dark colors from the white, I asked her where the Olsen's elevator was and who lived behind the other door I noticed on the other side of the hall at the top of the stairs.

"The other door goes to an apartment for Dad's assistant minister. Remember the young man who thought you were a ghost? He was going to take the job and would have lived there, but after you gave him such a fright, the poor fellow decided he'd find a different place to work." I saw her eyes start to get twinkly like they do when she's about to laugh, and then we both did because who in the world would believe I was a ghost.

"Dad has found another assistant to help him. His name is Richard Smithson. He'll move in tomorrow. You might have heard him yesterday bringing some boxes up those stairs."

"But why didn't he take his elevator like we do?"

"He doesn't have his own elevator. Dad told him he could use ours, but he didn't want to bother us."

"Then why doesn't he use the Olsen's? That would be closer than ours."

"They don't have one either. The people who live in these apartments have to get off at the third floor and walk down the hall to those stairs."

That didn't seem fair to me, and I told Mom so. "It isn't, Anna. Lots of things aren't fair."

"But why don't the Olsens and Mr. Smithson get mad about it?"

"Because if they want the jobs here and the apartments that go with them, they have to accept that they'll be using the stairs."

"I don't care. I'd still be mad."

I thought about that while the washing machine sloshed around the white sheets until they were ready to go through the ringer and get rinsed and go through the ringer again so we could hang them up, but I couldn't figure it all out. Mom says that Joey and I have to always play fair, so why should we have the only elevator? I'll have to see what Grandma says about it.

But I liked the laundry room. It had a nice big window where you could see the top of a tree that grows behind our building. I liked being there with Mom, sorting out the clothes and helping run them through the wringer. It made me feel grown up.

But I liked the *Dragon* best of all.

We hung the sheets and stuff on the rods and when there was no more room, Mom turned on the gas burners on the bottom of the Dragon and it swooshed just like a dragon should when it's breathing fire. You could see the flames through the holes in the Dragon's bottom. Then we started on the next load of wash, while the first one cooked dry like those batches of noodles Grandma sometimes makes that dry over wooden rods.

When we went back to our own door, there was a man just unlocking the door to the second apartment.

"Hello, Richard," Mom said. "How's the move going?"

"Fine, thanks, Mrs. Mackenzie. I don't have lots to move in – just my clothes and books from seminary."

"Well, call us if you want to use the elevator."

"Thanks, but I don't want to bother you."

"It's no bother. Why not at least use it for the heavy things?" Then she introduced me to him.

"Anna, this is Dad's new assistant I told you about, Reverend Smithson."

I knew he was nice because he squatted down so he was the same height as me. When he said, "Hello," I could see his eyes real good and they looked like he laughed a lot.

Then he helped Mom and me carry the laundry all the way to the linen closet near the kitchen, so Mom invited him to stay and have a sandwich. When he left, I asked if he had any children I could play with, but she said he didn't have a wife yet so there weren't any. I wished there were. They would be nice and laugh a lot just like him, and be funny and absent-minded like he was. I've never seen anybody so absent-minded. Take that first day when we were eating lunch.

Dad and Mom and I were sitting at the kitchen table, and Mom put out slices of bread and ham and cheese and stuff to make our own sandwiches. Dad and Rev. Smithson started having a sort of argument about something they called an *extra-Jesus* in the Bible. Rev. Smithson got so excited that he buttered a piece of bread and then turned it over and buttered the other side with mustard and got his hands all dirty.

I had to giggle when I saw the surprised look on his face. Then he started to laugh that really nice, funny laugh, and we all did while Mom made his sandwich for him.

Then one Sunday morning when I was in my room getting ready for church, I heard a knock on the black door and someone talking in Rev. Smithson's voice but sort of funny.

I went back and opened the door. He was standing there with his front teeth in sideways. "Anna, could you please ash your mother to thee if shtee could help me. Ith my teeth."

"Come in," I said and ran to get her.

Mom and Dad both came quickly down the hall. "Richard, what happened? Are you all right?"

"Ith justh my teeth. I wash cleaning them and when I put them in, I thilpped and they went in sidewaths."

"Well," Dad said. "Let's see if I can loosen them. Emma, could you go downstairs and see if Jack Byers has come in yet? He's ushering in the balcony today."

I wasn't too happy about that 'cause Dr. Byers is our dentist, and I was sort of naughty last time we went to his office. But after he came up in the elevator and saw Rev. Smithson's teeth, he was so interested in how they got that way, that he didn't seem to remember that I'd grabbed that water-squirter thing and said not to come near me again or I'd squirt him with it.

When Rev. Smithson told us how he'd lost his front teeth, Dr. Byers shook his head and said, "Young man, you're one lucky fellow it was just your teeth. You could have broken your neck with a stunt like that."

It turned out that Rev. Smithson worked in the kitchen at seminary to help pay for going there. It was hot that day and he decided to take a swim when he got through doing his chores. So, he snuck into the pool at the seminary.

"…didn't turn the lights on. Forgot it was the day they were draining the pool to clean it."

So anyway, Rev. Smithson gave the sermon he was supposed to give, and when he came up for Sunday dinner we wondered about how he'd have done it with his teeth in sideways. I think Joey did the best imitation of that.

Rev. Smithson's gone now. He went to join the Army as a chaplain. He was so jolly. You never knew what was going to happen when he was around. The night he went away, Dad was talking about what a loss that was for the church because he was a good pastor.

"The Army's gain's our loss. Hope God keeps his eye on that young man."

Mom agreed, but then to cheer Dad up, she said with a smile, "But Heaven help the enemy. Richard will probably wander off behind their lines and get the Japanese so muddled they'll bring him back and surrender."

They laughed because they really liked Rev. Smithson. Every night at dinner Dad prays for his safety when we say grace.

But the back apartment wasn't empty for very long.

About a week later, Grandma and I were playing a game of *Fish* in her bedroom, which is right next to that apartment. There were lots of thumpings and bumpings, and then the sound of a trumpet came through the crack in the locked-off door that divides our apartment from the other. The sound was heavenly, like I think the angels must make on those golden trumpets.

"That must be the new music director your mom and dad were talking about last night. He's pretty good on that horn, isn't he?" Grandma said.

"It's really pretty," I agreed. "I'll bet his children really like to hear him play."

But again, I got sad news. Mr. Hummel didn't have any children either. I guess I'll never find a playmate behind the black door.

But even without children, Mr. Hummel was not a disappointment. There was always something going on with Mr. Hummel around.

Take the way he directed the children's choir.

Sometimes singing in the children's choir can be real boring. Just ask any kid. Practice!

Practice! Practice! It's as bad as piano lessons.

But not with Mr. Hummel because Mr. Hummel could move his face around like nobody I ever knew. When he wanted us to sing louder, he would raise his eyebrows so high they almost touched his hair. When he wanted us to sing soft, he'd lower them so low his eyes almost went away. But the best thing was when he wanted us to stand up. He would wiggle his ears. I mean really wiggle them like they weren't even stuck to his head. Really! He could move them around like a cat or a dog. None of us ever wanted to miss that, so we never took our eyes off of him.

Best of all, he loved to give parties for our choir. He would get hotdogs that his wife would cook and bring downstairs to the choir room on the second floor. Sometimes he'd ask Mrs. Olsen to bake cookies, too. That was really fun.

Then one day, Mr. Hummel read about how you could make your own root beer. So, he bought root beer-making stuff and took it up to his apartment and made root beer. He put it in bottles and put the caps on them. Then he took the bottles into the storeroom in the back hall, and later brought some up to his apartment and shared it with us.

"Y'see," he said solemnly, "Root beer has to age to be good. Wait 'til you taste it."

"Not bad," Dad and Joey said when Mr. Hummel took us into the storeroom to taste the result. Mom made a face and excused herself because she said she had clothes drying in The Dragon.

Grandma and I drank our root beer back in her room so we could work on our crocheting.

She had been teaching me to crochet some of the squares like she made for Baby Grace's brother's blanket.

Grandma took one sip, then emptied both glasses into the bathroom sink.

"Ugh!" she said. "We fed better tasting stuff to sick horses out on the farm. If that's root beer, I'm Martha Washington."

But Mr. Hummel thought it was wonderful root beer and at the next choir party served it to the choir. Lots of the kids took their glasses and went out to the water fountain in the hall.

They didn't have any root beer when they came back. See, they really liked Mr. Hummel and they didn't want to hurt his feelings about how awful the stuff tasted.

That night we were all asleep when there was a series of bangs like gunfire going off, then the tinkle of glass breaking. In seconds, we were all out in the hall in our pjs to see what had happened. Joey thought it was an air raid. Mom said, "It's the Dragon. I knew it would explode someday." But Grandma, who never gets fussed about anything, said, "Storeroom," and started in towards the back door. Dad and Joey stopped her.

"Emma. Mother. Anna. You women go to the kitchen where you'll be safe. Joe and I will take care of this," but we followed them anyway. This was too good to miss.

You should have seen Hummel's side of the storeroom – broken glass all over the place and a river of root beer running into the drain in the floor. Poor Mr. Hummel stood there in the mess saying, "Now there won't be enough for next week's choir party. I'll have to buy some ready-made." And there wasn't enough, so he did have to buy some Hire's Root Beer for the party. We solved who got to drink that by drawing straws.

Mr. Hummel said, "Now those who have the shortest straws will have to drink the store- bought root beer. I'm sorry. There was a little accident with the rest. I'll make some fresh for the next party."

What he never knew was that the kids with the short straws thought they were the lucky ones, and some got as high as a nickel to trade with holders of the long straws.

But now the apartment's empty again. There's not enough ministers that aren't chaplains and stuff that Dad can hire as an assistant.

The new music director's something called *4-F*. He lives with his mom in an apartment closer to the college where he works when he's not here at the church. I sort of hoped he might come and bring his wife and some children with him, but Dad says he will stay with his mom because he doesn't have a wife and isn't interested in getting one. I guess I'll just have to give up on having a playmate close by.

I'm sorry Mr. Hummel's gone. He was sort of like a big kid himself, except that I wasn't allowed to call him Warren like I would have been able to do if he really was a kid. So, it's boring with him gone. He went and joined up in the Navy band. They really wanted him because he played a good trumpet and could lead the band. Mrs. Hummel carried all her things through our apartment to our elevator when she moved out. I saw tears running down her face and she look mad and sad at the same time.

At dinner last night, I heard Mom tell Dad that Mrs. Hummel had filed for divorce because Mr. Hummel didn't tell her he was going. He just walked out and signed up. I think he shouldn't have done that because I heard Mom say something about there was a baby on the way. I sure would have liked to have a baby to play with that I could babysit with and stuff.

But everyone's going off to war now. There aren't hardly any men younger than Dad or older than Joey left. Mom's getting worried that the war will last so long Joey may have to go, too.

MARY, MARTHA, AND MOM
May 1944

Right after we moved here, some of the church ladies told Mom that she was "expected to have a maid." She didn't like the idea very much. She had Grandma and, when she had time off from her job at the big house on the lake, Aunt Marie would come and help. And she had me. Before I was even six, she and Grandma were always teaching me cooking and setting the table and polishing silver.

Besides, Mom and Dad had to buy lots more furniture. The stuff we had in Champaign looked like something from my dolls' house in those great big rooms. And you couldn't have parties with no places for people to sit down.

Two men Mom and Dad knew from Mom's hometown lived near us. They were something called *inferior decorators*. They knew lots about furniture and curtains and stuff so they were helping pick out things that would look good in the apartment. Uncle Gus, who built furniture out in Iowa, helped Mom and Dad, too, and pretty soon the apartment looked real nice.

When that was all done, Dad said to Mom one evening, "They're beginning to wonder why we don't have a maid to live in the maid's room behind the kitchen." I didn't know who "they" were and why what "they" said was so important, but that's who Dad said was asking him when he was going to get a maid for Mom.

"I'm sure we can find someone, Emma. Money's tight down in Coal City with this depression having gone on so long. I'll bet there are lots of farm girls who'd jump at the chance to come to Chicago and work. Why not write Cousin Stanton and ask if he can recommend someone?"

"Money's tight here, too, Mack. How can we afford a maid? Your salary's stretched enough without having another mouth to feed and wages to pay."

"We'll manage. They expect us to start entertaining soon. They say there's a room for a maid and we should take advantage of it."

So, Mom wrote her Cousin Stan and he wrote back:

Dear Emma,

I'm sending you the address of Josh Larson's daughter, Mattie. She's a sweet girl and a hard worker. Josh has been having a real hard time of it with four daughters to raise up and him with a really bad back. Mattie's just finished high school with top grades. I think you'll like her.

Yours truly, Stanton

Dad picked Mattie up at the Greyhound Station two weeks after that and brought her up to the apartment. She had a little suitcase. She looked kind of nervous. I knew how she felt. I felt that way my first day here, too.

Then Mom got a letter from Mrs. Olympia Olmstead. Mrs. Olmstead owns the house where Auntie Marie works and has lots of maids and stuff because the house is too big to keep clean by herself like Mom and Grandma have to do.

The letter came in a real pretty envelope with Mrs. Olympia Olmstead and the address in nice curlicues in the back.

It said:

Dear Mrs. Mackenzie,

I am delighted to hear that you have secured the services of a maid. I'm sure you will find her a great help in the manse. May I suggest that when you go to Marshall Field's to purchase her uniforms. Give Miss Waterson in the domestic's uniforms department the enclosed card.

She knows me well and will be delighted to serve you.

Sincerely,

Mrs. Olympia Olmstead

It was spring vacation, so Mom took me along to Marshall Field's as a treat. I love to take the train to Marshall Field's. You get off at their very own stop and walk right into the store.

When we got there that day, there's this man with a red carnation on his coat who greeted us. He looked down at us when he talked, which was strange because he wasn't even as tall as Mom.

"May I help you, Madam?"

"I'm here to purchase uniforms for my maid," Mom said like she did that every day. "Of course, madam. That would be one floor up on three. Please take the escalator on your left."

I like to ride on those moving stairs they call escalators. You can see all sorts of pretty things starting at their bottoms and then going to their tops

75

while you ride up to the next floor. Then you turn the corner and do the same thing again. So, I was sort of sorry it was only one floor up.

When we got to the top of the stairs, we found those giant dolls they keep in tall glass cases were wearing dresses with little, useless-looking aprons and really cute hats. I thought that Mom ought to get one, because she'd look good in it.

"I'm Miss Waterson. May I help you?"

The saleslady was really tall and stood very straight, like our principal at school. When she talked, she sounded like she knew everything right to do and everyone else didn't.

Mom showed her Mrs. Hastings' card.

"Ah, yes!" said Miss Waterson. "Mrs. Hastings…so knowledgeable. And for how many maids will you be needing uniforms?"

"One. Here are her measurements."

"We shall start with the morning uniforms, then, shall we?"

Miss Waterson brought out two sets of uniforms made of a sort of crinkly striped stuff. One was pink and one was blue. They had white aprons with pretty trim that was the same color as the dress and these little headscarves that tied in the back and covered your hair.

Mom said, "We'll take one of the pink."

"May I suggest that you buy two…for when one is in the laundry."

"Of course. I meant two of the pink."

"Very good. And now for the afternoon uniform." Miss Waterson sounded like Mrs. Daniels, my first-grade teacher, when I get my sums right. "Would you prefer the maroon or the gray?"

When Mom answered "Maroon," Miss Waterson laid two of the pretty, dark-red outfits onto the pile without asking how many.

"And now for the formal uniform…" she led us over to the doll I had watched coming up the escalator. I had fallen in love with her dress and decided if I got to wear that every day, I would become a maid myself.

It was made of soft, satiny, black cloth with a tiny, square, white apron trimmed in white lace. There was a crown for her hair, too, all lacy and stiff and grand – she looked like a princess wearing it.

Miss Waterson started to put a second one of these on the pile, but Mom said in the voice she uses when you're not going to change her mind, "One of those will do nicely, thank you."

"And how will you be paying for these, Madam?"

"Charge, please," Mom said, and gave the lady a small, oblong, leather purse.

Miss Waterson took a flat piece of metal out of the purse, looked at it and said, "Very good, Mrs. Mackenzie. I shall put this on your account. Then she went off with the metal thing and came back with it and a paper for Mom to sign.

"The uniforms will be altered to your maid's measurements and delivered by the end of the week. Please give my best wishes to Mrs. Hastings. Good Day."

Mom looked at the paper, then folded it into her purse. I thought we were supposed to be going shopping for dresses for me, but as we got on the escalator, Mom sighed and took my hand.

"Let's go get a hot fudge sundae."

"I thought we were going to look at a new dress for my Sunday best."

"I'm afraid the person getting a new dress today is Mattie. Maybe next month…" But Mattie never even stayed long enough to get all her new uniforms soiled.

She hadn't known until Dad showed her, that our maids had to come in through the back door by the kitchen. She had to get off at the third floor and walk down a long hall to the kitchen stairs. Then she had to climb up the stairs past where we kept our garbage pails and let herself in with her key.

The building downstairs could be real spooky and dark. I only went outside the apartment at night if someone was with me because you never knew who might still be in there. Poor Mattie was more of a scaredy-cat than me.

So here's what happened. On her first day off, she went to a movie at the Bryn Mawr Theater down the street. The show was about some guy who turned into a wolf at night or something. By the time she got home, most of the people who came at night to use the gym and offices were gone, so the halls were pretty dark. But Mr. Krause, who was the Boy Scout leader, was still there straightening up after the troop meeting. Just when Mattie walked past the Scout room, Mr. Krause came out the door to go home.

Now Mr. Krause is really big. He even played basketball in college. So, when this big guy appears in the hall and says in his real deep voice, "Good evening, Miss," Mattie thinks he's the bad guy in the movie. She hollers so loud, she scares Mr. Krause. So, he follows her to apologize for frightening her. This scares her even more and she runs up the stairs to the back door and she's shaking so bad she can hardly put the key in the lock.

Next morning at breakfast, she's gone back to Coal City on the Greyhound bus. Mom read her note to us while we ate our oatmeal.

Dear Mrs. Mackenzie,

Here is my key. I liked you fine. I hope I did OK but I'm going back to Coal City where people don't jump out at you in the dark. He followed me down the hall last night and I got in the door just in time. I near died of fright 'cause there wasn't nobody to help. All your pretty clothes is folded. I took the "L" to the Greyhound station.

Mathilda Larson

When she finished the letter, Mom sighed. "I knew I should have told her not to go to that show. *Frankenstein Meets the Wolfman*...! That would scare the daylights out of stronger souls than hers."

So in a while, we got another maid. She saw we wanted one in the newspaper. Her name was Lucille Hoogestradt. She was born over on Clark Street. Mom said she hired her because she wasn't a scaredy-cat and besides, she was able to wear Mattie's uniforms. I really liked Lucille.

She had me call her Lucy and she had the same pretty gold hair as Miss Hobart who used to stay with me back in Champaign.

Lucy let me come into her room where she'd fix my strait hair in all sorts of waves and curls so I'd really look pretty though she said I looked *snazzy*. And she let me try on her jewelry and listen to the records she played on her leather-covered phonograph that folded up into a little suit-case. They weren't hymns about God and being good, but songs about falling in love and dancing all night and things like that. Some even had a sound you just had to dance to – not square dance like we did at Sunday school picnics either. It was more wiggling, and we'd hold hands and spin around the kitchen if no one else was there.

But what Lucy liked to do best of all was talk about her boyfriends. They were all bad and tried to steal kisses. They drank beer, which I wasn't supposed to tell Mom about, and got fresh. I wasn't sure what that meant because I thought only things like vegetables and meat were fresh. She never explained how a person got spoiled. Can you smell it if they have? Anyway, sometimes she'd tell me she had to slap them for trying to go *too far*, but she never told me where *too far* was.

Lucy was always happy and a good helper for Mom and Grandma. We all liked her. It was like having the older sister that I always wanted.

Then I noticed that her uniforms were getting tight and heard Mom tell Grandma that she thought Lucy was in trouble, so I asked her if she was and she started to cry.

"Oh, Anna," she said. "I have to go away. I'll miss you." And then I started to cry, too. It was all a mystery. Dad said, "What a shame!" And Mom said, in her real mad voice, "Men!"

Grandma started crocheting a new baby blanket, but when I asked her which of my aunts was going to have a baby, she never answered.

So Mom got the maid's uniforms cleaned and pressed and tried to find someone who'd fit them. Dad suggested asking Mrs. Hastings if she knew any trained maids. Soon Mom got this letter:

Dear Mrs. Mackenzie,

I'm sorry to hear that you have had a problem securing satisfactory domestic help. I do indeed have a suitable candidate for the position. My own maid, Elise, has a cousin who has just moved to Chicago from Des Moines. She is interested in fine cooking and is very well mannered and presentable. She was last employed in the home of a well- to-do physician in Des Moines whose wife speaks highly of her skills. Her name is Wilma Griffith. I feel confident that she will be an asset to your household.

Sincerely,

Mrs. Alice Hastings

So Wilma came to live in the maid's room, but she sure changed it a lot. She took down Lucy's pictures of Clark Gable and Tyrone Power and Betty Grable and put up a picture of grapes and oranges and bananas in a pretty dish on a table with a dead duck lying on it. The fruit was okay, but I wouldn't want a picture of a dead duck hanging over my bed like that.

She filled the bookcase with lots and lots of cookbooks and magazines like *Ladies Home Companion* and *Good Housekeeping*. I think she really thought being a maid was fun because I saw her in her room one day practicing little bows and putting on the lacy cap to that black outfit I liked and tilting her head to see how it looked.

But one thing that she did that I didn't think was such a good idea was telling Mom and Grandma how to cook and showing them stories in her magazines that said they'd been doing things all wrong. Everyone in the church knew that Mom and Grandma were really good cooks. Mom's roast turkey was the best and Grandma made doughnuts that made you think you were biting into a cloud.

"It says here," Wilma would say and show them a magazine, "that you should never cook potatoes without their skins on because that's where the vitamins are." Or, "You should try this recipe for devil's-food cake. It uses cold coffee and a hint of ginger to give it that special flavor."

Grandma had been doing that to her devil's-food cake all along and taught me to do it when I was five. But they didn't want to hurt Wilma's feelings because she could be what Mom called *prickly*.

But Wilma kept trying to change the way we lived, but we didn't, especially Dad and that was the problem.

It happened one Sunday when old friends from Champaign came up to Chicago unexpected and came to hear him preach. Of course, he invited them to dinner and Mom said, as she always did, it was fine with her, come on up.

Dad had brought some fat, red tomatoes at the Farmer's Market out on Ridge Avenue on Saturday. Wilma had read in *Ladies' Home Journal* that you had to heat fresh tomatoes over the gas burner so their skin would come off nice. When Mom came up from church and went out in the kitchen to check on her beef roast that had been cooking while we were in church, she found Wilma sitting on a stool by the stove roasting a tomato slowly over the flame of one of the gas burners. She'd stuck it on one of the long forks we use for toasting marshmallows and was turning real slow over the heat so it wouldn't burn in one place.

Mom said, "Hello Wilma. Is that the last of the tomatoes? We'll need them all because we've had some unexpected guests."

"The other one is already peeled and cooling in the refrigerator. This one has a few minutes to roast yet," she said, turning the tomato round and round."

"But we'll need at least six tomatoes. Rev. Mackenzie has invited some old friends from Champaign to join us for dinner. You'll just have to scald the others in hot water. Roasting them will take too much time."

"I can't," Wilma said, sounding real stubborn. "That will destroy some of the vitamin C. It's not healthy."

"Well, then, I'll take care of the tomatoes. You slice some carrots for the relish tray."

"Do you want them julienne?"

"Any way you want, just get them ready."

If Wilma was smart, she'd have known that sound in Mom's voice. But Wilma said, "I'll need to change my uniform if we are to entertain guests."

Then Dad came into the kitchen and opened the oven door and let out the good smell of the rib roast cooking in that special secret sauce Mom uses. "Boy, that looks good!" he said. "How long 'til dinner, Emma? The Ganzerts have to be back on the road by three because Larry's got to get his exam ready for class tomorrow."

Wilma let out a wail.

"Wilma, are you alright?" Dad said, looking shocked.

"I can't stand it," she blubbered. "How do you expect me to cook and serve you properly when you do this?"

Dad looked at Mom for a translation.

But Wilma kept on. "You're always bringing extra people for dinner and coffee and don't care that your tomatoes have lost all their vitamins. And I haven't even got time to change into the black uniform I should wear."

"What did…?" Dad started, but Mom shooed him out of the kitchen and whispered to me to go get Joe and Grandma to help."

As I left, I heard her telling Wilma, "Go get your face washed and put on your black uniform. I'll finish up here."

So, Grandma put the tomatoes in a pot of boiling water to loosen their skins like she always did and Joe got down the dinner plates, and I set out the silverware on the table like Wilma was supposed to have done instead of roasting tomatoes on a fork.

When Mom pressed the little hidden bell for Wilma to bring out the dessert, she came out looking like she'd been sucking lemons and made one of those silly curtsies she read about maids doing in a book she has.

"You rang, madam?"

"Yes, Wilma. We're ready for the dessert now. Anna and Joe will help clear."

Wilma walked through the swinging door to the butler's pantry like she was going to jail.

After we had finished slices of Mom's angel cake with some of her home-canned peaches, Mom rang for Emma to bring out the coffee. Nothing happened.

Mom went out to see what was the matter and found Wilma in her room, throwing her clothes into a suitcase. So Dad wrote out a check for the money he owed Wilma. Then he and Professor Ganzert drove her and her suitcases back to Mrs. Hastings' house. Mrs. Ganzert and Mom and Grandma did the dishes. They teased Mom about her bad luck with maids and imitated Wilma telling Mom how to peel tomatoes, so it wasn't really like work at all.

The next day, Mom and Grandma made the maid's room into a really nice sewing room, which they both wanted more than they wanted a maid.

But Mrs. Hastings and "they" were right about our apartment being too big for one person to clean, so Mom put an ad in *The Chicago Daily News* and Mary came into our lives.

Mary spoke Polish and couldn't read English, but she could speak enough so we could talk to her if we spoke real slowly and carefully like you were talking to a little child. I heard Mom and Dad say that Mary had to leave Poland, where they had lived, because of the war.

She had a nice husband named Vaslav who had read the ad to her. They had a dry cleaner shop on the West Side, but it wasn't making enough money, so Mary had to help people clean their houses. Mom asked her to please come once a week for the day and Mary said, "Fine."

Every Wednesday we all had to straighten up our rooms because every Thursday Mary was coming to clean and we didn't want her to think we were messy. On Mary's "day", Dad would spend the lunch hour with her at the kitchen table with my first-grade reader and then my brother's harder ones until Mary could read and write in English. Then one morning, Mom and Dad, and Mary and Mr. Vaslav went down to where people get sworn in to become citizens, and they got to be citizens and pledged allegiance to the flag and everything. Then they all went out to lunch to celebrate. Now Mary was happy and Mom was happy, too, but Mrs. Hastings often phoned her to see if Mom was still interested in hiring some distant cousin of one of her servants as a maid.

It was forgotten about my Dad driving Wilma crazy with extra guests until this Mother's Day when Dad got into trouble with Mom again. Joe said he saw it coming because every time Dad preaches about Mary and Martha, Mom gets mad.

The story goes like this: Jesus brings this bunch of men called disciples over to this lady's house whose name is Martha. Just like everyone who comes to our house, they're hungry. So Martha goes out into the kitchen to get them something to eat which, I guess, was pretty hard without a grocery store nearby, but she does it anyway.

But Jesus wants to preach to the men, and Martha's sister Mary decides to listen, too, so she sits at his feet like I do sometimes when Dad's in the mood to tell stories by the fire. So, Mary's sitting there and Martha's doing all the work and getting hot and sweaty and stuff. Jesus tells her to sit down and rest and listen to him. I looked up the story in the Bible. It goes like this:

But Martha was cumbered about with much serving, and came to him and said, "Lord, dost thou not care that my sister hath left me to serve alone? Bid her therefore that she help me.

And Jesus answered and said unto her, "Martha, Martha, thou art careful and troubled about many things:

But one thing is needful: and Mary hath chosen that good part, which shall not be taken away from her.

But it doesn't say who's going to get the food and do the dishes and stuff because it's all too much work for one woman. I'm sort of on Martha's side and so is Mom. Once I tried to get away with what Mary did when Dad brought up extra guests for dinner who told really good stories about being missionaries in China, but it didn't work.

Anyway, Mom says, "Why do you use that scripture on Mother's Day? Do you think Martha in the kitchen didn't want to sit down and listen, too – that what she was doing wasn't necessary and important? If Mary had helped, they both could have heard what Jesus had to say. Instead, Martha has to do all the work, shopping and cooking and serving, washing and cleaning up. And He scolds her for it. God forbid, the men could have gotten up and…" She kind of ran down after this. Joe says she's never won the argument, but every time Dad uses that text, she tries.

FIVE GENERATIONS

Marie Gerber
Grandmother

Nancy Jean Carrigan

Edith Hurrie Bohn
Mother

Caroline Carrigan

Brooke Anne Carrigan

Brooke's Song

I take you in my arms to dance with me
as nimble fingers of the March wind strum,
on silvered aspen harps, the melody
that each year calls the longer days to come.

Sere winter lawns are wearing snowdrop pearls.
Crocus rise to greet the warming sun
The gold-washed willows' every branch unfurls
a row of leafy banners. New brooks run

to celebrate the river's quickened pace.
Our captured earth has circled round its star
to birth you safely at this time of grace.
How did you learn, small pilgrim from afar,

to dance so well, to springtime's lively tune,
your dance of dawn that lights my afternoon?

The family in Dad's study.
Nancy holding Amber the white cat. Ralph sitting on the arm of the sofa.

Pretty as a Princess.

Princess and the pony.

Finally! Nicki: The pick of the litter.

Watch out!
Brother Ralph was arrested in Hattiesburg, Mississippi.
It was a dangerous time and place. Chaney, Goodman,
and Schwerner were murdered nearby.

Here comes the bride.
June 27, 1954

Shocking!
Wearing a two-piece bathing suit
on a Chicago beach.

Urbana renewal.
Residence during graduate school
at the University of Illinois.

On the wagon.
Touring through Germany in a VW.

Later in life, the Princess returned to rabbits. Rabbinia Hopinska front cover, circa 1998.

The Princess and Dick began to think about SETI while they were in New Mexico.

The Carrigans' home in Warrenville, Illinois.

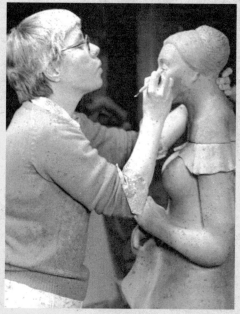

Nancy working in her studio.

An Aspen Anniversary.
Our 50th anniversary celebration with family on top of Aspen Mountain.

THE WHITE CARNATION
May 1945

This has been the worst week of my life. It started last Sunday which was Mother's Day.

Joe and Mom and I had red carnations to wear to church because we all have our mothers still alive. Dad wears a white one because his mother died when he was fourteen, only several years older than I am now. But I feel a lot older than that because on Mother's Day last Sunday…well…

I had a new dress to wear to church. It was a pretty pale blue, my favorite color. Mom bought matching blue ribbon to make bows for my braids, and I was in my room waiting for her to come tie them because Grandma was in Saint Paul and she always ties them for me. It was getting late. Sunday school would start in about twenty minutes. When you live just one story up from your Sunday school classroom, you don't have an excuse for being late, so I was getting worried.

Dad had gotten the red carnations for me and Joe and Mom and his white one already pinned onto his Sunday robe. What was taking Mom so long?

Then I heard her footsteps coming down the hall. Why didn't she hurry? We'd be late for sure. Mom's eyes were all red and swollen when she came into my room that day. I had never seen her look so sad. She took me by the hand and said Dad wanted to tell me something and that we were going to his study. I knew something really bad was going on, because on Sunday mornings we never go into Dad's study because he has to get himself ready for services.

When we got there, Dad put his arms around Mom and they both put their arms around me. Joe was sitting on a chair by the window, just looking out at nothing. I had never seen him like that. He didn't even turn around when Mom and I came in.

"Anna," Dad said, "We just got some very sad news from Saint Paul. Grandma Lowrie died in her sleep last night. Nobody knew she was sick, but she had something called an aneurysm that broke in her brain and God called her to Heaven. Uncle Henry said she had no pain and looked peaceful when they found her."

I had never heard anything before that I didn't want to hear as much. "But it's Mothers' Day!"

Nobody spoke for a while. Joe left the window and came over and we just stood there and hugged. Then Dad moved away and pulled on his black robe with the velvet stripes on the sleeve that he wears to preach like it was very, very heavy.

"I have to go, Emma. You know that Mother would understand, don't you?" Mom nodded. "What about the children? Do they have to go, too?"

"Only if they want to and think they can. It's hard on them, I know, but maybe going and being with friends might help get them through the morning. I can't let the congregation think that I don't believe in God's grace. They'll be looking up to us to see if we can handle our loss with faith."

"You go on downstairs," Mom said. "I know you have to. But we'll have to make up our own minds."

Joe shook himself like he was waking from a bad dream. "I'll go, too, Dad" he said. "Are you coming, Anna?"

I didn't know. Maybe if I pretended Grandma would still be coming home next week, like she promised. Maybe it wasn't even true. Maybe she was just still asleep and Uncle Henry didn't try hard enough to wake her up. Maybe my friend Ellen whose brother just got killed in a car accident would tell me what to do about having something so bad happen.

Maybe I should go downstairs to Sunday school and ask her because we always sit next to each other in the Junior class. That's it. I'll go down so I can talk to Ellen, and when I come back up maybe Uncle Henry will have gotten Grandma awake and it will all be something we'll laugh about at dinner.

So I went down to Sunday school… and Ellen was there. I sat next to her just like always and thought I'd wait until Mrs. Mitchell was through reading some Bible verses before I asked Ellen about…you know. But then suddenly I realized that it was true. Grandma was dead. I burst into tears and ran from the room without even saying I was sorry.

Mom was waiting outside the door. We got in the elevator and went upstairs to the apartment and talked and cried for a while. Then she said she had to go down to services because that was what "they" would expect her to do. When she left, she was wearing a white carnation Dad had found for her. That made me cry even more. She's braver than I am.

I just sat in my room and looked out the tall French windows and thought about Grandma–about how she was always there since I was real little, and how she was my best friend even when I was bad or had done something really dumb. I went into her room and got one of the butterscotch candies she kept on her dresser to give me when things went wrong.

Then I sat in her rocking chair and stared at the dictionary she always kept on the table next to her sewing box. She never let me just say, "I don't understand that word," when we were reading a book together. She'd say, "Well then, we'll look it up." And we did.

She's the reason I skipped a grade last year in school. They said my vocabulary and reading skills were at seventh grade or higher. Nobody asked why I knew all those big words. But Grandma knew, and so did I.

So I opened the dictionary and tried all the spellings that sounded like they were the word Dad said she died from. Finally, I found it.

Aneurysm: A morbid dilation of an artery, due to disease, or to a tumor...

Then I looked up *dilation* and *tumor*, but it still didn't explain why God had to take Grandma away from us. So I just sat and rocked until they all came up from church.

Uncle Henry brought Grandma's body back to Chicago on the train. It lay in a coffin in the church sanctuary so people could come and say goodbye to her and how peaceful she looked and things like that. I tried to listen, but that thing wasn't Grandma, and I couldn't stay near it.

The funeral was Thursday. All the relatives came. Uncle Henry went back to Saint Paul to get Aunt Louise and Grace and Billy. Aunt Mildred, took the train from California where she's a schoolteacher. Aunt Betsy and Uncle William came from Morris where they live in the house that's the same one Mom and her dad were born in.

Aunt Marie and her new batch of Bird Ladies served the coffee in the church dining room, and I guess everyone told Mom and Dad how sweet Grandma was and how much they loved her.

But I couldn't go. I didn't want to hear about God's grace and all. I wanted to just sit in her room for a while and remember her alive and not lying in that box. Some of the relatives got mad at my mother for letting me do that instead of going downstairs, but some understood. I think they would have liked to do the same thing but were scared of what other people would think.

Now a week has gone by. Joey is going to move into Grandma's room. Mom asked me what I wanted most from her room. I asked, "Can I please have her rocking chair and the table with the dictionary on it and the African violets?" Dad brought them in. He set the violets on the window-sill and the chair in the light that comes in from window across from my bed. I will keep that chair with me always so Grandma will never really be gone.

PETS IN A GOLDFISH BOWL
Summer, 1947

When you live on the top of the church where your Dad's the minister, pretty much everyone in the church knows what you're up to and cares about you. That can be really nice sometimes and a real bother some other times, especially when you're fourteen like I am.

The Bird Ladies won't recognize I'm almost grown up and am going to my first year of high school. Heaven forbid they should see me in lipstick. Then there are the other kids. The only guy I know who knows where I live and doesn't mind is Patrick who lives across the street. His building looks a little bit like a castle too, only smaller than the church. It was built for the French Consulate but was made into apartments a long time ago. Patrick's my buddy and sometimes we walk to school together. But he's a hotshot basketball player, and I'm into art and drama so our paths don't cross very much.

The kids in the church know too, but most of the time over at the high school, Joe and I keep it a secret. It's kind of hard for kids to be comfortable with the elevator and all. Lots of them live in elevator buildings like Uncle Robert's, but their elevators don't go right into their apartments like ours does.

Anyway, some of the good things are that you sometimes get nice things from the congregation, like a big, fat, fresh turkey from Mr. Stroski for Thanksgiving, or big boxes of oranges from Mrs. Martin when she goes down to Florida every winter.

Sometimes though, all that goodness cuts down on your choices.

Take, for instance, when I wanted to take ballet lessons in second grade and have a nice pink tutu like my friend Nancy. Dad said I could take modern dance lessons from Miss Megan who was Elder Megan's niece, but that we couldn't afford ballet lessons. I refused because you don't get a pink tutu in modern dance.

Then there was the matter of the dog. I really wanted a dog, especially after Grandma died because that made me really lonely.

We never had a dog in Champaign because we were always giving homes to stray cats who'd adopt us for a while, then go out the alley gate and never come back. Once I had a pair of kittens that the custodian found in the basement window well. They were really cute. One was all black so I called him Blackie. The other was all black except for a pure white spot under his chin so I called him Snowflake.

It was silly to think that if my parents said no to a dog when we lived in a house with a yard, the chances of getting one in an apartment on the fourth floor of a church in Chicago were pretty bad. But I tried anyway.

My parents pointed out that it would take a trip down four floors in the elevator to reach the real grass of the empty lot across the alley where a dog could be exercised. A dog, they told me, would be un-comfortable in an apartment. But what about Uncle Robert? His large, lazy, old bulldog seemed perfectly happy in a one-bedroom apartment on the seventh floor of his building?

They said that the parishioners might not like us keeping a dog in the manse. But Mr. and Mrs. C. had a spoiled, snappy Chihuahua in a fancy flat in the Edgewater Beach Apartments. Other members of the church had dogs. My dog would be the best of the lot. Why would they deny their minister the pleasure of dog ownership?

For several years my parents parried my every request for a puppy. Then they decided on the old "bait and switch" tactic. They tried a num-ber of tricks to get my mind off of wanting a dog. One or the other of the parishioners would help by coming up with something furry.

Then, when I brought up the dog thing, my folks could say we couldn't have one - because whichever parishioner-donated pet that was already in the house wouldn't like it.

The first of these was a pair of pink-eyed white rats from Mr. Heilmann who raised them for laboratories. I was only seven, so I said to myself, "Well, I'll pretend they're little, tiny dogs." I named them Rover and Silvercup and tried to get them to wear little collars.

Amazingly, Rover and Silvercup were kind of fun. They were really tame and very smart, especially Rover, who figured out how to open the latch of his cage if you didn't close it carefully enough when you fed him. Silvercup and he seemed to escape most often on Sunday morning when we were all in a hurry to get to church and got careless with the door latch.

Usually Joe and I got them rounded up before it was time to go down-stairs to church. But one Sunday when all the aunts and uncles and cous-ins were coming to celebrate Aunt Eleanor from Grand Rapids birthday, Rover and Silvercup were really gone. Dad had already gone downstairs to get ready for services. Mom was frantically getting a couple of pork roasts stuffed with apple dressing and tied into a roll so they could be roasting while we were in church. So, Joe and I ran all over looking for the rascals.

Finally, we gave up, washed the dust off of our hands and faces that we'd acquired looking behind doors and in closets, and went downstairs, too. Sunday school was pretty boring that day, so I daydreamed that Rover and Silvercup showed at dinner, maybe sitting on top of the pork roast or covered with icing from the chocolate birthday cake. That, I thought, might be worth all the trouble they had caused.

We let Robbie into the joke when he got there, and the three of us pretended that we saw the rats under the table or in the corner, which got Mom mad because Aunt Eleanor hates rats and Mom didn't want her to know they were loose. Rover and Silvercup never did show up. I wonder if their children are maybe still living down in the church somewhere.

Anyway, I started in on the dog thing again when the rats were gone for good and at Easter, I found a cardboard box by the elevator door with a pretty little rabbit in it. The box had "Stroski's Fresh-killed Poultry and Rabbits" printed on the side, but I didn't want to notice that. Oddly, this new pet was also white with pink eyes, as if he were related to Rover and Silvercup. I really loved him and I think he loved me, too. Dad and Joe built him a small house I painted bright red, and they put it in my sandbox on the balcony. Mom asked the grocer not to take the green tops off of her bunches of carrots, and Uncle Robert got the rabbit a bag of special rabbit food from the same pet store where he got Bulldog Dan's dog food.

I named him Tardy, for the White Rabbit in *Alice in Wonderland* who was always going around saying how late he was. Tardy got to be very big for a rabbit, but he was always sweet and loved to cuddle. He was very smart and never made a mess in the house. He got kind of spoiled and liked lots of attention.

Tardy still wasn't a dog, but he did lots of the funny things like climbing into the little stone arches of the concrete half-wall of the balcony so he could watch the traffic down on Bryn Mawr Avenue. I guess he found all those little creatures on the sidewalk down there really interesting. Mom didn't know about this trick until Miss Marigold McDaniel who lived across the street in the Lakeside Hotel called us. Her room is on the corner of the building just next to the K on the sign so it looks right down on our apartment.

"Oh quick!" she was kind of hysterical. "Quick! Do something!" she hollered into Mom's ear. "Your rabbit's about to commit suicide."

"What?"

"I just saw Tardy climb into one of the arches of your balcony railing. He's about to jump."

Mom put down the phone and ran to my room. "Where's Tardy?"

"Watching the traffic," I said. "Out there." I pointed to Tardy's favorite arch outside my window where Tardy's ears were twitching happily as he moved his head from side to side as he followed some interesting traveler or kept time to the hurdy-gurdy woman cranking music out of her old-fashioned giant music box on the street below. "He does that all the time."

Just then, Tardy backed out of the arch and hopped over to my window to come in for a snack.

Mom got a kick out of that and said, "I'd better go tell Miss Marigold McDaniel." She was laughing all the way down the hall to the telephone.

But I heard her tell Dad when he came home from calling on parishioners who were sick in the hospital, "Mack, I told you that woman watches our every move. I've seen the sun glinting off her binoculars. It makes me feel like a goldfish in a bowl. What are we going to do?"

Dad got that twinkle in his eye that meant he was going to say something I couldn't get away with. "We could get Tardy a cute lady rabbit so they can breed – really give her something to look at."

"Oh, Mack, you wouldn't," she pretended to be shocked, but I heard her stifle a giggle.

A few months later, Dad did bring home a pal for Tardy. He was not another rabbit, but an orphan from the tragedies of war.

One of the sad parts of being a pastor is when people have somebody in their family die.

During the war, the saddest time for Dad was when he had to go and comfort someone who's gotten that telegram that says their son or dad, husband or brother had been killed in the war. It happened a lot, and it was still awful each time.

Mrs. Freeman, one of our elders' wives, had called several years ago to say that her niece Laura, who lived with her, had gotten one of those messages.

I knew Laura Willenbrandt because she was just a couple of years older than Joe. Davie Willenbrandt had been in the Boy Scouts and was already an Eagle Scout when Joe and Robbie were Tenderfeet. Davie was always fun to be with and everyone liked him. The Scouts had a party for him when he enlisted in the Army and were real proud of him for doing his part to beat the Nazis.

Laura loved Davie like crazy. They held hands all the time, and I'd see them kissing when they thought no one was watching. They were real young to be married, but when Davie got orders to go overseas, Laura and Davie went downtown to the courthouse without telling anybody and a judge married them. Davie left the next morning, but he couldn't tell anybody where he was going.

Then there was the big invasion in France called D-Day. The newsman on the corner yelled it over and over again:

Extra, extra! Read all about it. Troops storm the beaches at Normandy. Massive casualties but GI's prevail.

But Davie Willenbrandt didn't. He was killed on the first day storming someplace called Omaha Beach.

Dad spent lots of time with Laura over at the Freemans' house, but when he'd come home he'd tell Mom she wasn't doing very well.

Davie had given Laura a pretty white kitten to keep her company when he enlisted.

"He'll take care of you 'til I get back," he'd said.

But he's never coming back and every time she looked at the cat, Laura started crying because she wanted Davie, and a cat would never take his place. Finally, Laura had to go to a hospital for a while. Laura's doctor thought that maybe the cat reminded her too much of her loss each time she looked at it, so one day he asked Dad if he could find him a new home. Of course, as he did with any needful thing, Dad brought the cat home to the apartment until Laura was well enough to have him back

"Good heavens, Mack," Mom told him when he walked in the door with an enormous white Persian yowling in a cat carrier, "We can't have that cat here. He'll eat Tardy."

"No, he won't," Dad said confidently. "And I promised to keep him, so I can't take him back. His name is Amber after the color of his eyes. Look at him. Isn't he a beauty?"

And Dad was right on both counts. Amber was a beauty and he never ate Tardy. In fact, they became inseparable friends, chasing each other around the house in an elaborate game of tag. First, Amber would chase Tardy up and down the hall to the bedrooms until he pretended to catch the rabbit. Tardy would play dead until Amber got bored teasing him, then he would chase the cat, hopping down the hall in a frenzy until they both got too tired. Then they would curl up together and go to sleep.

Then one day Tardy didn't wake up and Amber was alone.

So when the cat saw someone had left the door open to the reception hall landing, he slipped out into the church building to look for his friend. He was gone for two days, and we sadly thought that he had managed to sneak out the main floor door to the street and was gone forever.

However, one day Mr. Olsen came to the back door with a pitch-black cat with matted fur wrapped in a towel stained with soot. Only those beautiful amber-gold eyes announced that the filthy animal was our missing cat.

As soon as I got home from school, Amber covered my white blouse with soot as we had our happy reunion.

"That cat's got to have a bath," Mother announced. "Anna, go get your old clothes on. I'll run some water in the tub in the maid's room. Bring my kimono when you come, will you?"

So, I put on an old pair of slacks and one of Dad old white shirts and carried Mom's cotton kimono from her closet to the maid's room behind the kitchen. When I got there, Mom was swishing some lukewarm water around in the tub to make some bubbles for Amber's bath. I lifted the cat into the water while Mom stripped off her dress and put the worn kimono over her bra and panties so as not to get them wet.

Like most cats, Amber hated his bath. I think it was because he was so vain about his looks. All wet, he was about half his normal size, his beautiful fluffy tail looking more like Rover, the Rat's than a prize Persian cat's. But being a white cat in a city where everyone heats their homes and offices with either fuel oil or coal, there are times like this when a bath is necessary.

The cat made sounds I'm sure were cat words Grandma never would have allowed. But between Mom and me, we got Amber back to his original silky whiteness. We were both drenched, and Mom's kimono had come untied, but we wrapped Amber into an extra-large beach towel so we could dry him well to keep him from catching cold.

Now, a wet cat is slippery as an eel, and Amber slipped out of Mom's grasp and tore out of the maid's room. He skidded across the kitchen floor and out through the butler's pantry trailing soapy water through the dining room to the living room with me and Mom in hot pursuit. Just as the cat made the right turn into the reception hall, with Mom, kimono flying behind her and bra and panties in full view, Dad opened the elevator door and ushered Elder Freeman into the hall. Mom gamely waved as she ran past grabbing in vain for the belt to her kimono.

"Hello Bill, nice to see you," she waved and sprinted on past.

Elder Freeman did not return the greeting as he thought he had seen rather too much of his minister's wife already. He backed into the elevator without a word and pressed the down button before Dad could follow him. For some Sundays afterward, he blushed scarlet when he passed the collection plate to us.

I hinted to Mom that a dog would not have behaved as foolishly as Amber did that day, but my timing was not good.

Amber was forgiven his transgressions that time. Mom learned which of the vacuum tools best removed white cat hair from Dad's clerical robes. Joe began to tolerate the cat welcoming him home when he arrived late from a date. And Dad happily found a new hobby – upholstering furniture.

And the latter was the cat's downfall. My uncle in the furniture business had a lovely piece of French tapestry left from a custom order. Dad bought it and lovingly reupholstered an old sofa that became his pride and joy.

One day at Sunday dinner, we heard a horrible noise coming from the living room.

Before we realized what it was, the entire back of the sofa had fallen victim to Amber's sharp claws. Dad stared at the shreds of fabric hanging from the frame and I saw that this sin was not going to be forgiven. Soon the cat became the property of another member of the congregation.

By now I was in high school, so the dog campaign received a new twist. "A dog," I pointed out, "will be just the thing to keep you company when I leave for college."

Mom sighed. Her answer this time finally made sense to me.

"When you get married and have your own home, you can have a dog."

So, now I have a new idea about what sort of a man I want to marry. I will watch to see if he likes dogs and if dogs like him. That shouldn't be too hard. Everyone likes dogs.

When I did go to university, my boyfriends never knew that each campus mutt that came as we walked on the quadrangle was a kind of test. If the young man ignored the dog or, worse yet, was afraid of it, I crossed him off my list.

Then, one day, I was going out for coffee with a transfer student from the University of Florida who seemed to attract every pup we passed. And when he stopped to scratch every cocked ear or stroke a hairy back, I knew I'd found my man.

We bought the first of our four loving dogs on the first Christmas after we were married.

OUR OWN G.I. JOE
Fall, 1947

The war's been over for a while now, but they still are drafting guys into the service.

Joe's just about blind as a bat, so we never thought that he'd have to go into the Army, but one day a letter came telling him that his draft number had come up and he'd have to report for a physical. I think the army doctor probably thought that Joe was kidding when he said that he couldn't even read the first letter on the eye chart without his glasses. I guess they thought it didn't matter because he wouldn't have to aim a gun or anything like that since the shooting had stopped. There were still other things they needed him for so they passed him, gave him a pair of the ugliest eye glasses I've ever seen, and sent him off to basic training to learn to be a soldier.

Mom was real unhappy about that. She'd seen how many of the guys came back from the war and was pretty sad at what she saw. Dad, too, was worried that some other kind of conflict might start or something. Uncle Robert, who'd never been in the military, said that being in service would make a man of our gentle Joe. Why would training to kill 'make a man' of a guy? They never said that going in the WAC's made a woman of a girl. So I've always thought that's a pretty dumb excuse for learning to kill people.

Joe wasn't the only soldier in the family by then. Robbie Jr., as he wanted to be called now, had gone to a military academy in Virginia and went into the Army as soon as he was eighteen. Since he had ridden in their fancy equestrian troop and knew how to handle a horse in a parade, he got sent off to Washington to ride in the military parades there. Our other cousin, Tom, Uncle Gus and Aunt Betty's son who was the same age as Robbie Jr. and Joe, had volunteered to go into the Army when he was still in high school. As soon as he graduated, they sent him to basic and then to Paris where he was in a Graves Registration unit, kind of a heavy thing for an 18- year-old guy from Iowa.

But of course, it was Joe I missed the most.

The back bedroom was very quiet and lonely. First Grandma had died, and now Joe was gone. His old pump organ that *Oma* Marie had brought with her when she and *Opa* Mueller came over from Strasbourg sat silently gathering dust, since Joe was the only one in the family who had the energy to pump its old leather bellows. A year or so ago, he'd found an antique set of chimes he'd wired up to the keyboard of the organ somehow and played them at night after he'd done his homework. They stood silent too, gold-colored pipes waiting to sing again.

I missed that and the teasing of his friends Hal and Frank, who took more notice of me now that I was not just a little eighth grader. After all, I'm starting my junior year in high school and they don't call me *Peskyanna* anymore, and instead, tease me in other ways. Their numbers weren't called up, so they had gone off to college. Anyway, I was real glad when Joe came home on leave at last.

One afternoon he came over to our high school to visit some of his teachers he'd liked there. Well, my girlfriends suddenly wanted to talk to me and everything because Joe really looked spiffy in his uniform. But I dragged him off to the art room to show him some of my paintings, then followed him into the band room when he went to see Mr. Michelson who had gotten him started playing the French horn.

Joe wasn't the only soldier who came home on leave that weekend. When we got home from the high school, there was a man in an officer's uniform with a small, silver cross on the collar sitting in the living room talking to Mom and Dad.

I hardly recognized Richard Smithson, Dad's funny old assistant who'd knocked his teeth out in the swimming pool. He seemed taller, somehow, and his face had gotten thinner and his eyes…I don't know how to tell you how they were different, but they were. He hardly recognized me. It had been almost five years and I had gotten taller, too. Then his eyes twinkled for a moment and he said, "Thay, Misth Macthenzie, could you asthk your mother if sthe could help me? Ith my teeth," and I realized that he hadn't forgotten. I ran over and hugged him. We all laughed, because when Rev. Smithson was around, you knew laughter would happen.

Just then, old Mr. Steinberg across the street opened his window and started shouting. You never could tell when this was going to happen because Mr. Steinberg was pretty crazy.

"What's that?" asked Rev. Smithson. "It sounds like he's speaking German."

Dad went over to the window and opened it wider. "He is. Can you understand him?"

Richard went over and stood by Dad. He listened for a while and nodded, "Of course, I can. That's the most elegant German I've ever heard. Does he do that often?"

"Whenever the memory haunts him. Wouldn't you?"

"I feel like shouting out of a window myself sometimes. I was there, you know, with the troops that went into Buchenwald. It was…"

He didn't finish the sentence, but stood there and the new, sad look darkened his eyes.

Dad closed the window, but the wretched voice still echoed in our minds. I remembered what Dad had told me once about what Mr. Steinberg was doing when I complained that I couldn't study when he was going on like that.

"He's trying Hitler for the crime of killing his wife and her whole family and his own children in a concentration camp. He was a lawyer in Dresden before the war. From the eloquence of his speech, I suspect he was a very good one. He's speaking the kind of elegant German your Grandmother Mueller insisted I learn when I was a child. We must be patient with him. His memories have unhinged his mind and he can't help what he's doing."

Soon Mother called us in to dinner. She had made all of Joe's favorite things: roast turkey with cranberry sauce, candied sweet potatoes, fresh rolls, and creamed beans. Aunt Marie had made him one of her famous angel food cakes. It was a wonderful meal, but even though Mr. Steinberg had been called inside by his son, his voice hung over the table like a ghost.

"So, what about it, Richard?" Dad asked finally as he pushed away from the table. "Will you help me serve Communion Sunday?"

"I'd be honored," said Richard, and he meant it because Dad had helped him learn a lot about being a pastor when he worked with him.

After dinner, we all trooped back to Joe's bedroom and Joe managed to pump the old organ back to life. He played real well, too, because he was the organist at the army chapel where he was stationed and had kept in practice. We sang some of the old hymns in the harmonies we all loved. Mom sang soprano. I was alto, with Richard as tenor and Dad as baritone.

Then, Amber ambled into Joe's room and chimed in. I mean really *chimed in*. I'm not kidding. That cat had gotten fascinated with his reflection in the longest gold pipe of the chimes and had learned to hit it with his paw, which sent the whole row of chimes clanging. Richard Smithson watched the performance, then reached down and picked Amber up. I was amazed.

That cat never let a stranger handle him without a fight. Richard stroked the soft fur behind the cat's ears just like he knew that Amber loved to be stroked there best of all. Amber purred like a race car and tucked his head under Richard's chin, an ultimate sign of affection he usually reserved only for me. For that moment, my friend's eyes looked like they once were when I first knew him – warm and content.

At the services the next day, Richard looked very handsome in his dress uniform, and I noticed several of our unmarried single girls coming up to talk to him at the coffee hour. Elder Freeman came over to say hello, because he had always liked Richard. Then Mrs. Freeman came over with a very pretty young woman at her side. It was Laura Willenbrandt.

I had not seen her since Davie died because she had been sick and needed to go to the hospital. But now she looked well again. I heard Mrs. Freeman say when she introduced her to Richard, that Laura was going to the University of Chicago over on the south side and was studying political science and history. Richard and Laura shook hands and started to talk. After that, Richard seemed not to notice that the other women were still trying to get his attention. I just hope someday a man looks at me like Richard looked at Laura that day.

PUTTING ON AIRS AND OTHER SINS
October 1949

Now that I'm sixteen (and I have been kissed more than once), I can finally get an after-school job to earn money for Christmas presents and stuff. So, on Mondays, Tuesdays, and Thursdays I go to the Bluebird Dry Cleaners in a storefront shop of the Lakeside Hotel. I work at the counter taking in clothes and pinning on the ID numbers so we can get the orders together when they come back from the plant. It could be boring, but it's a good place for a writer or an actor to work.

You'd be amazed at what people leave in their pockets at the cleaners, and you can make up all kinds of stories about them from what you find. For example, I think I know who puts those wads of two-dollar bills in the collection plate every now and then, which tickles Dad.

"I wish everyone was as diligent about tithing as our anonymous gambler. Then I could finally get the church out of debt," he'd say when one of the ushers kidded about our gambler getting lucky that week. But I'm pretty sure that the "anonymous gambler" is one of two parishioners. Mr. Talbot leaves betting stubs from Arlington Racetrack in his pants pockets when he brings them in to be cleaned. Or it could be Miss Marigold McDaniel, who places a bet every week with Old Zack, who has the newsstand on the corner.

I once saw her give Old Zack a big hug when he told her she'd won something called the trifecta. Everybody had come into the shop to get out of one of those sudden showers we have in Chicago, and Miss McDaniel had forgotten I worked there. She was kind of embarrassed when she saw me cheering along with Mike O'Shaunessey, the cop on the corner, and my boss, Mrs. Gondelman who has me call her Mavis, and a couple of regulars who had come in to pick up their dry cleaning. When she remembered who I was, she got all flustered.

"Don't worry," I winked at her. "You don't tell Mom everything you see on the balcony and I won't tell on you."

She was so happy about her winnings that she even winked back.

"It's a deal," she said, and I knew that my boyfriend Larry and I could kiss on the balcony all we wanted from then on. Maybe Miss Marigold McDaniel wouldn't put her binoculars down, but she wouldn't tell Mom what she saw with them from then on.

I learned a lot at the Bluebird Cleaners – like that Officer O'Shaunessey knew that the news agent was a bookie, and Old Zack knew that O'Shaunessey sometimes took a bribe instead of giving someone a parking ticket.

And I learned about jazz from my boss, Mavis Gondelman. It seems that Mr. Gondelman used to be called *The Slide Man* before the war because he played trombone in a jazz band before he got drafted. After a shell exploded right near him in the Battle of the Bulge, he lost his hearing and had to retire from playing. But Mavis had some of the records the band had made. We played them on the little suitcase record player she kept in the back room when we were working. Best of all, she knew some of the musicians who played at the nightclub under the El tracks. I yearned to go to *The El Stop* to hear them play, but a jazz bar was strictly off-limits for the local minister's daughter. Mavis's "boys" loved to come in and chat about the good old days when there were lots of speakeasies that had house bands. As I listened to them, I thought that what they did for a living sounded like fun and not sinful at all like my Dad thought it was. And boy, when it came to setting my feet moving, sometimes I just had to dance if I was listening to those records while I was pinning those ID tags on Mr. Talbot's pants.

It's really nice being a senior because you feel more comfortable. Senn, the high school I go to, is big, with lots of halls and staircases going off in all directions. It took a long time just to find out where they all went and in which wing of the building places like the swimming pool and the gym and the cafeteria were.

Sometimes even the school people got confused. Like the time they called my mother and told her that my boyfriend Larry and I were running off together during school hours and that she should do something about it. But my Mom's a first-class mother. She just laughed and said, "I'm quite sure there is some mistake. Anna wouldn't do such a foolish thing. She's far too pleased at being in the *dramats'* homeroom with Mr. Mehlman and the other drama students."

"She's not in that program." the caller said firmly.

"Perhaps you don't think so, but I think if you go to room 121 and ask Mr. Mehlman, you will find that the drama coach will inform you that both she and Larry are in his room. But thank you for your concern. I will ask Anna when she gets home from school."

And she hung up the phone.

So, when I came home from school to drop my books off and get ready to go to the Bluebird Cleaners, she said sternly, "Well, young lady, what have you and Larry been up to?"

"What?" I tried to think of anything we could have done to get us in trouble.

"The attendance officer at the high school just called to say that you and Larry have not been attending classes the past few weeks."

"WHAT!"

Then Mom started to laugh.

"Of course, I didn't believe them and told them so. They said that mothers never believe it when their children are in trouble. At least the attendance office had the grace to apologize when they discovered that they had forgotten to change their records when you and Larry were transferred into the *dramats'* room."

Of course, I was pretty mad that they would think the worst. Larry and I both take our studies really seriously. We both have after-school jobs, and the days when we don't work we have play rehearsals. We don't have time to goof off even if we wanted to.

I can't decide what I like best — art or drama, or maybe physics. Dr. Crandall's got to be the handsomest teacher I've ever had, so I worked really hard in his class. But I'm not so good in math, so maybe that wouldn't work.

But I do draw really well, and I have the lead in next play. We're doing *Our Hearts Were Young and Gay*. It's about two lucky girls who are taking a trip to Europe. It's lots of fun thinking about what that would be like. Even Dad and Mom have never gone to Europe. My best friend, Barbara, plays Cornelia Otis Skinner and I play Emily Kimbrough. Larry and Jeff, who is Barbara's boyfriend, are our boyfriends in the play, too. A lot of the girls are jealous, because the guys are both so cute, but they don't know how long those rehearsals are.

A few of the girls like Dolly Smith are also mad because this is the second play I've gotten one of the lead parts in. Dolly Smith doesn't like that one bit.

"What makes you think you're so good? You're just Mr. Mehlman's pet," she said while we were putting on our coats after school. "It's not fair. You're no better than I am. Besides, you're too short to play next to Jeff and Larry. You look like you're still in sixth grade. It's ridiculous. My mother's going to complain to Mr. Mehlman about it."

I got to thinking about it. Maybe Dolly was right and I was hogging the spotlight like Dolly said. So, I went to Mr. Mehlman and told him that I felt I was getting more than my share, and I'd give up the part to Dolly.

But Mr. Mehlman just laughed. "Whatever put that silly idea into your head? Do you know why I gave you the part of Emily? Because you are the best person to play it. Those girls are nice kids, but they really can't act as well as you can. Now go back to getting the blocking straight in your mind for act two. We have a rehearsal after school today."

But it wasn't as easy as that. When Mrs. Lichtenberg called my parents into her office when I was in grade school, she told them that I tested pretty smart. She was looking for six students they thought could do the work to do double track so I could skip a grade the next fall. Dad wasn't sure that this was a good idea because he had skipped not one, but two grades and didn't like it. The other kids were bigger and older, and it was hard for him to be the youngest all the way through college and seminary.

So, he and Mom called me in to Dad's office when I got home from school that day and told me what Mrs. Lichtenberg wanted me to do.

"Some people will be jealous of you if you do this because they didn't get a chance to do it. They may make fun of you as a 'brain'. But your brain is a gift to be used, not wasted. On the other hand, you are never to feel superior to anyone. Everyone has something to give and will have talents other than yours."

Mom added, "I know sometimes it is hard being a PK, Anna. Some *Preacher's Kids* really feel set apart and think they have to be either too good or too bad to be accepted. But you've got to make up your own mind about what you want to do. If being younger than your classmates will make you feel still more set apart, tell us."

Of course, I couldn't wait to get to the next grade and I said, "Yes, I want to do it."

But I'm uncomfortable that their prophecy has come true. I really want those girls to like me. I don't think I'm "stuck up" like they say — at least I don't think so because that was one thing Grandma wouldn't allow. If I were, I'd still hear her voice calling me "Miss Smarty-pants", even though she's been dead a long time. What she and Mom called *putting on airs* was as forbidden as using swear words.

But why should someone who says they like you want you not to be good at things you're good at? People who are good at things are lots more fun to know. They can show you how to do things you don't understand. Aunt Lillian taught me lots about sewing. My friend Jake, up at Dad's fishing lodge up in Wisconsin, taught me how to play Mumblety-peg with a jackknife, and my friend Jeanne's mom showed me the secret to her super fudge brownies.

Anyway, Dolly's jealous of everybody so she says nasty things about them. She says Joanie Hamlin's stuck up about her collection of cashmere sweaters, and Betty Svenson's blonde curls makes her look too cutie-pie. She's even tried to steal Barbara's boyfriend, Jeff. And she's jealous of my cashmeres, and they're hand-me-downs Mom got at the church rummage sale. I guess everybody would have to give up too much to be friends with her. Maybe that's why Dolly doesn't have any. But I've got to admit, I'd really like a new cashmere sweater for once, and would trade my straight, brown hair for Betty's blonde curls in a minute.

Besides being a *dramat*, the neatest thing I get to do is take Bulldog Drummond onto the field at football games. Our school team is called "The Bulldogs." They didn't have a mascot. So Uncle Robert went to the coach and asked if he would like to use Bulldog Drummond, the nice brindle bulldog Uncle Robert got when Bulldog Dan died two years ago. Since I knew how to handle Bulldog Drummond from walking Dan since I was about six, Uncle R. suggested that I should be the one to be Drummond's handler at the games.

Coach Albertson said, "Okay." So Aunt Lillian, who can sew anything from sails for their little sailboat at Belmont Harbor to a copy of some fancy French design she'd tried on at Marshall Field's 28 Shop, made Bulldog Drummond into the best-dressed mascot in our league. She made him a green flannel coat in the school colors with "Senn" in big felt letters on the side. And to top that all off, she made me a dark-green pleated skirt like the cheerleaders wear and got me a sweater to match.

Mom could sew and cook too, but Aunt Lillian was special. She'd come over to show me how to sew my own clothes. She knew things like how to preshrink wool and cut velvet the right way and things like that. Mom mostly used cotton and wool. Aunt Lillian used silk and lace and always looked really spiffy. Mom said that she was *putting on airs*. But I thought Aunt Lillian looked like a million dollars. She even colored her hair so that she looked like the movie stars she'd seen in Hollywood when Uncle Robert went there to try being an actor.

Ever since we moved to Chicago, Uncle Robert and Aunt Lillian have spoiled me. They gave me all of Robbie's books and hand-me-down toys, like the sidewalk bike I found waiting one day after kindergarten in the long hall that ran from our kitchen to the reception room. It was a red boy's bike and not blue like a girl's bike is supposed to be, but I loved to ride it up and down that hall on rainy days.

They also gave me the complete set of *My Book House* books that Robbie had finished. The pictures in those books are what made me really want to be an artist, and I spent hours studying them.

When I told my art teacher about them, he told me that some of the most famous illustrators in the country had drawn them.

Once Robbie (well, he was Rob Jr. by then, but I never could call him that) got some new riding boots and gave me his old ones. That gift was nearly the death of me.

As I said, Robbie really knew how to ride a horse. The military academy he went to had this horse troop that was in parades and everything. All I ever rode on were the horses on the farm some cousin of my Aunt Betsy had down near Morris where Mom came from. Once a girlfriend and I rode Duchess, a big old Belgian plow horse bareback out in a field at her farm in Michigan. That was like riding a big, flat coffee table. Sometimes my friends and I took a streetcar to the end of the line where there was a stable near the bridle path in Harms Woods and we would hire horses by the hour. That was not very often.

Anyway, the Saturday right after I got my new hand-me-down boots, Larry called me up and wanted to go out there.

"Hey, Annie, want to rent some horses from Mercer's stable out by Harms Woods and go for a ride? It's a great day for it. You call Jeanne and I'll call Jeff."

"Mercer's Stable is way out in the country. I'd like to try Gruber's over on Clark Street. They take the horses over to that bridle path that goes along beside the Outer Drive – you know, the path that runs from the Saddle and Cycle Club on Foster all the way along the lake? My cousin Rob used to work there so I've met Mr. Gruber. I'm sure he'll give us some good horses."

Since I've been a little girl, I've watched members of the Saddle and Cycle Club start out on their beautifully groomed and outfitted horses from their stables on Foster Avenue onto that bridle path. Saddle and Cycle horses always looked as if they'd been polished from head to hoof as they trotted elegantly down the path, their riders dressed in the finest of equestrian wear. Now I had riding boots just as fine as theirs. I pictured one of them passing me on the bridle path and saying, "My dear, look at that beautiful young girl on the chestnut gelding. Doesn't she look elegant?" Well, they looked at me all right, but that's not what they saw. That ride was an illustration for Pride-Going-Before-the-Fall for real.

Larry, Jeanne, Jeff and I had met at the streetcar stop at Clark Street and rode south to the stable.

The stable boy greeted us with, "Mornin' folks. The name's Wayne. I'll be your guide on your ride. You ride English or Western?"

The others all said, "Western."

But I knew better than to ride a clumsy western saddle in boots as fine as mine. Cousin Robbie had told me so. I said in my most confident tone, "English, please."

Wayne went into a stall and saddled a fine-looking bay who acted as if he'd been drinking strong coffee with his oats. The horse danced inside his stall as the guy threw a flimsy piece of leather over his back and cinched the girt tight around the horse's stomach. Then, to my horror, he kneed the animal in the gut. The horse responded with an "OOOOF" and blew out a huge puff of air.

Wayne tightened the girt a little tighter.

"What a thing to do!" I told him indignantly. "You'll hurt him!"

"Not as much as you'd get hurt if you fell off him because the saddle was loose. He's sixteen hands high. You ought to know that's a long way down."

"Sixteen? I thought he wasn't more than ten," I said, not having a clue how many inches a 'hand' was. Wayne laughed like I'd made a joke.

"Hell no, he's really twenty, but we don't like to admit it."

He led the horse out of the stall and tied the reins to the hitching post.

"Come on, funny girl. I'll give you a hand up," and he laced his fingers together. I put my left boot in his hands like Robbie had said to do, and Wayne flung me up onto the horse's back. I grabbed for the saddle horn to keep from going over the other side, forgetting that I, vain fool, wasn't in a western saddle. But Larry, who was watching my act with a puzzled expression from the comfort of his hand-tooled, saddle-horned perch on a horse called "Lazy Boy", reached out and caught me before I disgraced myself.

"Okay. You folks all ready?" said Wayne as he sprung neatly on to a jazzy-looking black horse with a white blaze in the middle of his forehead called "Stardust" and turned its head toward the park just across the street.

"I forgot," I called. "What's my horse's name?"

"Dynamite," Wayne called over his shoulder. "He likes to explode."

Dynamite? That nag was ambling so slowly we barely made it across Clark Street before the traffic light changed. Larry and Jane and Jeff, whose horses were moving at a gentle trot, laughed. Dynamite straightened out his neck, shook his head until the tack jingled and laid his ears flat back and slowed up even more.

We fell farther and farther behind. I was well seated, as Robbie would say, and had my heels down and was trying to post just like Robbie had taught me, but I looked pretty silly trying to move with my horse since the horse was barely moving at all. So, I gave him a little kick with my heels.

Dynamite shied and then blew up. My right boot slipped out of its stirrup as I felt the horse suck in his breath and the girt loosen. I slid side-ways in the saddle and flung my arms around the horse's neck to hold on. I knew I had to get my left foot out of its stirrup before I fell or I'd be dragged like one of those trick riders you see in Tom Mix movies.

The trees in the park went past in a blur and I glanced over my shoulder to see a little girl looking out of the window of a car driving by on the Outer Drive. The silly kid was clapping at what she thought was a bit of

122

trick riding. Finally, I got my left foot free and let go. Dynamite was half-way back to the stables before I hit the ground.

I rolled over and sat up in time to see a distinguished man I had often seen riding out from the Saddle and Cycle Club. He was coming up from behind me, his beautiful, white steed at a brisk canter. I know white steed sounds pretty fancy, but that was a pretty fancy horse. The rider drew his horse up to a well-bred stop and looked down at me from a great height. (How many hands was that beast…about forty?)

"Are you all right, Miss?" he asked.

I jumped to my feet, and laughing gaily, brushed the dirt from my aching backside. "Just a little tumble," I said in my best Katharine Hepburn voice. "The groom will have caught my horse by now."

"Very good, then" he said, tipped his black riding hat at me, and rode on, posting perfectly, his rising and falling in harmony with his perfectly mannered steed in the perfect afternoon sunshine. I hated them both.

A few minutes later, Wayne came toward me from the other direction, leading my mount who was foaming at the mouth. Wayne was whistling *Yankee Doodle*.

"Look what I found," he said with a wicked grin. "Old Gruber's going to be mad you got this gentle horse into a sweat. Get back on. You've got to ride him back."

"Not on your life!"

"Get back on or you'll never be able to ride again."

"That's fine with me," I said.

His voice changed. "Get back on. I mean it. We've got to have Dynamite cooled down before we get back or we'll both be in trouble."

That was probably the first time I ever used one of those forbidden words. Mother would have washed my mouth out with soap if she'd heard me.

"Tsk, tsk…such language from a lady," said Wayne as he gave me a hand up. "By the way, I tightened the girt. Dynamite played a trick on me, I guess. He didn't let all the air out back there at the stables, so the girt was loose."

"Thanks for telling me that," I growled. "My backside feels much better."

Larry, Jane and Jeff were waiting at the stable yard when we returned. Larry rushed up and gave me a hug that, in the condition my body was in, was not the best idea he ever had. And it seemed that the streetcar hit every bump on the way home.

I had one of my nightmares that night. I was riding a horse whose bright-red body was a stick of dynamite with a lighted fuse for a tail. His tail streamed out behind us as he ran headlong towards a giant streetcar with a pure white horse inside. The horse stuck his head out of the window as we flew by and said, "that's all right then," as I felt the heat from the lighted fuse on my back. Then Grandma stood between me and the streetcar, her arms folded across her chest like she always did when I was bad. She was shaking her head and muttering, "putting on airs again." Then I heard the click, click of the streetcar wheels going over joints in the rails, and woke up to the sound of my teeth chattering with fear.

Robbie got his boots back the next day and handed them down to an incoming cadet at his military school who thought they were the greatest boots in the world.

That night, I heard Mom and Dad chatting in the kitchen as Mom washed the dishes while Dad dried, something they often did just to have a little time by themselves.

"It's too bad those boots didn't work out for Anna. After all, Robert bought them with money you gave him to outfit Robbie when he went off to that fancy school."

"Now Emma, you know that was just a loan. Robert will pay it back."

"Ha! Rob will get out of debt to us when Chicago gets a Republican mayor without an Irish brogue."

"…whose favorite pastime is cheering for the Cubs in every World Series," Dad laughed. "Listen! Joe has to have shoes from Payless and Anna has to do with rummage sale sweaters so your nephew can strut around in those fancy uniforms at the Academy. When will you ever learn?"

I quietly got the glass I'd come to the butler's pantry for before I started eavesdropping. Then I went back to my room and thought about what I'd heard. I suppose that if it was true, I should have been mad. But then I figured that Dad probably paid for the coat for Bulldog Drummond and my fancy cheerleader's skirt and sweater that I liked so much. I knew Mom would never have thought of my being the trainer of the school mascot or known how to make a coat for a bulldog. Uncle Rob and Aunt Lillian did. That's why it's always exciting to be around them. But I'd like to thank Mom and Dad for paying for it all, like I thanked Uncle R. and Aunt Lil for doing it. It doesn't seem fair not to, but I can't let on that I was eavesdropping during their private conversation.

BACK TO CHAMPAIGN
November 1950

It has been twelve years since Dad and Mom left the church in Champaign and packed our family off to Chicago to live in what Uncle Rob calls *The Castle*. That change was pretty hard sometimes, but I got used to it. Now I'm back here in my home-town – one of those college women I used to look up to when I was little. I miss Mom and Dad and Joe. My brother got out of the Army this summer and went back to Northwestern to finish up his degree. He's living at home, so Mom and Dad won't be lonely.

Amber's not there anymore. When Richard Smithson, Dad's old assistant, married Laura Willenbrandt, they asked my folks if Amber could come and live with them. That cat loved Richard even more than he loved me and Laura felt like that meant Davie forgave her for getting married again. So, they're really happy and Amber is right where she belongs.

This has been a pretty exciting year for me. I graduated from high school in June. I was eleventh in my class and on the National Honor Society so I didn't have any trouble getting into the University of Illinois down here. It's kind of funny being a college student instead of a PK in pigtails. Professor Ganzert is still teaching agronomy in the agriculture school. I saw him the other day and he hardly recognized me. Of course, I forgot that while I was getting older, so was he and we both looked different. But when he hugged me and said how proud he was of how I had "turned out" it was just like being a kid again. I love that man.

Anyway, high school graduation was lots of fun. There were over four hundred of us in the class. We had a fancy prom at the Edgewater Beach Hotel on Lake Michigan. The moon was full and Larry and I danced outside and walked out onto the pier. I wore a really pretty, strapless dress of pale blue taffeta with a full skirt and an overskirt of tulle. Some people said I looked like June Allyson. I didn't mind that a bit.

Larry looked like Jimmy Stewart in his tux. He's really handsome, and I hated to see him going off to Yale. I'm sure there are lots of pretty girls out East. I've never been there. But Larry's dad went to Yale, and I guess if your dad's gone to Yale, you go there, too. He's going to stay on Cape Cod for the summer, so it will be a long time until I see him again. We talked it over and promised to write each other every day.

Several of my classmates who were also in the Honor Society have come here to Champaign. Sadly, Barbara wanted to go to a smaller school so she's gone off to Knox College in Galesburg. Jeff's here though, and Patrick from across the street. Joanie Engelmann pledged to the Jewish sorority on the other side of campus, and we see each other often. She invited me to dinner at the sorority house, and I sure wish our dorm had their cook. But of course, I'm staying at a house run by the Presbyterians. Mom's on the board, so you can guess how much room that gives me to kick up my heels (and how often they serve liver and onions).

The girls in the house are nice. They assign you a "big sister" to help you find your way around for a couple of weeks. Mine is a senior named Ruth. She's really sweet, though she did shake her head and roll her eyes when I missed the top step coming down to the lobby from the registrar's office and bounced part way down the stairs on my backside. I grabbed the first thing I saw to stop my fall. When I looked up, I found I was clutching the arm of this really distinguished-looking man and I blurted out, "I'm sorry. I thought you were the stair rail." I felt like a klutz, but the man just laughed and said, "That's the nicest thing anyone's said to me this morning. Now, may I have my arm back?"

"Nice going, Anna," Ruth whispered. "You just met the Dean of Students."

But after that bumpy start, things are going smoothly.

There are lots more guys than girls because ex-servicemen from the war are still around studying on the GI bill. They're older, of course. Some have lost limbs and are wheelchair bound. Many have that same look in their eyes that Richard Smithson gets when someone mentions Dachau or Auschwitz. I wonder what they see when that happens. They look like they are watching a horror movie that's playing somewhere in their brains. That may be why they stay pretty much to themselves, because those of us who weren't there can't see that movie, too.

Anyway, college is lots of work. In high school, people like Barbara and Jeff and Larry and I were among the best students in the class. Now the best students from all the schools in Illinois, and even around the world, are here. You've got to work really hard to keep up, instead of being the one everyone else is trying keep up with.

I found this out when I went to the auditions of *Romeo and Juliet*. They nodded their heads and said, "Very nice," and offered me a part in the crowd watching the fight scene between Tybalt and Mercutio. Boy! That was a comedown. I didn't want to attend all those rehearsals and stuff to be part of the crowd in one scene of the play. So, I said, "no thanks," and left. I was miffed but Ruth said, "You turned them down! You surely didn't think that a freshman who isn't even a theater major was going to get more than a walk-on at best, did you?" I told her I had decided it would take too much time away from my studies, but she knew that was fudging because that was exactly what I'd thought. The only good thing that came of that was when Professor Kane in my rhetoric class gave us an assignment to write about what we had learned in the first months of university. I wrote a story called "The Fallen Star" in which a dumb freshman auditions for a production of *Romeo and Juliet* and gets miffed when she isn't asked to play the lead. The whole class laughed at how vain she was, and I deserved that. But I did get an *A* on the story. I even sent carbon copies to Barbara and Larry as a joke on myself.

Barbara wrote back and said she'd done things like that, too, though with the classes so small, her chances are better to get good parts and she's going to play Nina in *The Seagull* this winter.

Larry didn't write back at all. In fact, he hasn't answered my last two letters. I think he's got a new girlfriend. He wrote about a girl named Bunny in his last letter and how she was going to attend Mount Holyoke in South Hadley, Massachusetts. That's one of those fancy women's colleges they have out East. I don't care. There are plenty other fish in the sea. Oh heck! I guess I do care because he's also smart and fun and dances like Fred Astaire. I wish he would write.

But there's this guy on the freshman debating team with me who has asked me out for coffee. He can convince you that *up* is *down*, he's so smooth. He's cute, too. His name is Daniel Webster. His parents must have guessed when he was born that he'd be a real talker. He's asked me to go to the Sigma Chi Fall Fling. It's formal and everything. I'll wear my blue prom dress again. I wonder if he's as good a dancer as Larry.

Ruth, my "big sister" thinks Dan's a little too smooth, but it's not like I'm going to marry him or anything, for Heaven sakes. If Larry's not going to write, I'm not going to sit home on Saturday nights.

This weekend is Dad's Day on campus and all the fathers are supposed to come for the football game. Dad can't stay for Sunday dinner at the dorm like the other fathers can because he has to be back home Saturday night so he can get ready for Sunday service. But I got him and Mom tickets for the big game with Purdue, and he'd never miss that. I'd better clean up my half of the room before they get here. Ruth says it's about time I did that anyway. I'm not used to having so little space of my own. Ruth and I share a wardrobe that's not even half the size of the closet in my old bedroom.

I really like Ruth. She has been like a real sister since I got here. Being away from home, even if I was coming back to where I was born, was a kind of uncertain thing to do. Mom had spent the first part of the drive down here giving me all sorts of advice about studying and behaving myself and boys and things like that. Finally, she sort of ran out of steam and said, "Anna, I've spent seventeen years trying to teach you all these things. If you don't know them by now, it's too late to teach you in the next couple of hours. Dad and I will always love you and be there for you, but you're going to be on your own here. If you do things you know you shouldn't, it will not be someone else's responsibility. It will be yours."

And that was that! So I was really lucky when Ruth came up to me and said, "Hi, Anna. I'm Ruth Mayfield. I'm your roommate for the year and your "big sister" while you go through registration and get settled in."

Ruth was studying to become a high school math and science teacher. She was smart and really patient with my fumbling around. The campus was so confusing to find your way around in. Classes are so large it takes an auditorium to hold them. Everyone seems so sure of themselves. Even the rules at The Presbyterian Dorm for Women were a mystery. But Ruth always laughed when I messed up, and I thought how lucky her students were going to be to have her as a teacher.

But sometimes when I went up to the dorm on the fourth floor where we all slept, I could hear Ruth crying softly in her sleep in the bunk above me. And I never saw her go out on a date, pretty and sweet as she was.

Finally, I asked her best friend Millie why?

"She was to be married in June when she graduated. Hal had already graduated and had a good teaching job in Springfield. They were both home in Chicago last summer when it happened."

"When what happened?"

"They'd been out on a date and Hal had to drive back to Uptown from Ruth's house in Beverly on the south side. It was late and Hal had been up since six because he was working on a road crew for the summer. He fell asleep at the wheel. His car ran off the road and hit a bridge abutment. He was already dead by the time the police got to the scene. Ruth's still mourns for him, though she's better now. She was pretty bad this summer – had a sort of nervous breakdown, and her folks weren't sure she'd come back to school this fall."

"I never knew. Here I go chattering about dates and how I feel about losing Larry to that Bunny from Cape Cod. What a dope I've been."

"Actually, it's been good that you're kind of a klutz. The first time I heard Ruth really laugh since it happened was her telling me about you calling the Dean of Students a stair rail."

"Anything to help," I shrugged and we both laughed about that.

But how I wish I could just put my arms around Ruth and tell her that I'm so sorry about what happened. Would it make her sad and burst into tears? I wouldn't want that to happen.

Or maybe I'll just try to fix her up with someone, just for fun – nothing serious. One of Joey's best friends, Frank O'Malley, is here in graduate school working on a PhD in astronomy. I think I'll work on that…

DECISIONS, DECISIONS!
October 1951

I wonder if the lady I sold a size 40 pair of lime-green pedal pushers to last summer really wore them outside her house. Or if the lady who bought that hat with twelve of the ugliest silk cabbage roses on God's green earth on the brim ever did find a hat she liked. That's what happens when you work in retail like I did all summer vacation. It makes you wonder why people make such screwy choices.

Of course, when I came back to Chicago at the end of my first year at the University, I was a PK again. I probably always will be. But this time it was an advantage. Mr. Peters, one of Dad's fishing buddies and a deacon in the church, is the personnel manager of Mandel Brothers department store on State Street. And now that I am eighteen, Dad asked him if there were any jobs there I could do for the summer.

Mr. Peters said I could apply for work as a roaming clerk. I didn't have a clue what that meant but I went down and filled out the forms and the job was mine. I loved working in the Loop for the first time. I was an honest-to-goodness strap-hanger as I rode the "El" train from the station at Bryn Mawr to the store. There I was, clinging like a monkey to one of those leather-bound straps hanging over my head as the crowded train carried me to another day on the selling floor as a roaming clerk.

That job was harder than it sounds. Roaming clerks don't stay in the same department every day so they can learn the stock and where it all is. Instead, each day they will be sent wherever someone was on vacation or sick or something like that. I sold ladies' hats, sportswear, men's shirts, cookware and just about anything else where they were a clerk short.

If I were going to be a writer, I'd do that every summer. It's a great way to meet people and, like working at the Bluebird Cleaners, I found out lots about what makes them tick. Take, for instance, the lady in the lime-green pedal pushers. I guess she saw my face when she came out of the dressing room to ask me how I thought they looked on her. To be honest, her legs looked like she was wearing two enormous zucchinis stitched together. I even wondered if the size 40 was large enough and feared for the merchandise if she should sit down. But then she said, "I know what you're thinking. *Why would she pick out lime green…a woman that big?*"

"Well, I…"

She let out a shout of laughter as big as she was. "Of course, you were, honey. See, I'm a big girl. I ain't gonna be one of them Powers models. But I got me a good man, and he likes big women and he likes lime green. So do I. I'll bet there won't be anybody buys from you today will have more fun with what they take home than I will. So wrap it up, Tiny." Then she slapped me on the back, let out another shout of laughter, and went back to the dressing room to change.

And you know, I think she was right about having fun with your clothes because the lady who bought the rose-covered hat in the hat department the next day sure didn't. She was small and far too thin. Her face was just cranky-looking somehow. She sat in front of the mirror and had me fetching hats for her for almost an hour.

"What makes you think I would like that one?" she asked when I brought her a little copy of a cloche by Lilly Daché. "It will make me look like a flapper." The straw bonnet was too "cute". The velvet beret was the wrong color, even though it matched the trim of the expensive raincoat she had slung over the chair. The brim of my next selection was too large, the one after that not large enough. She finally settled on the cabbage-rose number, though she was way too small for that hat. It needed a tall, willowy woman and the little lady wearing it completely disappeared under its rampant blossoms. Then, as I put it in a hat box and wrote her bill, she said disapprovingly that our stock of hats was wanting. She was going to check Marshall Field's and return this one if she found something better there. I guess she was just one of those people for whom nothing is good enough. She returned the hat on Monday, and I'm willing to bet she wore it to church on Sunday.

My job was over as soon as the clerks I had been subbing for came back from their summer holidays. I'm back here in Champaign starting my sophomore year, with money in the bank for a change.

Now I have some choices to make, too. My advisor says I have to declare a major by spring so he can get started figuring out what courses to advise me to take. I have "speech major" written in my files, because that sounded like the closest thing to acting, though I wasn't really sure what "speech majors" did when they graduated. Dad knew, however. He said I could make a living at it, unlike drama. That was o-u-t! Uncle Robert's misfortunes trying to make a living in Hollywood made that a no-go. He and Aunt Lillian had come home broke, and Dad and Mom and Dad's sisters and brothers have helped pay their bills ever since. Majoring in art, which I really wanted to do, was even more "out" than drama. The term "starving artist" was very real during the depression in which I had grown up. Mother, who had to give up college and go to work when her father died suddenly, was convinced that it was important that a woman be able to support herself and not waste time on frivolities, like making pictures. So, I had been just muddling along trying to figure out what to major in.

There was also the question of the men in my life. With a statistic like seven-and-a-half men on campus to every woman, I could really pick and choose. Though all of us joked that most of our blind dates were the "half" in the statistic, there were a lot of good guys looking for dates.

All the girls in the house have more than one fellow on the line. At the moment I am writing this, I have three.

As I mentioned, the first guy I went out with here was Daniel Webster. He was a freshman like me but tried to look like one of the professors – all scholarly in tweed jackets with leather elbow patches, and a pipe in his coat pocket that he would take out and go through that 'loading the tobacco' ritual. My friend Joanie Engelmann calls that his *schtick*.

Dan's majoring in political science and tells me he'll be governor of Illinois someday. And he might. He's a good debater. I'm glad he's on our team so I don't have to compete with him. The best thing about him is that he really likes to debate, and if he is getting smoochier than I like, I bring up a subject he's more passionate about than he is about me. Senator Joseph McCarthy's tactics can distract him in a minute. One night he was getting too insistent on going farther than I had any intention of going. I pushed him away and told him he was as pushy as McCarthy at a Senate hearing. Now that obviously doesn't work on most college men, but Daniel took his hands away, sat up straight and snarled, "That's not fair. It's hitting below the belt." Well, since he was aiming in that direction himself, I felt it was not only fair but sheer genius on my part. The only trouble was I had to listen to an hour-long harangue on the Communist witch-hunts, which wasn't really a debate because we both were against them.

The second guy in my life is Jack, the jock. He's on the Varsity Football team and he's a real hotshot tackle. He's not stuck up about being a football hero, but sometimes he falls asleep in the movie when we go to the Coed Theater on Sunday afternoon. Jack is also BIG. When we dance, he towers over me like a giant, and he forgets that when he gives me a hug, he's got about a hundred-pound advantage on me. It's like being mauled by a bear.

I feel sorry for some of the guys on the other teams, but Jack says some of them really play dirty and it's hard not to do the same thing. But he's really sweet, when he can stay awake and hasn't got an arm or ankle or some other part of his body in a cast or taped or something.

Jack was my date for the Homecoming Dance this year. I was really looking forward to it, but during the game somebody didn't get up after a goal line stand and guess who it was?

They say Jack's thigh bone should knit in about six or seven weeks, and the concussion should not leave any permanent damage. Ruth and I went to see *The African Queen* at the Coed on Homecoming night since Ruth still isn't in to the dating game yet. Maybe I'll get to wear my new formal someplace else.

Now I like sports but hearing every play in the game I just saw at the stadium played over and over that evening at Katsina's can get a little dull. There's a cheerleader who lives over at the Delta Gamma house whose got her eye on Jack. Maybe I just drop out of the picture and let her have him. I don't think we really have a lot in common, Jack and me. He deserves better than someone who really doesn't care much about where the tight end goes on a fourth-down play.

Then there's Sven Elfstrom. Sven's an engineer. You can tell because when he gives you a hug, he always forgets to take his pens and slide rule out of his shirt pocket. Sven reminds me of a big old Golden Retriever my Uncle William used to have down in Morris. His hair's about the same color and tousles over his forehead in a way that makes you want to push it out of his eyes. He's quiet and enjoys sprawling in front of the fire in the living room of our dorm and just holding hands and looking at the flames. He loves being an engineer and talking about how you build bridges and roads and things. He's very good at drawing elevations of plans and making things that are pretty dry and dull sound interesting. Sven's also a guy who gets really devoted to a girl. He brings me flowers and candy and opens the door of his light-blue Mustang when we go out on a date. That Mustang's really neat. Since students aren't allowed to keep cars on campus, he's really lucky his Aunt Gennet lives in Urbana and lets him keep it in her garage. Sven's sort of safe – you know, the kind of a guy you could bring home to your mother and she'd start baking cookies for him and planning what she'll wear to the wedding.

Last Saturday he asked me over to the Triangle house where all the fraternity members are engineers like Sven. They were having their annual Apple Cider Party. I couldn't wait to go to the party. I love apple cider and doughnuts when the air starts to get crisp and the leaves on the paths in the quadrangle crunch under your feet on the way home from class.

We could smell the wood smoke from the bonfire in the yard behind the fraternity house as we drove up in the Mustang. There was a vat hanging from a tripod over the fire and the hot cider with clove-studded apples floating in it smelled like something you should bottle and sell as a perfume labeled *Autumn Magic* or something like that.

Sven went straight to the bonfire and ladled out paper cups of cider, then brought them and some doughnuts to a blanket he'd laid on the lawn. It was perfect. Sven leaned back with one hand behind his head and the other caressing my shoulder. It was all very romantic, complete with full moon and one of the "brothers" playing *September Song* on his guitar.

Finally, Sven got to his feet. I started to get up, too, but he said, "Wait there. I'm going to get more cider."

"And more doughnuts?"

"Okay. Be right back."

But instead of going to the vat over the fire, he went around the side of the house and disappeared. I was perfectly happy on the blanket listening to the music, so I didn't notice where he'd gone.

"Got us some of the special house cider," he grinned and handed me a cupful.

Now I'm the original *lips that touch liquor shall never touch mine* girl. Both my Mother and Grandmother were members of the Women's Christian Temperance Union. They weren't exactly disciples of Carrie Nation and her saloon-destroying ax, but we didn't dance with the 'demon rum'. One time when Mom was sick, the doctor prescribed a couple of teaspoons of brandy in some hot water every two hours. Mom said she'd rather die first and got well immediately.

The first taste of the applejack just tasted strange. After a half of the cup, there were several bonfires and two Svens. I realized first, that this was not my mother's mulled cider; and second, that I had no stomach for alcohol, especially 80-proof apple brandy drunk on an almost empty stomach. Fortunately, the brandy and I parted company almost immediately, and whatever Sven had had in mind for the rest of the evening went with it.

Thank goodness everyone in our house slept upstairs in a common dormitory. I was able to sneak up to bed and sleep it off before the house-mother saw me. It would have been just my luck to be caught by that paragon of virtue with liquor on my breath. She'd be on the phone to Chicago in a minute.

But the other good thing about that night was that my mother would never have to worry about a drunken daughter getting into trouble when she was away at college. Mother Nature took care of that because I swore I'd never feel like that again. A lot of the other girls thought it was a way to spend the evening, so I was always the one who had to hold their heads as they got rid of a night's indulgence into the toilet.

I heard later that Sven finished off a good share of the apple-brandy brew those engineers had made in their attic still. I found out that everyone on campus except me knew about the Triangle still and the Apple Cider Party. I guess I've led a sheltered life.

But ever since I met Mrs. Olsen in the back hall by the laundry room, I've had a weakness for Swedes. Sven called up the next morning and apologized for not knowing that I couldn't drink booze, which I hadn't known either. I did make another date with him. And so, he continues to woo me in his taciturn, Scandinavian way.

I love that word "taciturn." It was one of those hundreds of words Grandma made me look up in the dictionary when we were reading books together. But when it comes to a date, it can cause some heavy going. Sven expects me to supply all of the conversation when we go out. That seems to amuse him, but it's a lot of work. Sometimes I wish he would joke or tell me what he thinks about things other than how much weight a truss can hold on a bridge. He even seems to structure our kisses like he's designing in his mind where our noses should go and how he will compensate for the differences in our heights, and he still keeps a slide rule in his pocket just in case he needs help doing it.

So, the fall is slipping into winter and I figure Mr. Right is still out there someplace because he sure isn't Mr. Right Here.

But I have finally found a major. I'm really interested in writing and design. The place where those two skills go together is in the field of advertising. At Dr. Wilson's suggestion, I've decided on a journalism major where I can hone my writing skills and pursue my art without Mom and Dad thinking that I'll starve to death without Mr. Missing Man of My Dreams.

BUT DOES HE LIKE DOGS?
November 1951

Maybe it wouldn't have happened if I hadn't just gotten a letter from Larry last Thursday telling me that he and Bunny were engaged and all former girlfriends (What! Why plural?) are to understand that the Rabbit had an exclusive. I don't know why I was surprised, or even why I minded. We hadn't seen much of each other during vacation last summer. Larry had gone to Cape Cod again, and our letters had been dwindling to almost nothing. But still, you know how it is. Sven was out of town. Dan was dating a poli-sci graduate student, and the coach wouldn't let Jack date until he got his grades up to snuff. My latest back-up boyfriend was an ag student who, when he found out I was a city girl, told me he could only date girls who would want to become a farmer's wife.

Anyway, I had sworn off of men that week and so had no date after the pep rally the night before the game with Ohio State. A group of us who lived in my dorm and in the Phi Gam house next door were standing around in the alley between our two houses sort of joking around in the dark, when someone came up the alley literally whistling *Dixie*.

141

"Here comes the Old Seminole," laughed Jake. "Hey, Antonio, come on over here. I've got some of the women next door who are dying to meet you."

"No more than I am dying to meet them," the singer said, and ambled over to where we were standing.

So, Jake introduced Tony to me and Irene and Ellen, my roommates.

It was impossible to see his face in the dark. I just liked the sound of his voice and that southern drawl. But he took each of our hands and sort of nodded his head over them like he might kiss them. It wasn't hammy, just sort of different, sort of *Gone with the Wind*-like.

"Would one of you ladies care to accompany me to the movies tonight? I hear that the film at the Coed is really terrible."

"Wow," said Irene, "How could a girl refuse unless she'd seen the movie last night with her steady boyfriend like I have."

"Sorry, but my guy Bill and I are going out to Katsy's for something to eat." Tony looked at me.

"Why not? I've sworn off men, but not movies, just so you know where I stand."

"I can see you're really enthusiastic, Miss…Anna, is it? I'll call for you in ten minutes. Shall you be waiting in the parlor?"

"No, I shall be waiting in my room for you to ring for me."

Now there was a good reason for this. There was a closet on the landing from which we could see our blind dates before they saw us.

That gave a girl time to have her roommate go downstairs and tell him you had come down with some communicable disease if he didn't come up to snuff.

When Tony came to pick me up, Irene, who was doing look-out duty for me while I was combing my hair, came up from the closet to my room and said, "Go! If you don't, I will," which was a big joke as she and her steady Mike were practically engaged.

The movie, as Tony had predicted, was truly terrible. The acting made me cringe. The writing was worse. Everyone was snickering half the time, and it wasn't supposed to be a comedy. When the heroine came on the screen and the hero turned and drew her to him while the camera closed in on his lecherous gaze, Tony said, in what I later found passed as a whisper for him, "Sex rears its ugly head." Everyone around us burst out laughing. It was that southern drawl that did it, and I had to admit to myself that I maybe wasn't really going to give up men after all.

After the movie, we went down to the local coffee shop and got coffee and a doughnut and talked until I noticed the clock on the wall.

"Oh, boy! We've got to run or I'll be locked out."

He got me in the door just as the housemother was coming down from her apartment to lock up. He gave me a quick kiss and said, "Tomorrow? After the game? Steak and Shake?"

"Okay."

"I'll phone you up in the morning."

He gave Mrs. Hammerschmidt one of those little, courtly bows and got out of the door before she slammed it in his face.

"Who was that young man? I don't recall seeing him before?"

"Tony? He lives next door. Just transferred up here from Florida. He's nice."

"Tony. Does that mean he's Italian?"

"I don't think so."

"Well, good night."

Mrs. Hammerschmidt locked the door and watched me go up the stairs to my room.

I was seething when I got to my room. That woman is the snoopiest person I know. She seems to feel that she ought to know every single detail of my life so she can report to my mother. We wouldn't want my mother to hear that I might be dating an ITALIAN! That might mean he might be CATHOLIC. Oh, my goodness! What would the Mackenzies say if she let that happen! I'll bet she was wondering right then whether she should call Mom and Dad and tell them that their daughter was on the verge of going to the Papists.

Why would it matter if he was a Catholic? Grandma was a Catholic before she married my Scottish-Presbyterian grandfather and they were very happy. Besides, Tony's full name is Anthony Paul Herrington. He was raised an Episcopalian, and we had a date to go to the Presbyterian campus church next door on Sunday

But that was Mrs. Hammerschmidt. She was always jumping to the worst, wrongest conclusions. Take last week, for instance. Melody Allen had a really bad fight with Luke Douglas, the guy she is engaged to marry. She came home in tears and I asked her what had happened. "I don't want to talk about it," she sobbed and ran upstairs to the dormitory to have a good cry. The dormitory is a good place for that on Friday night because almost nobody goes to bed early on a date night. So, all the bunks up there were empty, and it was the most private place in the house then.

Melody wore herself out weeping and fell asleep with her clothes on and that was the problem. No one saw her come in except me. She hadn't called her roommate Gloria to sneak her in the side door after lock-out time, so Gloria got worried because it was an hour after curfew and Melody's clothes weren't strewn all over the room as they always were when she came home from a date. So she looked in the closet, and the dress Melody had worn wasn't there.

The other house members she talked to didn't know where Melody was, so Gloria went to Mrs. Hammerschmidt to see if she had heard from her.

Mrs. H. hadn't seen Melody either and jumped to the conclusion that the naughty girl and that lecherous Luke had run away together. So she called Mel's parents at about 1 a.m. to warn them that every mother's second worst fear had come true.

I'd had an art project due on Monday, so Tony had dropped me off early so I could finish it. But the hubbub in the halls interrupted me. Gloria was standing out in the hall crying. The other girls were standing around her looking serious.

"What happened?"

"Oh Anna, didn't you hear? Melody's run off with Luke. Now she won't graduate. And her parents are really upset and everything."

"When did this happen? I didn't see her come down from the dorm, and I've had the door open all evening."

Dawn breaks slowly after midnight. "Dorm?"

"When?"

"Let's go look."

Gloria was the first to reach Mel and wake her up. Melody was really puzzled to see all the girls in the house chattering around her bunk.

"You better go down and report to Mrs. Hammerschmidt," Gloria said. "She's going to be really mad."

"What did I do?" asked poor Melody, who was one of the best-behaved girls in the house. "She'll explain," someone said, pointing at me as the rest of the girls scurried downstairs and prepared for bed as quickly as possible.

The next day, Melody was still mad and I was along with her. I remembered how furious I was in high school the time they called Mother and told her that Larry and I had run off when we'd been in class the whole time. When Luke heard, he was mad, too. Then he took Melody in his arms and said, "Running off? What a terrible idea to put in our innocent young minds!"

That cracked us all up. I slipped away while they settled down to some serious making-up. But Mel's parents didn't see anything funny about being awakened at 1 a.m. with such a story.

They wanted her to move to the Lincoln Avenue dorm, but she said she didn't want to leave her friends. Mrs. Hammerschmidt never forgave Melody and me for getting her into trouble over the whole thing.

You'd have thought that she'd have learned to lighten up after that, but she was watching from her post in the front parlor when Tony picked me up for church. She had to be impressed by his nice gray dress suit, white shirt and gray and blue stripped tie. One of Dad's elders couldn't have looked more proper or, in my eyes, more handsome. He said good morning to her. But I was so tired and still mad at her, I just nodded, took his arm and went out the door.

"Trouble?"

"No, just miffed." And I told him the story.

"Too nice a day to be miffed," he said. "Let's forget church and take a walk."

"But…"

"She'll never know the difference. The guys at the house told me she's really an Episcopalian like me. Didn't you know that? Haven't you wondered why you never see her in church?"

"I guess I never noticed."

"And why do you think she's so proper? Didn't you say you had to wear formal gowns to dinner every Wednesday night to learn to be a lady? That's the kind of thing my mother would have wanted for me if I'd been a girl."

Tony minced down the street as if he were wearing high heels and a long gown. He looked so ridiculous, I forgot to be mad, and burst out laughing. Then he took my hand and we ambled off down to the quad to scuff up the autumn leaves falling from the giant elms arching over the sidewalk.

We talked and talked – not like Sven and I did, but each having something to say and sometimes saying nothing as the dry leaves crackled under our feet. We came to one of the benches lining the walk and sat down. Tony put his arm on the back of the bench and I laid my head on his shoulder and watched the leaves drifting down onto the lawn.

The dog was one of those indiscriminate mutts that somehow always find their way onto the quadrangle, and occasionally onto the football field during the games. He was part spaniel with long, silky ears; a ridiculous, out-of-control tail; and big, brown spaniel eyes. In his mouth he carried a battered tennis ball, which he rushed up and dropped at Tony's feet.

"Hi there. This what you want?"

He patted my shoulder, removed his arm from my back and took the ball in his hand. "Go get it, boy!"

The ecstatic dog loped across the leaf-strewn grass, brought the ball back and adoringly dropped it at Tony's feet again. I watched to see what would happen. Tony picked up the ball and tossed it again, over and over until the dog laid down panting at his feet. Tony got out a clean handkerchief and wiped the doggy spit off of his hands.

"Sorry," he said, "I'm a sucker for dogs. Now, where were we?"

"Right here," I said as I put his arm around me again and reached up and kissed him.

147

THE END OF THE BEGINNING
January 1953

It's my birthday tomorrow, and Tony and I are going out to the Illini Union where the food science chefs practice their craft by staffing a nice restaurant in a corner room of the building. The food's really good. It's a special occasion place for us.

We both worked all last summer, so there is a little for nights like this.

I had a job at an insurance company in Uptown reading claims. Each one of those claims was a little novel in the making. I loved to make up stories about people like the man who crashed his car into the west wall of some Methodist church downstate when a hornet got in under the cuff of his pants and worked its way north. But it got mad as a hornet does when someone slams it between his legs to keep it from reaching the North Pole, so to speak. You had to feel sorry for the guy.

And there was the lady who…but I'm getting off the subject.

Tony was assigned to Sheppard Air Force Base in Texas learning to fly. He'd done well in his studies in the Air Force ROTC and was supposed to be there for the whole summer. So I was surprised when he called me up in July and said, "Hi! Want to go out on a date tonight?"

"How? Where are you?"

"I'm home at the folks. I got discharged."

"Discharged! Why?"

"They saw in my records that I was asthmatic. They've decided not to let anyone stay in the AFROTC unless they can fly and asthmatics are disqualified. So here I am."

I'd known that Tony was asthmatic when he was young, but since he had come north the climate seemed to cure him. And now with a medical discharge…

"So that means you won't be drafted?"

"I think so. I've been discharged. Besides, that mess in Korea is winding down. I don't think we'll be involved much longer. Now how about I drive over, unless you've got another date." He paused.

"Are you kidding? How soon can you get here?"

We had a lovely reunion. It was a Saturday night, and I didn't have to get up at the crack of dawn to catch my bus to go to work the next morning. The time slipped by so fast that it was well into Sunday morning when he left to go back to his parents' apartment on the south side.

By the next Monday, Tony had gotten a job as an orderly at the hospital where his mother worked and we settled into a nice summer routine.

One night, Tony finally asked me to wear his fraternity pin. Since I had known almost from the minute I met him that he was the man for me, I of course, said, "yes." From then on we were committed to each other.

Sven was decidedly chilly when I picked up the phone the next day. He asked if there was "someone else" and had more to say during that phone call than in the whole time we were dating.

So, the summer passed in a nice, summery way with Tony coming over to have dinner on the balcony where Dad had set up a barbeque and the flower boxes on the railing were bright with red geraniums and blue ageratum. Tony and I would sit outside on the porch where he would tell me about the latest excitement at the hospital.

Would you believe that one of his jobs was to swat the flies that got into the operating room? I will not go into the stories of the brain surgeries he explained in detail, the excitement clear in his voice. I was afraid he might become a doctor, which would be a bad fit for me, with my phobia about doctors, dentists, and any place involving shots, drills, and distasteful medicines. The fact that these stories were accompanied by the smell of the ether that had permeated his clothing during the day did not endear me to the idea of becoming a doctor's wife.

But he returned to campus in the fall eager to get back to his true love, Dame Physics, and I got into my new major/minor in the journalism and art schools, which turned out to be a good fit for me.

Everything was going great when the letter came. It was a cheery greeting from Tony's draft board in Florida where he had registered when he was eighteen. The letter announced that his number had come up and gave the date when he was to report for his physical for induction into the Army. And what about that medical discharge? Apparently, it was just a piece of paper and he was classified 1-A. Right at the beginning of his senior year, he was being drafted.

It turned out that he could get a deferment until he graduated and that's why he's still here to celebrate my birthday.

But what about summer? They'll just be waiting for him. I have decided to see if I can go back home and go to Northwestern. I've had just about enough of Mrs. Hammerschmidt who tracks every moment of my life here. She's worse than a whole flock of Bird Ladies.

At the U. of I., you can take your senior year away and still get your diploma from the University, so I asked Mom and Dad if I could come home and go to school at a university nearby. I've never really gotten away from being a PK here at the Presbyterian House. With Mrs. Hammerschmidt, and the minister at the church next door being a buddy of Dad's, I might as well go home and be a PK there. The food's better and Mom's a lot more understanding than Mrs. H.

But for tonight, it is snowing one of those drifting, fairyland snows that makes halos around the old-fashioned street lamps lining the walks of the quadrangle. Tony's in one of his mellow moods, having just been asked to participate in a graduate seminar in Optics. The basketball team's set to win the NCAA. The Illini football team won the Rose Bowl. Life is good.

When he brought me home just at curfew, Mrs. Hammerschmidt was at the door locking up. Tony did his Southern Gentleman thing and she melted, as she usually did. Since she found out that he'd been an Episcopalian altar boy and had nice manners, she's decided that I am not good enough for him, rather than the other way around.

I had just gotten up to my room and was brushing my hair, when I heard myself being serenaded. The voice sounded well-oiled and the words of *Fiji Girl* were a bit fuzzy around the edges. Knowing Tony's penchant for bursting into song at odd times, I thought the worst. But Tony had said he was going to study tonight for another exam, so he'd be up most of the night.

Certainly, the romantic singer was not he.

I peeked out the window and saw Jake, the guy who had introduced us. He was standing in the swirling snow proclaiming that I had not been properly serenaded since I'd been wearing Tony's fraternity pin and he was curing that slight. Such a thoughtful, off-key gesture! I was quite touched.

Mrs. Hammerschmidt was definitely not. I heard her coming up the stairs and down our hall proclaiming in her best housemother voice, "Does anyone up here know that young man? His behavior is quite unsuitable and if you know him, I suggest you tell him so before I call the authorities."

We all shrugged and said we didn't have a clue who it was. Of course, everyone including Mrs. H. knew I was the only girl dating a Phi Gam. After Mrs. Hammerschmidt left, I heard Tony's voice gently persuading his friend that the concert was ill-timed and that he'd ask the brothers to serenade me properly. Mrs. H. heard all this and Tony rose yet another notch in her estimation, especially since she had been told that his mother was actually born in England. I threw that in when she was prying into his background. Mrs. H. is a hopeless Anglophile.

But this will be my last semester of real college life. I have already applied for a transfer in the fall and will have my interview in a few weeks. My grades are good and my dear advisor, Dr. Westerfeldt, supported my decision with a glowing letter of recommendation. He and his wife- to-be had been separated during his service in WWII, and he knew my feelings about staying here without Tony. But we have no idea how long he will be gone or where he will be stationed.

Korea is not a finished story, and it is still dangerous over there.

LIFE AMONG THE STARS OF STAGE, SCREEN AND BASEBALL
Summer, 1953

Tony is in his last week of civilian life before he reports to Ft. Campbell in Kentucky to begin basic training as a soldier. We are spending as much time together as we can, but soon he will be gone.

After graduation, Tony took a draft-deferred job in some research project at Firestone Tire and Rubber Company in Ohio, while I moved back to Chicago. He was there just six weeks when the Army drafted him. We had just a week together before he left for basic training.

Though the Korean War was winding down, men were still being sent over there to fight. Who knew where he would be sent? So we spent as much of that week together as we could.

Every evening after I got off work at the famous Edgewater Beach Hotel on Sheridan Road, he'd come pick me up at the mail desk where I was the clerk. It would have been a dream job if I hadn't known he was going away. I was the mail clerk at one of the most glamorous hotels in Chicago. The Edgewater Beach Hotel and its companion building, the Edgewater Beach Apartments, occupied several blocks of choice real estate facing the shore of Lake Michigan near the posh grounds on which The Saddle and Cycle Club has its very elegant and very private clubhouse and stables. It was there, as you remember, that the antihero came on his blasted white horse to observe my ignominious unseating off of Dynamite, the horse from hell.

At intervals along a shoreside path between the two buildings are comfortable benches facing the water. From the benches you can see a wooden pier built out into the lake from the hotel. This is the famous Boardwalk with its curved iron lampposts blooming with softly tinted glass pendants in the shape of lily-of-the-valley blossoms, which cast a romantic glow on the elegantly dressed couples taking a break from the dancing taking place on the shore.

Since the apartments are kitty-corner from the church, and since Dad and the hotel manager know each other, it was inevitable that I would interview for a job there this summer. I was given the assignment of clerk at the mail desk where the guests came to collect their messages and mail.

Working at such a famous place has been a dream job for me. It is better than the dry cleaners for studying people, the rich and the famous who come to visit or perform at the Boardwalk, or the ballplayers who stay at the hotel when they are playing the Cubs at Wrigley Field. And it had some lovely surprises.

One afternoon a couple of guys from the Milwaukee Braves were standing by my desk flirting as usual.

"What'd you think of the game today? We was pretty good, huh?"

"Did ya see Charlie and me pull off that double play in the bottom a' the eighth…"

"And Big Max's homer that won the game top a' the ninth."

"Yeah! You should come and see us play."

"It's the least you can do, babe," said Big Max as he leaned on the mail desk and grinned what I was quite sure was a well-practiced smile.

"You are our hostess, ya know."

"Can you get off for the afternoon tomorrow? I've got two tickets in the players' box right in front of first base." He took them out of his pocket.

My boss overheard this exchange and since he was a real nice guy he said, "Go ahead, Anna. I'll cover for you."

So I called Dad's office.

"Are you busy tomorrow afternoon?"

"I've got to work on Sunday's sermon and meet with Jim Freeman about…"

I broke in, "Some guys on the Braves team who are staying at the hotel stopped at my desk just now and gave me two tickets in the players' box for the game tomorrow. Mr. Madison's given me the afternoon off. Can you come?"

"What's game time?" he asked.

I guess even a dedicated parson can be tempted in Chicago. Dad and I had a great time just being ourselves together, a rare occasion because it seemed that Dad was always on call to answer the needs of what he called *his flock,* considering that his calling was as much *pastor* as it was *preacher.*

Another delight of my job was listening to the tales of Conan Ahern, the house detective. Conan and I ate lunch together in the staff cafeteria.

I loved listening to his stories of goings on at the hotel and he was a born storyteller. There was one about the newlyweds who managed to make off with their honeymoon mattress. There were other tales of spectacular parties, lewd behavior and downright crime, tales of indiscretions that later often made the gossip columns in the newspapers the next day.

My favorite was the story of a famous ballplayer whose wife shot him when she entered their room to find him in bed with his mistress on game day.

Mrs. X had been shopping in the men's department at Marshall Field's for some new underwear for the guy when she heard her husband's name mentioned.

"Shame he couldn't play today. That slide into second in the fifth yesterday must have been worse than it looked."

Slide into second in the fifth? Not playing today? "Honey, can you go down to the Loop tomorrow and get me some of those undershirts I like at Field's?"

Well, the lady put one and one together and decided she'd better get back to the hotel. The fool had made three errors that day: first was the mistress, of course; second was the lie about the game; and third was having bought his wife a small "lady's" handgun that he urged her to carry on the tough streets of Chicago.

Luckily, she was so mad when she got back to their suite and found the lovers together, her aim was bad and nothing worse happened than a bill from the hotel for shooting down one of their chandeliers – and the fact that her husband wouldn't find it too easy to slide into second for a while.

Lots of famous people come to dine in the hotel restaurant, the Marine Room. And on the outdoor stage by the Boardwalk, Tex Beneke and the late Glen Miller's band played all the Glen Miller favorites for dancing. Mr. Beneke once asked me to the rehearsal for opening night. The rehearsal was held in a small meeting room near the kitchen. Wow! It took the rest of the day to get my hearing back after listening to that big band playing full out in that tiny space. I wondered how the musicians do it all the time, but I wouldn't have missed it for the world.

Xavier Cugat came for a couple of weeks with his Latin rhythms. He and his wife, the singer Abby Lane, were staying in one of the nice suites and were really sweet when they came to get their mail. One sweltering hot day, Abby came to pick up her mail wearing a full-length mink coat, which she clutched around her as if she were cold. When she reached over to pick up the mail, two Chihuahua pups peeked out from the fur. She tucked them back into her famous bosom with a sheepish smile.

"I know dogs aren't allowed, but they're so tiny. You won't tell, will you?"

"What dogs?" I said, "I didn't see any dogs."

She beamed at me, and when their gig was over, Mr. Cugat gave me a nice tip.

Great aerial view of the Edgewater Beach Hotel

Members of the teams playing the Cubs stayed at the hotel if they were white. I didn't realize that the black players had to stay at another hotel on Clark Street until the Teachers' Union booked a luncheon in the main dining room one day. I heard a fuss in the lobby and watched the teachers group protectively around a well-dressed African-American lady, while their leader had a heated discussion with Francois, the maître d' of the Marine Room. Then the whole group turned and marched angrily out the front entrance of the hotel.

I asked Conan at lunch what had happened.

"Well, now, lass, those teachers didn't know when they made their plans to have their luncheon here that the hotel don't let colored folks into the dining room except as busboys. But that Negro lady you saw was one of their officers and they said either she stayed or they'd go, and Francois said she couldn't come in so they left."

I'd never heard anything like that. One of my favorite people was Miss Molly, the cook at the Reid's apartment in the Edgewater Beach Apartments. Mr. Reid was one of the largest contributors to the work of the church, always ready to help someone in need or contribute to some special emergency fund when the church needed one. This gentleman, chairman of a large oil and gas company, once took the afternoon off when I had the mumps as a little girl, went to the toy department at Marshall Field's and brought me a charming little doll he had bought.

But Mrs. Reid is an awful snob. A fading photograph of *Courtland*, the family plantation in Virginia, hangs in the most prominent spot in their living room. She considers that this makes her some sort of an aristocrat in the state of Virginia, and she never lets you forget it. I think she even looks down on her sweetheart of a husband who, in spite of his enormous wealth and his generous philanthropic interests, she sometimes disdainfully calls her "hardscrabble husband."

Whenever we were invited for dinner, I would get nipped by her obnoxious little rat terrier while she would retell plantation stories in her gracious southern accent that never seemed to fade despite living in Chicago for thirty-five years.

Ah just had the cutest ol' pig when Ah was a girl like you. Mandy *had the run of the house. Ah dressed her like a darky woman with a shawl and a bandana on her head. She wuz just the smahtes thang there was. Smahter than some of the field darkies, ah declarah. But they wah loyal, both the hands and the house nigrahs. Did y'all know Miss Molly wuz the dautah of mah nanny. We wuz raised up to gethah.*

Now Miss Molly was one of my favorite people in the whole world. She reminded me of Grandma and when Grandma died, she helped me come to grips with my loss. Even when she was in the midst of making some of the best dinners in the world, she loved to chat as I sat on the kitchen stool. And she really seemed to care what we were talking about – school, cooking, songs, whatever.

Her speech was much less hard to understand than that of her mistress, musical, sort of.

I was devastated last winter when Dad got the call from Mr. Reid that Molly had died of a heart attack suffered when she was cooking dinner. Mrs. Reid had this to say about her faithful servant:

Ah just knew thair was something wrong when she came into ma livin' room an sat down. She would nevah had done that in her raht mand.

Now my Aunt Marie was the cook at the Smithfield's and she didn't eat with them, so I hadn't found it strange that Miss Molly didn't eat with us at the Reid's. But the idea that she couldn't sit down in the Smithfield's living room at any time, let alone a dire emergency, or eat in a restaurant if she wanted to, was a surprise.

I guess I should have known about things like that, but Dad and Mom entertained people from all around the world and would never have thought of excluding someone because of the color of their skin.

I remember the day of the annual spring Women's Luncheon Benefit for some missionaries in Africa when Mom came upstairs in one of her "exasperations" as Dad called her snits about people who were acting foolishly.

"Amelia Lou Reid drives me crazy with her thoughtless ways. Why is she still living in the North with that plantation mentality? Her daddy may have raised her like a lady to the manner born before he had to sell *Courtland* to pay off his gambling habit, but he forgot to teach her the manners of a lady."

Mom's exasperations always amused Dad a bit because Mom was small like me, but in an exasperation she'd be six feet tall.

"What did Amelia do today?" he asked.

"Well, the luncheon was a big success. We raised about four hundred dollars for the mission. When those of us on the committee were finally able to sit down in the kitchen to eat, I called Louise Daniels and Mrs. Olsen to leave the rest of the cleaning up and come to the table and have their luncheon while the dishwashing machine finished cleaning the last of the dishes.

"When Louise sat down, Amelia stood up, took her food and marched out into the dining room. She ate there by herself at one of the empty tables. She told me later it was because Louise is colored. She said I should not have put her in the position of "havin' to sit at a table with a nigrah or leave."

The nerve of her! I'd rather eat with Louise any day.

But back to the hotel. For a while we had a resident elephant living out back in quarters right on the beach. The beast was part of one of Dorothy Hild's extravaganzas on the Boardwalk.

The Dorothy Hild Dancers are quite famous, and people come from all over to vacation at the hotel and take in the nightly shows at the night club.

One of the things that had baffled me since I started working at the mail desk was the cubby hole across from the mail desk and about halfway down the huge lobby. Against the wall, near the signature four-sided fireplace, some hand-carved wooden screens were arranged into a small room-like space. The entrance was screened by large potted palms so the people entering the space had a furtive look about them.

A man came in every Tuesday, Thursday and Saturday dressed in an authentic Scottish Highlander kilt, white shirt and black tie, flawlessly brushed sporran and a Highland jacket. The fellow would disappear behind the screen for most of the day, but I never knew what he did there.

Then one day, I noticed my very favorite resident of the hotel, Mr. Reckinger, come out of this mysterious hide-a-way. He looked as if he might have been weeping, but he smiled when he saw me. He made his way to the mail desk as he did every afternoon. He handed me, as he did every day, a single red carnation that matched the red one he always wore in his lapel.

"For you, my dear," he said, handing me the flower.

I thanked him and gave him his mail, most of which was, as usual, related to his apparently large interest in a chain of restaurants scattered throughout the metropolitan area. He laid an elegant leather-bound book he had been holding under his arm on the counter while he went through the mail, handing me unwanted brochures and notices that I would discard for him.

While he was sorting his correspondence, I glanced at the title of the volume. The title, stamped in gold, read:

Reaching Across the Divide
How to contact loved ones
Who have passed over.
By Reverend Stuart Maxwell

"He's quite wonderful, you know," said Mr. R, noticing my interest.

"He has put me in touch with my son, Paul, who passed over during the polio epidemic.

Ah! You would have loved Paul. He would be just about the age you are now."

"The name, Stuart Maxwell, sounds familiar to me. Do you know him?"

"You don't know who he is? He has that little chamber over there," he answered, pointing to the structure of palm-hidden screens.

"Reverend Maxwell is the most renowned medium in Chicago. He has not only let me communicate with my dear son, but recently he has reached my beloved wife, Maude. She died last year still mourning the death of our Paul. He was our only child, for after he came she could never have another.

"Maude tells me that she often talks with Paul. He is happy there, she says. The two of them watch over me and miss me as much as I miss them. Sometimes I wish…"

He paused, and I didn't want to know how he would finish that sentence. Then he sort of shook himself and brightened up.

"They have said that I should help Reverend Maxwell in his work so that he can help other people have the joy of communicating with their departed. That's why I financed the publishing of that book," he said gesturing at the one on the counter.

"It's a beautiful piece of work. May I have a look inside?"

There was no doubt that the Reverend had spent a considerable amount of Mr. R's money in the production of the volume – endpapers were of the most elegant Italian marbled paper; the type was handset type and printed on archival paper.

The last page of the book contained a photograph of the man in the kilt, white shirt and brushed sporran I had seen going into the cubbyhole.

He had the thick, perfectly-silvered hair of so many Scots. An errant lock fell engagingly over one eye. His deep, blue-green eyes were dark and penetrating, almost mesmerizing and strangely familiar.

Mr. Reckinger continued, "The good Reverend is fitting out my place in Highland Park to become a Center for Study of the Paranormal. I haven't lived in the house since Maude died.

Twenty empty rooms and all of them haunted. Too big and lonely for an old fellow like me. Living here in the hotel I have company – the dining room staff, the housemaids, a lovely mail clerk to give carnations to, and of course my dear Reverend Maxwell. He will inherit my worldly goods when I pass over. It will be the least I can do.

"You really should meet him. He is a remarkable man. Come along with me. He'll be ending his three o'clock session in a few minutes."

I locked up the mail, left a note on the counter and followed Mr. Reckinger down the long-carpeted lobby. Entering the palm-sheltered booth was forbidden to the employees of the hotel, but Mr. R. was everybody's favorite and no one bothered because I was with him. The Scotchman looked up from shuffling papers from his recent client.

"Stuart, I'd like to introduce my lovely mail lady."

"But I have already met Miss Mackenzie a very long time ago. It is lovely to see you again. I hope all of the family is well."

"Very well, thank you, and yours?" I used the PK's ploy of throwing the question back at the questioner while you try to remember who in this great world he is and why he knows all about you and you can't remember a single thing about him.

So, we chatted for a few moments about plans for the Center and I praised the elegance of his book.

"It looks so interesting. May I borrow a copy to show my father?" Mr. Reckinger spoke up quickly.

"I will do better than that. I would be delighted to give you one. Reverend, would you sign a deluxe version to Miss Mackenzie for me?"

Reverend Maxwell did so with a flourish and handed it to me. "Do give my best to Dr. Mackenzie."

That night at dinner, I showed Dad the book and asked who Stuart Maxwell was and how he knew who I was. Dad laughed and said, "I wondered when you'd meet him. You changed that rascal's life, you know."

"How? I don't even know him."

"Ah, but you do. Do you remember one night when you were little going into our bedroom when you were having a nightmare?"

"And I pulled his nose. His screaming was worse than the nightmare. It scared both of us half to death? How could I forget?"

Tony, who was having one of his last dinners with us before he had to report for his physical, laughed when he heard the story.

"Bet my Mom would love Maxwell's book. She can tell the creepiest ghost stories and I'll swear she believed every word she's saying. One of them is about an old rocking chair in her family home in Chester that rocked all by itself on nights when the moon was full."

Tony slipped into a British accent.

"Creeeek, creeeek!" he moaned. "The chair would cry like the voice of a dead child. And when you felt the seat, it was always warm, as if a living body had been sitting there. I've had a phobia about rocking chairs ever after," he said solemnly and we all burst out laughing.

It was a funny story, of course. But as the laughter died, Dad got an angry look on his face. "I knew that rascal was after Reckinger's money. What a cruel racket!" I almost felt sorry for Rev. Maxwell. When Dad gets that crusader look in his eye, somebody's in for a hard time for sure.

Tony watched Dad carefully, surprised at the changed look on his face.

He's been in awe of my father since the first time they met at a basketball game not long after our first date. My folks drove up about noon in the big, black Cadillac sedan Dad drives, so he claims, to be able to give rides to mourners at funerals. He got out of the car dressed in a plaid wool shirt and knit tie. Tony stared at his short, muscular body, the black overcoat over one arm and the Cuban cigar clamped in his teeth.

Raised on stories of Chicago gangsters driving murderous, black Cadillacs, he turned to me and whispered, "I thought you said your Dad was a Presbyterian minister." We still laugh about that day when he thought he had been conned into thinking a hoodlum's daughter was the daughter of a man of the cloth.

But now Tony's gone.

We write every day, but I did not see him until Thanksgiving, when his mother and I went down to Kentucky to visit when he was given a day's leave. Mrs. Herrington, usually a rather subdued person, had a sparkle in her eye and was acting very mysteriously. She never let her purse out of her sight and clung to it when she dozed in her seat on the train.

We took a cab to the post and checked into the guesthouse on the grounds of the Army base. After working at the Edgewater Beach, it was, to say the least, a come-down. The walls were Army drab, the window shades drooped, and the beds were iron-framed cots. But Mrs. Herrington didn't seem to mind. Tony got off guard duty at four o'clock and came right over to see us.

They say a uniform does something for a man. Even though nothing really fit him, Tony looked wonderful to me. Mrs. Herrington looked the other way while we kissed and then slipped something into Tony's hand. Tony kissed her and said, "Thanks, Mom."

Mrs. H. gave an exaggerated yawn and said, "I'm going to my room for a nap. That train ride was exhausting."

Tony went to the window to pull down the blind. It fell off in his hands.

"Well," he said. "So much for privacy. Come here," and he wrapped me in his arms and whispered, "Boy, have I missed you."

When we came up for air, he took the small package his mother had given him and undid the wrapping.

He sat me down on the rickety chair by the rickety desk and got down on one knee. "Miss Mackenzie, will you marry me?"

"Private Chesterton, I never thought you'd ask."

He slipped a diamond ring from the box and made our engagement official. It wasn't the Edgewater Beach, but it was good enough for me.

Mrs. Herrington tapped gently on the door and said, "May we go to dinner now? I'm hungry." Tony looked at me and winked.

"Aren't we all."

When Tony was finished with his basic training, he was sent to another army post to wait his permanent assignment. This could have meant anything from a posting as an infantryman in Korea to stateside technical work. The policy is that the army would look at each man's qualifications and decide where the service got the most for their money from the draftee.

There were a group of newly graduated physicists and engineers in his group and one man who had just finished his degree in Classical Languages. You can guess who got sent to Korea and who got sent to the large missile proving ground in New Mexico. I wonder if any of the Koreans got a chance to learn Latin and Greek.

HERE COMES THE BRIDE
May 1954

It's almost over. Finals are coming up soon and my undergraduate life is nearly finished. It's been almost a shock, coming back to the Castle after three years away. Life as a commuting student is a lot different than living on campus. There is, of course, none of the campus Rah!

Rah! stuff. It's pretty much: *Get up, dress, eat breakfast, walk to the "El" and get on the train, get off the train, walk to the campus, go to classes, come home, study, write Tony, go to bed.* Repeat daily until weekend arrives. When the weekend arrives the only thing that changes is no class, just homework.

I wasn't really bored, though. I was carrying a heavy class load and both the art courses and the journalism classes had a lot of homework. I had to adjust to a new set of professors and fellow students. My classes at Champaign, however, had prepared me well. Some of my teachers had studied there. In fact, the textbook on typography had been written by the same professor who had taught me at the University of Illinois. Nonetheless, I had gotten off to a rocky start when I applied to transfer to Northwestern.

When I went in to the admissions officer, he sat me down and looked at my grades and the listing of the extra-curricular activities in which I had participated at the University.

"Hmmm. Your grades are good…and you were inducted into Torch, I see," he said, mentioning my membership in the honorary society that welcomed active students with good grades.

"I see you did some theater work as well…managed Star Course and acted on the campus radio station. Do you like acting and things like that?"

"Yes," I said. He frowned at that for some reason.

"And I see that you're wearing a fraternity pin. Are you planning to get married?"

"Yes, when I finish school."

There was a long pause while he shuffled some papers. "Well, I'm afraid I will have to deny you admission."

I was flummoxed. My grades were good. I was "well-rounded" in my activities. I had good recommendations from my professors.

"Why?" I asked when I found my tongue.

"Because I don't feel that you are a serious student."

"Because I'm planning to get married? Is that it?"

"Well…"

"Do you ask your male applicants if they are planning to get married?"

"It doesn't matter with them."

I jumped out of my chair and gathered up my material.

"And it doesn't matter with me either," I said and marched to the door. I'm afraid I slammed it as I left.

When I got home, I stomped back to my room and slammed that door, too, I guess rather loudly because Dad heard it all the way in his study. He came and tapped on the door.

"Anna, is something wrong?"

"Go away. I don't want to talk to any men right now…even you."

"Anna, what happened? It can't be that bad."

I opened the door. "It's bad as can be. That jerk denied my application."

"Did he give a reason?"

I told Dad what had happened.

"He has no right to do that to a woman student," Dad said in a voice that I hope he never uses to me. "I think I'll make a phone call or two."

"No! I'm not going to pull strings. They either take me as I am or I'll…"

"Now listen to me," Dad said. "He gets away with that kind of thing because no one calls him on it. Who knows how many other good women he's denied entry because he thinks they might marry. He's still living in the last century, and it's time for him to get into the twentieth."

"If you decide not to go to school there, fine. But that practice should end, and end now." Dad walked out of the room. This time it was he who slammed the door.

A few days later, I got a call from someone from the journalism school asking me to come back for another interview. I told Dad I wouldn't go. But he used the same *if he gets away with it with you, he'll keep doing it to other women* argument and finally talked me into going.

Everyone was sooo nice, I should have been pleased, I suppose. But...
well, I went and I'm finishing my year there, but I'll remember that first
interview for a long time.

But Dad had been right. I heard from my roommate in Champaign
that she also had an experience somewhat similar to mine. I got a letter
from her with a return address in Carbondale, home of Southern Illinois
University. It read:

*You know what that fossil who heads the Paleontology Department told me when
I went in to register for classes in his department this spring in Champaign?* "There
will be a woman in this department over my dead body."

I said something like, 'Don't tempt me,' *and stomped out. They're a little less cal-
cified down here and I decided to transfer so I can major in paleontology like I wanted."*

I sure hope if I have a daughter, she won't be treated like that.

But I've got other things to think about now that my wedding day is
only a month away. I wonder if I'll recognize Tony when he gets here
for the big day. He's been living out in the desert in New Mexico testing
rockets. Will he have changed? Surely there's been nothing in his letters to
show that he has, but still, it was Thanksgiving when I last saw him.

He writes me about his life, like the fact that he and his buddies have
to eat old C-rations left over from the last war. The cook throws them into
hot water and boils them until they're hot. And this is a man who hates
even SPAM.

Or, about one of his Army buddies who tried to smuggle a prostitute
he'd met in Juarez across the Mexican border back to the base to what
purpose one could only guess. Tony wrote:

*Jack got drunk on tequila in a bar in Juarez last night. That nut claimed that,
being trained as an experimental physicist (at least that was his excuse), he should experience what the lady was selling. The hooker looked like a kid if you didn't look too
closely. She told him that she was supporting her family in a poor farming village nearby*

and that without her 'fees' her ancient grandmother's chickens would die of starvation because she wouldn't have money for grain. That broke Jack's heart.

"She's so young ... so beautiful," he cried into his shot glass. "I can't leave her in this sordid place.

"I know!" he says, all bright-and-bleary-eyed. "We could put her in the trunk of the car. No one would look for her there. Come on, guys. Don't you have a heart? Don't you want to save her from this life?"

The idiot was making a scene and we saw some MPs heading our way. So, Charlie and I frog-marched him out to the car and high-tailed it across the border to the base.

Lucky the only result of our night in beautiful Juarez was that Jack was late for roll call because he put earplugs in his ear to quiet what he called, "those damn, screeching crickets yammering outside my windows all night."

And he didn't want to be reminded that he was dumb enough to think no one would look in the trunk of the car. We'd have had better luck strolling arm-in-arm with her across the bridge.

I can't wait until you're here with me so a night out will be dinner at "La Posta" and...

Love you, Tony

So, while he was eating ancient Army C-rations and experiencing the bars in Juarez, I was going to school and planning our wedding.

A PK's wedding is not a private affair. News of our engagement has activated the Bird Ladies into a frenzy of ideas, which they generously share with my mother, my Aunt Marie, and anyone else who would listen.

Of course, Mrs. Olsen will not hear of anyone else doing the buffet to be served in the church dining room after the ceremony.

No one conceived of the idea that they might not be among the invited guests.

There were the various out-of-town aunts, uncles, and cousins on both sides, old friends from Dad's other pastorates and Dr. Herrington's lab friends, fraternity and army buddies of Tony's, my classmates at Presby Hall, and on and on it went. The potential guest list was burgeoning into the hundreds, with possibly two-thirds or more of them showing up. The idea made Mrs. Olsen ecstatic. A wedding buffet like that would be the fulfillment of her culinary dreams.

The only problem was that, while Mrs. Olsen's *hors d'oeuvres* were the envy of Presbyterian kitchens all over Chicago, the table better be large enough to hold Mrs. Beyer's tri- color ribbon sandwiches and Aunt Marie's Mexican wedding-cake cookies. Mrs. Smithfield, whose cook was a rival of Mrs. Olsen's, insisted on making her delicate, tiny cheese puffs and the Ganzerts promised a lug of prize strawberries, for which their garden on the farm outside of Champaign was famous. Mary, who had been a member of the family ever since she replaced our useless maids, was bringing a poppy-seed cake. The list grew with alarming speed.

A family meeting was called for. When Joe and his wife Jessica married three years ago, things seemed simpler. I don't know why, but of course during the planning stage of their wedding, I had been away at school and probably just missed all the fuss. Now they were missing mine. Joe was studying for his PhD in religion and philosophy at New College in Edinburgh so they were living in Scotland and couldn't get home for the ceremony.

Anyway, Dad and Mom and I sat down and tried to figure it all out. There were two solutions. The first was to let it be known that the wedding would be a private affair for family members only. This would be simplest, but would get lots of people mad, including dear old friends who could not be included if you wanted the excuse that it was strictly *Family Only*, because others for whom there was no room would find out.

"Shall we just elope?" I asked.

"That's easy to say, but it would leave me in a hornets' nest of disappointed ladies who have looked forward to a nice wedding, and I'd have to live with that forever," sighed Mom. "Besides, even if you did, we'd still have to throw some sort of a party when you got back and there'd be more of the same with that."

Dad, who loved a party and the bigger, the better, came up with the second solution. "Just invite everybody and let the chips fall where they may. Have Mrs. Smithson get the Ladies' Association to form a committee to work with Mrs. Olsen. They can decide how to split up the food. We'll order the cake from Signe Carlson's bakery so that's out of the picture, and Lillian can coordinate the decorations."

This was appealing for two reasons. Signe Carlson's bakery was the "Wedding Cake Bakery" in our part of town, which included the Swedish enclave known as *Andersonville*.

Everyone knew this, and even the most skilled amateur would know they couldn't compete with them.

Aunt Lillian had made wonderful table decorations and favors for some of the most elite charity affairs in Chicago. Though she never had much money after she married Uncle Robert, she was the adopted child of a wealthy railroad baron in Chicago. When she married Uncle Robert, the railroad baron saw to it that she inherited only a single dollar. However, she remained popular in the high-society environment. She knew what beautiful decorations were, and how to make them as economically as possible. She also could charm the birds from the trees, even if some of the birds were of the crow variety. Her critics always ended up as helpers.

Our family would give the church a reasonable donation for the costs of the festivities and everyone could participate.

Dad can be very persuasive, and Mom really thought it was the best solution. I didn't really care because I realized that Tony and I will be just the marzipan bride and groom on everyone's wedding cake. Dad prevailed and plans are going relatively smoothly.

So I am just going with the flow and working like crazy to finish up the quarter so my diploma will arrive by graduation day, which, because of scheduling problems, is the same day as the wedding.

You can guess which affair I will attend. Mom says that if that diploma doesn't arrive the Saturday before the wedding, it's all off. Hollow as that threat has to be, Mom feels very strongly about that piece of paper. The untimely death of her father had denied her plans for a college education and she wasn't about to let my diploma get away from me.

Mother's sister, my Aunt Grace, just arrived to "help" and caused quite a family flap by announcing that her husband, after carrying on a flaming affair with his secretary for most of their married life, had succumbed to his mistress's demands and filed for divorce.

So, Grace is ensconced in Joe's old bedroom and has thrown herself into the wedding preparations to assuage her grief. Of course, she and mother are not quite on the same page. Those two have been having this *my sister, pro-and-con* relationship since, I suspect, Mom was three and Grace was an infant. They think alike yet are convinced that the other is spoiled and headstrong and/or doesn't know what she is doing.

Take the episode of the hat for the wedding, for instance. Uncle Bert, Grace's soon-to-be- ex is a wealthy land developer and spoils both Grace and his mistress. So, it was only natural that Grace would show up with a charming little flower-covered confection by Lilly Daché to wear with her fancy Chanel suit. When she popped the hat out of the signature hatbox (complete with dangling price tag) my poor mom didn't know whether to laugh or cry.

She had bought an exact copy of the original at Carson Pirie Scott for a tenth of the price. It would take the wisdom of Solomon to divide up that baby. Grace suggested that Mom wear the original hat. "A daughter's wedding was not the place," she said, "to wear a cheap imitation."

Then Mother hid the price tags, mixed the two hats up and defied Aunt Grace to identify the original. Grace said that was silly and picked the wrong one. Dad came in and asked, "Which one of you ladies is going to get in the car and drive down to Marshall Field's and buy another hat? Now!"

They both did, but Mom still plans to wear the copy at the wedding.

THERE WENT THE BRIDE
Late June 1954

I'm an old married woman now. I've been Mrs. Anthony Herrington for over a week, but it still sounds wonderfully new to me.

The wedding went, as Dad predicted it would, in a lovely, disjointed way and a good time was had by all. The only anxious moment for me was when Dad asked Tony if he would *take this woman to be your lawfully wedded wife*. My normally soft-spoken husband must have been more nervous than I realized because he belted out "I DO!" so loudly that Dad jumped and then started to crack up. It's a problem when the clergyman/father of the bride starts laughing out loud. But Dad does have this easily tickled funny bone. I got him under control just in time when I hissed under my breath, "Don't you dare!"

Of course, dancing at a wedding in a Presbyterian Church was O-U-T, as was drinking a champagne toast to the happy couple. This was always a puzzle to me. If the first miracle Jesus performed was the turning of water into wine at a wedding, where did that "no wine" rule come from?

Anyway, the service was soon over. Mrs. Smithfield kept the Bird Ladies in line and Mrs. Olsen outdid herself at the buffet. The cake was a masterpiece and delicious to boot, living up to the expectations of all concerned.

Everyone I ever knew in my life, and lots whom I had never laid eyes on, passed through the receiving line in one big blur because I was too vain to wear my glasses. But they were all so nice, I just pretended I knew everyone. Tony was a real trooper and charming to everyone.

Finally, the crowd settled down to demolish the delicious, church-social buffet. No one even noticed when we went upstairs to the apartment to change into our travelling clothes.

There was a pile of unopened gifts up there that we saved to open when we got back from our whirlwind honeymoon. With rice in our hair and, it turned out, in our luggage, we headed off to Wisconsin to spend the three days Uncle Sam had allowed us for our wedding trip. The cabin was supplied, of course, by one of the parishioners.

We were driving through Highland Park when I said, "Are you hungry? The only food I've had today except a boiled egg at breakfast was that chunk of wedding cake you fed me."

"Am I ever hungry! All that great food, and I never got a bite," he agreed.

"There's a really nice inn here where we used to go for birthdays. Let's stop before I fall over."

So we stopped for our first dinner together as man and wife. As he slipped his hand into his pocket to get his billfold, Tony remembered that someone had given him an envelope as she passed through the receiving line.

Inside the bright, pink envelope were a dozen $2 bills and a note which read, "*Wedding Cake* paid off in the second race yesterday. Have a nice dinner on me. All the best, Miss Marigold McDaniel. PS: Old Zack didn't take his cut, so some of this is from him."

Sometimes being a PK is a real pain with everyone expecting too much of you. But sometimes I feel like a real princess with more fairy godmothers than anyone has a right to have.

And so, after a wonderful meal courtesy of Zack, the bookie, and Miss Marigold McDaniel, I got into the car with my prince and headed north to be alone with him at last.

Those three days seemed like three hours after being apart so long. But we had only three more days to get back to Chicago, pack up the most practical of the wedding gifts and get Tony back to the base in New Mexico before his leave ran out.

Our new blue and white Chevrolet was a generous wedding gift from Tony's parents, who have been very sweet to me. I was used to car trips to Wisconsin, Michigan and Iowa to visit family. But driving to New Mexico was a real adventure. Midwestern to the core, any place farther west than Davenport was cowboy country to me. The expanse of the sky, the distances between towns, even the music on the radio were all new to me. I had no idea what to expect in New Mexico, which hadn't even been a state until 1912, a scant forty-two years ago.

Our last night on the road, I realized how far I was from Chicago. The thunderstorms started in the Texas panhandle east of the New Mexico border. I had never seen lightning like that. Great ribbons of brilliance struck the prairie as if to crack it in two. Thunder rolled in waves across endless fields and grazing lands. Tumbleweed rolled, ghost-like, in front of the car. And the wind… in Chicago we have wind, but it seems more civilized somehow.

The storms surrounded us. Left, right, in front and behind! It was like the "Twilight of the Gods" done over the top, as the drama students would say. I was scared silly. Tony laughed when I hid my head under the dashboard before he realized that I am truly frightened of lightning.

"Do you want to stop for the night?"

"Where? We're in the middle of nowhere." I said, peering into the sheets of rain sluicing down the windshield.

"Hey! There's a red light down the road. It may be a motel."

"If it is, it'll be the first one since dinner. Let's take it. Please."

The proprietor looked as if he'd stepped out of the set for one of those corny cowboy movies my Dad, who was born in Kansas, was addicted to on television. The man was tall and dusty, made taller by the heels of his worn cowboy boots. There was a wad of chewing tobacco in one cheek. His hair was in serious need of a trim, and he made a clam on dry land seem downright chatty.

Evenin'

Hi! My wife and I would like a room for the night. Do you have a vacancy?

Yup.

How much?

Ten bucks.

I'll pay you eight.

Nine.

Okay.

This was a side of my dear Tony I had never seen. Bargaining for a room on such a night as this! What if the man had said no? I was not going out in that storm again, and I'd have given him half our wedding-present money for that room. Tony counted out four singles and a five.

The guy pocketed the bills, took two threadbare towels and two grimy washcloths from under the counter and drew water from the tap into a blue-enameled pitcher.

He jerked his head at us to follow him and stomped out into the storm. We followed him to a small, rough log cabin. He went in and turned on the 25-watt bulb in the overhead fixture, set down the pitcher and turned toward the door.

"You want to wash, just pump that there handle. Water's okay to wash in, but ain't no good for drinkin'. Use the pitcher."

And he stomped out.

We hooked the door locked, sat down on the edge of the bed and immediately rolled into the sunken center of the double bed where we threw our arms around each other.

"Well," said Tony. "Guess if we can't drink the water and the light's too dim to read…"

The next morning, I woke before Tony did and decided to look out the small front window of the cabin to see what the countryside looked like. I have always wanted to use the word *sere* in a sentence and this is a perfect chance. The only thing moving in the sere, sun- glazed landscape was a dusty ball of tumbleweed cartwheeling across the lonely road. It was the color of an old sepia photo left in the sun to fade. I pictured the moon as having more life than this, so I ran to the back window to see if the view was more encouraging. The tumbleweed continued past the side of the cabin and disappeared into the far distance while I stood watching it rolling towards my future home.

I don't know how long I'd stood staring out that back window. I do know that Tony has been able to read my thoughts from the day we met and mine were pretty low that morning.

"It's really kind of pretty when you get used to it," he said.

"I guess I'll find out," I said as I pumped cold water into the basin to 'bathe'.

So, we packed up and got back out on the road. Seeing the motel in the daylight only confirmed my impression of the night before. It looked like a cliché set for a Saturday afternoon Western, only worse, plunked for real in the middle of nowhere. The only other sign of life was a single gas pump rusting in front of a tumbledown shack with a big, faded-red Coca Cola cooler next to it.

So, we drove on to try to find a place to get breakfast. In about half an hour we reached Clovis, New Mexico, a pretty town with two lovely motels and a clean, bright café that served up a breakfast of sourdough flapjacks with maple syrup, generous halves of sweet grapefruit and coffee. It was our first meal in New Mexico. There wasn't a tumbleweed in sight, and the water was pure and sweet.

I was a new woman. It was fun driving on the uncrowded highway past grazing land where rust-red cattle with white faces browsed on grass still green from the spring rains. Calves released from the branding pens gamboled with their playmates, their patient mothers grazing nearby. In the bright sunlight, the small white clouds seemed to be frisking, too, chasing each other across the endless blue sky.

Late that afternoon we passed a sign that said *Mesilla, New Mexico*. The population on the sign was less than my high school graduation class.

"Almost there," Tony said.

"There? Meaning close to here?"

"Yep, pardner, meaning close to here. Turn on the radio. You'll see what I mean."

On the first station, a sexy-sounding man was belting out a lively tune in Spanish accompanied by a trumpet, guitar and accordion. I changed the station and got an evangelist shouting at his listeners to send *what evah*

God's grace enables ya'll to send to further our mission heah on earth. A quick run up and down the dial revealed that Spanish or Bible-banging were the two choices on the airwaves. I chose the sexy man and his merry band.

Outside the window of the car, a small, sturdy woman in a long, full skirt was carrying a basket of laundry on her head, posture correct, waist-length braid hanging like a plumb line down the middle of her back. She entered one of the tiny houses lining the road, each of which had a red or pink climbing rose bush arching over the lintel of the door and a string of bright chilies hanging from a peg. The houses were so close together that they looked as if you took away the one at the end, the whole block would fall down like a set of dominoes. Doors hung less straight than the woman's braid, which appeared to be the only thing in the whole village that was plumb.

Children were everywhere, chasing mongrel dogs, playing marbles or catch in the dusty streets. We passed a cantina where men were drinking beer under a trellis where a bougainvillea provided dense, rose-tinted shade. A parrot in a cage hung from the trellis squawked his welcome to anyone who passed, greeting the women with a lewd whistle and the men with a virulent spate of what had to be Mexican profanities. Three saddled horses were tied to the hitching post, ears and tails twitching away the flies as they waited patiently for their masters.

"Does our house look like those?"

"Maybe a little better?"

"I hope at least it's got indoor plumbing,"

"Yeah," Tony grinned. "And screens too. We're going first class."

In twenty more minutes down a graveled road, my husband pulled into a sandy driveway on the right side of a cement-block building with two doors in front. It was one of four such duplex buildings that appeared to be set like Monopoly pieces on the treeless desert landscape.

When we drove up, we saw a woman about my age standing three or four feet back from the door of the other apartment. She was tossing pebbles against her front door.

Tony got out of the car and went up to her. They chatted for a minute. Then he came back to the car laughing.

"What was that all about?"

"That's Helen, our next-door neighbor. There's a big tarantula sitting on her front step.

She's trying to get it to move so she can go in. Come on out and meet her."

"Meeting Helen and not the tarantula, I hope."

We had arrived at our first home together.

ART GALLERY

The Queen of Night Steals the Sun

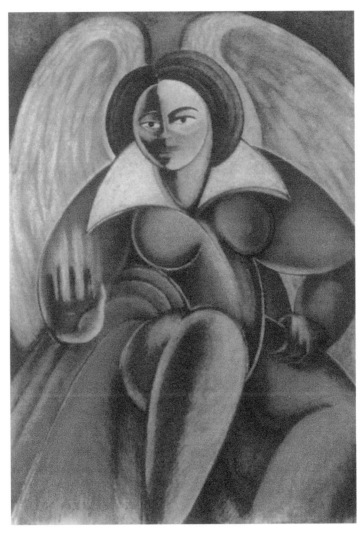

Angel with an Attitude

The Burden of the Phoenix

Paso Doble

Ancient of Days Takes Measure of Chicago

Il Chino e la Sirena

La Mexicana

Persian Madonna

Nancy Jean Carrigan ©1997

41" x 32 3/4"

The Virtual Pharaoh

Acrylic on Linen affixed to Board; Computer components, Hammered Brass, Miniatures

The Virtual Pharaoh

The Warrior and the Cockatoo

NOT A REAL EPISCOPALIAN
August 1955

At last! Corporal Anthony Herrington has his discharge from the U.S. Army, and we are on our way back to Champaign so he can start work on his PhD in physics. It seems almost like a lifetime that we have been here in Las Cruces. I have had three jobs, sewn corporal's stripes on my husband's uniforms, fed dozens of dinners to hungry buddies on C-ration nights, tried my hand at being an Episcopalian, and finally got the dog ("Nicki") that my mother promised me fifteen years ago.

About the only job I could get when we got here was as a data processor at New Mexico A & M, the state college here in town. The work involved sitting all day in an oven-like Quonset hut in the desert with dozens of other army wives calculating raw data from the missile shoots going on at White Sands National Proving Ground where Tony was stationed. We used a recalcitrant Marchant calculator to triangulate (whatever that was) the numbers in the columns they gave us. I wrote down the results on a ruled pad of paper, which my boss would then give to the "draftsmen," three or four women who plotted the numbers by hand on graph paper. It was boring, sweaty work, but it helped pay the rent.

"I hear you have art training," my boss boomed in my ear one afternoon as I sat punching numbers in that infernal machine and trying to stay awake in the heat.

"Yes, ma'am, I have an art minor."

"Then go up to Dr. Gardiner's office in the main building. She wants to talk to you." Anna Gardiner was the director of the Physical Sciences Laboratory. She was gracious, fair, and motherly to the scores of young Army wives who passed through her employ. And (God love her!), she took me out of that Quonset sardine can into a real office with a real window. I will always be grateful to her for that.

"My office mate's real nice," I told Tony at dinner a few nights later. "Her name's Patsy Tombaugh."

"Wow! Do you know who her husband is? He's Clyde Tombaugh, the astronomer who discovered the planet Pluto."

"Well, she's sure friendly, and she loves to tell stories about the setting up of the proving grounds and funny, odd things that have happened here. Did you know we once shot a missile into Mexico by mistake?"

"I've heard about it. What's the story?"

"Well, she says she was outside taking down the laundry when she glanced up at the sky and saw a rocket crossing the moon. Took her a few seconds to realize it was going south instead of north, but when she did, she called Clyde Tombaugh, her husband, right away. The Mexicans were pretty mad when they found a rocket nose down in one of their churchyards."

"Wonder if the guys who programmed that one backwards are still around."

But in the short time I worked as a draftsman putting small pencil marks on graph paper, a tremendous change took place. Across the hall from my office several large rooms were being cleared out, state of the art air conditioning was being installed, and mysterious boxes and crates were being unpacked. The Marchant girls in the Quonset hut were on their way out. PSL had acquired a machine that would make them obsolete. It was a conglomeration of blinking lights, boxes and huge rolls of tape. It swallowed up huge amounts of data, did all the calculations so fast it also swallowed up the jobs of the Marchant girls. But the cruelest cut of all was that, while we had parboiled in a Quonset hut, the machine rated the latest air-conditioning equipment available.

I had really liked working with Patsy and our boss, Liz. We remained in touch, and Dr. Gardiner gave me a hug when I left and we promised to stay in touch. But I was being transferred again, this time to be editor of the alumni newspaper for New Mexico A & M.

At last, I was able to use the skills I had worked so hard to learn, proving now that mother was right about my more practical journalism major coming in handy.

I wrote, edited and produced a monthly publication that was enormous fun, except when my printer's assistant would get caught wading across the Rio Grande from his home in Juarez to El Paso and have to spend a few days in jail. The printer would call up to say that the edition would be a little late. It turned out that this was to be expected and so I learned not to raise a fuss. That would have been impolite.

But who'd have thought this city-bred PK from Chicago would find herself writing about how to read cattle brands and how to rustle good beef from a rancher? The idea for the feature came from the head of the alumni association who just happened to own one of the most famous brands in the state. He put me in touch with the cattle inspector who, he said, could help me with the background.

Cal Timpkin was straight out of Hollywood's central casting office. He filled the whole door to my office and had to duck to come inside. He wore a large, silver rodeo buckle on his belt and had a fringed, cowhide jacket that looked just exactly as it should.

"You Miz Herrington?"

"That's me."

"Cal Timpkin," he said, extending a paw as big as a bear's.

And I actually said, "Howdy," a word I had never uttered in my life.

Cal didn't bother to conceal his smile, and we got along just fine. He taught me how to read a brand, how to "run" a brand with a hot iron, meaning to change a brand in some way to conceal the real owner. Best of all, he seemed to know all of the ranchers' brands in the state, and some in Texas and Colorado. That story is still one of the most favorite I have ever written.

In addition to finding a job when we moved to New Mexico, we had to find a church. And so this Presbyterian Princess found herself attending an Episcopalian mission church with her Episcopalian consort.

We fell in love with the charming little white church in its grove of cottonwood trees, and once we met Father Bill Farthingale, there was no other place that we would call our church. To make matters even better, Father Bill had also been raised a Presbyterian. He never said why he made the change, but he had a cheery, comfortable feeling about us and our "mixed marriage."

Tony, of course, knew the liturgy and walked me through it, or rather stood me up, sat me down, or made me kneel at the right time. We often had Father Bill and his wife Betsy over for coffee or dinner, and they became two of our favorite people in New Mexico.

One evening at dinner, Father Bill asked me for help. The woman who had been teaching the four-to-six-year-old Sunday school class was leaving to follow her husband to a new job as a professor of physics up in Albuquerque.

"No-one's come forward to take her place, and that is a rather, hmmm, shall we say, an 'active' age. Didn't you say you taught the summer Bible school to the little ones at home?"

"I did. And they wore me out. I'd fall asleep right after lunch every afternoon when I finished. They're little perpetual-motion machines, especially the brightest ones. I had to keep ahead of them every second."

"So," beamed Father Bill, "you're just the person to take over the class. There are twenty kids signed up, but not all of them come every Sunday."

"There's just a small problem. I'm not an Episcopalian."

"Doesn't matter," the good rector laughed. "You're not going to teach them catechism class, just keep them in line so their parents can go to services. You know how far these people have to drive in from the ranches. They have to bring their kids and they expect a Sunday school class to be there for them."

"I hate to see a grown man beg," Betsy chimed in, "but Bill's really in a bind. If you don't say 'yes,' he'll be down on his knees."

Tony and I laughed at the image of six-foot, six-inch Father Bill on his knees. That would make him just about my height (5'3") standing up. It was too much, so I said I would give it a try while he looked for a more permanent teacher for the class.

Thank goodness for the New Mexican weather! For much of the time I taught my twenty Sunday schoolers, we were able to go outside and have class in the shade of one of the towering old trees. Father Bill was right about one thing. Four-to-six are active ages. But he was wrong about another thing. None of the twenty children enrolled ever missed the class.

Having a fairly good grounding in scriptures and children's bible songs, it was no problem being an Episcopalian Sunday school teacher and we got along fine. There was the occasional centipede down the neck of the little girl in the pink ruffled dress. She was so pretty as to bring out mischief in little boys. But Milly Esterman won my complete admiration. Every time Luke or Zeke or Adam did the centipede thing, she'd reach calmly into the back of her dress, pull out the offending creature and say, "Oh, it's just a centipede," then flick the insect into the nearest sagebrush.

I thought that the parents would be pleased when I taught the children that, while God loves them, he doesn't always say *yes* to every prayer. Sometimes, just because he loves the children, the answer to "can't we have an elephant in the barn?" has to be *no* so they can learn how to cope with real life. Maybe my originality was what got me in trouble.

Father Bill called me into his office one Sunday after church.

"I've had a complaint about you teaching the children's class in Sunday school." I looked at Father Bill in dismay.

"What about?" I asked. "I thought everything was going fine. Who complained?"

"Well," he said, looking unusually somber, "Mrs. Milton (She's the one in the dark blue hat with the two-foot long peacock feather that nobody likes to sit behind in church.) and Mrs. Gregory (The hat with the little stuffed wren nesting on the brim. She always sits just off to my left. She's so tiny that whenever she cocks her head slightly, the wren looks as if it will just fly out the window or something.)."

I knew those hats. Had the old Bird Ladies of Champaign and Chicago just changed hats and names?

"But they're about a hundred years old. They don't even have kids in the class," I protested.

"Milly Esterman is Mrs. Milton's great-granddaughter, but that's not the point. They were very disturbed that I had put a Presbyterian in charge of the class. They told me that I have to protect the purity of the doctrine taught in an Episcopalian Sunday school. They never can forget that I was a Presbyterian once myself and feel compelled to keep an eye peeled to see if I'm backsliding."

"I don't want to get you in trouble. I'll resign. I'll miss the kids though. I was just getting all their names straight. Milly Esterman's the centipede girl I told you about."

"Ah! I'm not asking you to resign. Most of the parents are very pleased you're brave enough to teach the class," Father Bill suddenly burst out laughing. "Besides, I've solved the problem. I just told Mrs. Milton and Mrs. Gregory how delighted I was that they were coming in to volunteer to take over the class and handed them the lesson plans for the next month.

"They headed out the door so fast, a feather flew off of Mrs. Gregory's wren!"

And so I stayed a fake Episcopalian until last week when I got hugs and kisses from twenty of the dearest little people in New Mexico, and turned the class over to a new, real Episcopalian, newly arrived from Atlanta, Georgia and above doctrinaire reproach.

Now we are due back in Chicago for a quick visit, and then off to Champaign-Urbana where Tony has been accepted in the graduate program in the Physics Department. The car is almost packed and Nicki can't wait to go. Every time we open a door to put something more into the back seat, he hops in and settles firmly on top of the suitcases to make sure he is coming with us.

Nicki is like that, completely in charge of his destiny and of our lives.

Until he came, our pet was a charming little brown lizard named George. Every day, we swept George up into a dustpan and Tony would dump him far into the desert behind the duplex. And every day, he appeared again, sunning himself on the screen above our dining room table.

He disappeared after we got Nicki. I choose not to think why.

We bought Nicki last December from a breeder of dachshunds in El Paso, who advertised a litter of puppies for sale just before Christmas. I had forgotten to tell Tony that my mother had said that as soon as I had a home of my own, I could have a dog. He also did not know that on our first or second date when that spaniel fell in love with him, it had sealed his fate to become my husband. It was love at first sight, but if he'd been mean to that dog, I'd have had to rethink the whole thing.

Anyway, when I asked him in November that didn't he think it was time we got our dog, he seemed a little puzzled.

"Dog? Who said anything about getting a dog?"

"I just did. It's something you do when you have a home of your own."

"But…"

"You once said you always thought dachshunds were fun dogs."

"Well, yes, but…"

"And there's a litter at this breeder in El Paso. If we don't go down right soon, they may be all sold."

"I don't…"

"Please? We don't have to buy one, just look and see if they are nice dogs."

So the next Saturday, we got in the car and drove the fifty miles south to El Paso. All the way down, Tony lectured me on how we were going down to LOOK at puppies, not BUY a puppy. By the time we drove up to the neat white ranch house with the neat white sign *Dachshund Puppies for Sale* in front, I had given up hope that at last I would have a dog.

Four pups were bouncing all over their big pen in the family's living room, watched over by their pretty dam, Mitzi. She was a fine black and tan specimen with a sweet disposition, and so friendly that when Mrs. Meeks, the breeder, brought us into the room, Mitzi sat up on her haunches and demanded to be petted.

Mrs. Meeks reached into the cage and picked the pups up one by one and put them on papers spread on the living room rug.

"Just look them over and see what you think," she said and left for the kitchen to get us some lemonade.

Smart woman! She knew that you don't sell puppies. Puppies sell themselves. I sat down on the floor and Tony, being aloof, sat in a chair nearby. The puppies tumbled over themselves to have a look at us. Then three of them bounced away to play tug-of-war with an old sock. The fourth marched directly over to Tony and sat down in front of him, looking him over as a stockman might look over a calf for sale. Then he toddled over to Tony's shoes and neatly untied the laces. Having immobilized and amused his victim, the pup sat down in front of him and cocked his head.

The next thing I heard was Mr. *We are not, understand, **not**, buying a puppy,* saying, "Hey, there. You want to come home with us, do you?" as he reached into his pocket for his checkbook. I always knew I had picked the right guy. Nicki and he have been pals from that day on. I'm just allowed along for the ride.

DOES GOD HAVE A FUNNY BONE?
January 1956

It's strange being back in Illinois after New Mexico. Nicki, Texas born and bred, thinks we have brought him to a low-slung dog's version of damnation. The first time we took him out into the snow, he glared at the alien stuff and refused to pee. Needless to say, that didn't last long, but he still rushes back to the door as soon as the necessaries are complete.

We, however, are glad to be back and started on the next phase of our lives. I have found a job as an editor/business manager of a trade journal, and Tony is settled into his studies. The two years he was in the Army he had taken physics classes at the graduate level at New Mexico A&M, now New Mexico State. He became determined to get his doctorate during that time. The G.I. bill was available, and with my salary, we are doing fine.

Of course, I have returned to the Presbyterian fold. Tony's mother may have been an ardent Episcopalian, but her son is rather indifferent to which church he attends, if any. His father was a dedicated scientist and spent the Sabbath in his laboratory, often taking his young son with him.

My father-in-law, in fact, was the first person I had known well who did not go to any church. In fact, he seemed to feel that he didn't need to, not because he felt that he was perfect, but because studying the secrets of this wondrous world was spiritual inspiration enough. Dr. Herrington is one of the nicest people I have ever met. He doesn't see people as Catholic or Jewish, Presbyterian or Baptist, rich, poor, black, yellow, red or white, or any mixture thereof. Such labels mean nothing to him. He is much like Henry Higgins in the play *Pygmalion,* but much nicer. He would treat a washerwoman like a princess and a princess like a washerwoman. This generosity of spirit is sometimes a little naïve…like the time a panhandler asked him for money at the "El" station near their home on the Illinois Institute of Technology campus in Chicago.

The guy's story was that he needed the fare to visit his ailing mother at a hospital on the other side of town. Dad Herrington not only gave him the money and then some, but helped him up the stairs to the train tracks and personally saw that he got on the right train to the hospital the beggar had described.

"He seemed very confused when I put him on the train. I almost had to push him aboard before the train started. Odd fellow, he was. Even started pounding on the door as the train took off. Shook his fist at me, in fact. Seemed to have a broken middle finger. It wouldn't bend."

This wonderful *Candide* truly has become my second father, except that he spoils me more than Dad does. But he is also very serious in his love of the wonders he has glimpsed in his studies of chemistry and physics. They seem to affect him the same way discussions of religion and philosophy affect the men on my side of the family. My dad, grandfather, three clergymen uncles, and now Joe, who has finished his doctorate in philosophy and also been ordained in the Presbyterian Church, are all clergymen. Their discussions are far from those Tony and his father have about quantum mechanics or molecular structures of soils or who got the latest Nobel Prize in physics or chemistry and for what. Sometimes, I think that the two scientists are speaking another language, but I'm getting used to it.

Anyway, we have started attending the Presbyterian Church on campus again. To my delight, I found that Dad's former assistant, he of the sideways teeth, Rev. Richard Smithson, was now the pastor there. He is slightly gray now and has the kind of *gravitas* you might expect from someone in that position. He and Laura have three lively boys, all of them with the same charm and good looks as their parents.

I was glad to see him and he grinned and gave me a hug when he realized who I was. "Thay, Mthess Herrington, ith great to thee you."

Thank goodness! Under all that *gravitas*, the rascal still lingered. I wondered if God was still playing tricks on my old friend and sure enough, He seemed to be.

It was a Communion Sunday and The Day of Giving. The highlight of the service was a collection for the Missions work of the church. For that reason, the day's scripture lesson was Matthew 6: 19-21. The first reading of the passage was by a devout student who hoped to become a clergyman. He read:

Therefore, lay not up for yourselves treasures upon earth, where roth and must doth corrupt,

There was a smile or two, but the young man gamely finished…

For where your treasure is, there will your heart be also.

There was a sigh of relief from the fellow's girlfriend, who I knew was sitting next to us.

The guy sat down, hoping nobody had noticed the slip.

The scripture was repeated by Rev. Smithson's new assistant pastor, a young Ethiopian exchange student recently graduated from seminary. He stood tall in his clerical robes, walked up to the podium and read:

Therefore, lay not up for yourselves treasures upon earth where (I held my breath) *roth and must doth corrupt…*

This time there was a titter or two as the two clergymen moved to the Communion table set with the usual stacks of silver trays of Communion bread and slotted trays holding small glasses of vintage Presbyterian wine (called grape juice by the vintner from Welch's).

Rev. Smithson gave the prayer before the passing of the bread and 'wine'. Why he felt that he had to revisit that scripture passage, only God knows. Perhaps it was a test.

And so, Dear God, let us remember not to lay up for ourselves treasures upon earth (Here came the pitch!) *where roth and must doth corrupt; to remember that it is more blessed to receive than to give…* (Strike three *and* an error!)

Tony and I, sitting in the last row by the vestibule could hear the ushers waiting to serve the Communion choking back laughter. Richard, now his endearing flustered self, signaled his assistant to join him in removing the silver lids with the seven-inch silver crosses on top from the stack of trays. Each man put one of the lids on his pulpit chair behind him, passed the trays to the waiting servers, then backed up, and sat down…and stood back up again very quickly.

Tony said afterwards that he had thought that Presbyterian services were pretty stuffy until that morning. Richard almost made a Presbyterian of him that day.

"God works in mysterious ways," I told him, "Just look at the duck-billed platypus if you think He doesn't have a funny bone."

When we went home for Christmas, God's funny bone came up again. Joe and Jess had arrived home for New Year's, the Christmas services having been successfully completed at Joe's pastorate in New Hampshire and left the New Year's prayer service in the capable hands of his assistant. But just before he had left, he had been asked to do a pro bono service for one of the members of the community who was a notorious drunk and womanizer.

"When I got to the *ashes to ashes* scripture," he said, "I got as far as *ashes to ashes and dust to dust*…then my mind went blank and all I could think of was *ashes to ashes and dust to dust…if the gin don't get you, the ladies must.* Did I really say that out loud? Where in the world it came from I'll never know. I just stood there, head bowed like I was contemplating the untimely passing of the deceased. But I was really praying as hard as I could that no one noticed the slip and that God would stop playing jokes with me. It didn't do much good because the laughter, though muffled, sounded like shouts to me. The rest of the service is a blank, but the widows, of which there were five, told me how much I had caught the spirit of the old reprobate."

"I love God's little jokes," Dad said. "Next to Adam's rib, God's funny bone is the most important piece of anatomy in religion. I think it's there to keep us from getting too puffed up and serious. Without Tony's yelling *I DO!* at your wedding, for instance, I'd probably have gotten all blubbery at the idea of our little girl getting married and moving away. That *I DO!* saved the day.

"But my most humbling moment was during an Easter service in the era of those hats women wore that were about as big around as a truck tire…you remember them, Em. Your sister Grace had one that looked like a giant turkey platter with cabbages on it."

"I remember those. Mom had one, too," said Tony. "Her's was only dinner-plate size, but one Easter, she nearly poked Dad's eye out with a spray of artificial lilacs when she kissed him goodbye as she left for the sunrise service. I often wondered if it was an accident or on purpose because he was going to go to the lab on Easter Sunday instead of going to church."

"Then you know the kind I mean.

"Well, this Easter, Mrs. Smithfield came to church with one of the truck tire ones. The brim was woven to look like a peppermint candy... an enormous swirl of red and white. Now, Mrs. Smithfield always sits just behind Emma so she's right in my line of vision. The roses were like no roses God made. They were about the size of Texas grapefruit...that swirl of red and white was something I just couldn't take my eyes off of.

"Remember now, Mr. and Mrs. Franklin always sit in the pew just behind Mrs. Smithfield. The Franklins are both short and deaf as posts, so they lipread the sermon. Mrs. F. was behind Mom so she was okay, but Mr. F. couldn't see around the Smithfield hat. If Mrs. Smithfield tipped her head slightly to the right, I could see Mr. F. peering around the left side of that confounded hat. If she tipped the other way, he'd pop up on the right. I tried not to look, but those blessed red roses were hypnotic.

"Left, right, left, right...why didn't the silly woman hold her head still? It was like watching a pendulum. I was getting closer and closer to losing my train of thought and my dignity with it.

"But Mr. F. didn't give up until finally, Mrs. Smithfield dozed off, her head dropping so that the truck tire was straight up and I was staring directly into the swirling circle of the brim. I saw Mr. F's left eye and the top of his head appear on the right side of the hat, then the right eye and the top of his head on the left side of the hat, and then, God help me, he must have stood up and I saw just the top of his head and his eyebrows appear right in the center above the brim just like Kilroy."

Dad started to smile at the memory. "He made one last effort, a little hop above the brim and then he just wasn't there anymore." And he laughed until the tears came to his eyes, and we all joined in the fun.

When we had calmed down, Mom shook her head. "Really," she said. "Those hats weren't that bad. I thought they were pretty."

But I knew she could never have bought one of those extravaganzas. They were far too expensive and frivolous for the minister's wife and besides, we never wore new clothes at Easter. That would have been *putting on airs.*

IT'S DOCTOR HERRINGTON NOW, THANK YOU
June 1962

At last, Tony is through graduate school. That piece of paper with his name and the words granting Anthony Paul Herrington a Doctor of Philosophy in Physics is tucked away somewhere in one of his files.

He accepted a job at Carnegie Institute of Technology in Pittsburgh. We love our new home in Pennsylvania. Both sets of parents wished we had moved to Chicago, however, because they hated having the grandchildren go so far away.

Margaret Anne was born during finals week the last year that Tony had course work. Bad timing, I guess, but who was thinking of final exams when a gibbous moon was shining through the branches of the golden maple outside the window of our little graduate school house in Urbana, and it's warm enough to have the windows open so you can hear the music of a dance band playing for Octoberfest way over on campus, and you're celebrating the seventh anniversary of the night you met. Hey, we couldn't afford the luxury of going out to Steak and Shake, and he'd just had his thesis topic approved, so life was going pretty well.

When Meg arrived, she did so conveniently on a Saturday so Tony really didn't miss any of his exams after all.

Joey arrived twenty months later. He also timed his arrival with his father's needs in mind. Tony was deep into his doctoral research project and the betatron was closed for a maintenance check on the Wednesday Joey was born. His father was at the hospital for the delivery and, having worked a twenty-hour day before, sat by my bed to hold my hand and promptly fell asleep. The doctor marveled at how relaxed he was, but I knew he was just exhausted.

That was the way it was all through graduate school. The field of high-energy physics is a demanding one, because the subject is so intriguing and the machines necessary for the research are so expensive to build and run. The rule is, *The Machine Rules*. It's easier to get a man away from a mistress than to get a physicist away from his machines. A baseball player's family life revolves around baseball season, and a teacher's family, around school holidays. Tony's life revolved around a betatron. I can see how unlocking such basic secrets of the building blocks of all creation could be the ultimate fascination for those lucky enough to understand how to do it. But sometimes it was hard to ignore that even we, his nearest and dearest, often were playing second fiddle to a machine.

But when the *Eureka* moments happen, it's worth it all.

I know this sounds rather awestruck, but Tony's work is really fascinating. It's hard for me and my relatives to understand what exactly my husband does for a living. In a family where most of the men are Protestant pastors, the mystery of the meaning of life is best solved through detailed study and discussion of the Holy Scriptures. Oh!

They know *for now we see through the glass darkly*...and all that, but pastors are mostly too busy caring for their flocks to worry about mesons and muons and all of those unknown, unseen elementary particles that are spinning around each other all the time.

Of course, in seminary, the ministers-to-be study Greek and Latin and Hebrew so that they can read the scriptures in the original languages. But what's really all Greek to them are Alpha particles and Beta decay. They are baffled when Tony has to leave a family dinner to run over to the cyclotron because some colleague has seen an "event."

There were mid-dinner calls in my own family's history except that a mid-dinner call to Dad might be to go to the bedside of an accident victim just arrived at the hospital, or to console a family whose daughter has gone into severe depression and sliced her wrists.

Living next door to the church for the first five years of my life and above the church before my marriage meant that not only was Dad "on call" all the time, but that everyone in the family was.

One night as I kissed Tony goodnight in the hall after a really nice date during spring break, the telephone started ringing. Mom and Dad were already asleep, so I picked up the receiver.

"Hello there," I said with a smile in my voice. "I do hope you're having as lovely an evening as I. What may I do for you?"

"Please," the voice on the other end sobbed, "Please, call your father. Mother has had some sort of a seizure. The police are here and they say they can't find a pulse. They're taking her to Edgewater Hospital. Please! I need to talk to the Reverend. I don't know what to do."

It was Marianne Mitchell.

"Hold on," I said and ran to wake Dad. Sadly, Mrs. Mitchell, who lived with her unmarried daughter, passed away before he even had time to get to the phone, but Dad dressed quickly and went out into a blustering spring storm to help Marianne cope with the shock of her mother's sudden death.

I never again let my own euphoria show when answering the phone at the manse.

Dad never knew what was waiting for him downstairs when the call box up in his apartment office rang. One night it was a hoodlum with a gun who was involved with a drug gang and wanted help extricating himself from the whole awful business. Another was from an unbalanced woman who had become obsessed with Dad. She called to say that she had a sweater she had just finished knitting for him against his wishes. She wanted to deliver it to him immediately. It was dinnertime and Mom took the call, and told the woman that Dad was not available. But the woman called and called and eventually Dad had to lodge a complaint about her to the police. Then she got so mad she sent Dad a bill for knitting the sweater and the yarn and threatened to tell the newspapers that she had been seduced by a prominent clergyman on the North Side.

Once, when I was little, I asked my Mom if anybody was happy. Dad had to deal with so much sadness in other people's lives. And there were no mathematical formulas or physics theories to help him. Every case was different. Often, especially in domestic problems, Dad turned to my pragmatic, no-nonsense mother. She could see through fraud like Superman sees through walls.

One young woman walked out on her husband and young daughter and left the neighborhood to go to Siam and work at an orphanage there. Dad was shocked. At dinner the night after the husband had come to him for help, he told mother the story.

How could she do that! Harold is the salt of the earth. Never misses Sunday service.

Never misses teaching the Junior class at Sunday school. He does a great job. I've listened in to a couple of his classes and he's spellbinding. He treats little Emily like she was a goddess.

Never saw a father as good to his child as he is. What more does she want?

Mom had a different view of this paragon.

Perhaps Elise was tired of being corrected every time she opened her mouth. If you were so smug and proper and know-it-all as that pompous twit, I'd have left you years ago. As for the child, haven't you ever seen how Harold is turning her into a brat. He countermands every suggestion Elise has about how to raise the girl? And that mother of his scoffs at her in front of the child — nasty remarks like, "Oh Elise, let the child alone. Don't you know children outgrow that 'jumping on the furniture' stage." Then she'll go on about the latest 'stupid' child-rearing mistakes Elise has made.

And did I mention that while that dandy wears the best clothes Marshall Field's sells, Elise hasn't come to church in a new dress since I've known her. The last thing she had new was a housedress I saw her buy at Woolworth's.

What a pill that man is!

Mom paused, though I suspect she had only just started on Harold Nitchske's faults as a husband.

Dad put down his knife and fork and looked in surprise at the tiny pieces he had made of his steak as he was listening to Mom.

"Don't think much of him, do you?" he observed.

"You asked." she responded.

"Well, what should I do? He really loves her, or says he does. Should I tell him to go get her and bring her back, or maybe have the child write her a plea to come home, or should he just file for divorce?"

"How about telling him to cut Mrs. Nitchske's apron strings and *cleave unto his wife* as the Bible says. Write Elise a letter. Tell her he misses her wonderful patience and caring. Say he wants her to come back and make their house a home again."

Dad was not controlled by Mom but he always listened to her, then he would go back to his study, think over her observations and find a solution that usually included her suggestions.

Of course, I can't help Tony that way. What high-energy physicist would listen to the ideas of a woman whose only physics was at the high school level and who only took that because of the handsome Dr. Crandall. The only thing I'm good at is letting Tony rant on and on about some problem that has come up at the lab and ask him questions when I'm totally lost.

Then he goes off to the lab and figures it out while I go to bed because we have two kids under three. There isn't enough sleep in the world to get me through the day with them around if I'm not in bed by ten o'clock. Maybe Mom and I aren't too different after all.

But I wouldn't trade Tony and Meg and Joey for the world. Just before we left Champaign, I met one of my former art teachers at an exhibition on campus. Much to my surprise, she remembered me and my work and asked eagerly what I was working on now.

"Taking care of two kids and helping my husband get through graduate school. I've just finished proofreading his thesis, so there's not much time for art," I said, then added so as not to look as if I were a lost cause, "I do keep working when I can, though."

She looked at me with a mixture of scorn and pity. "What a shame!" she said, and turned away.

I don't know which of us was sorriest for the other.

JUGGLING ACTS
November 1963

O ur life here is not much different from graduate school. Tony is juggling teaching duties at Carnegie Tech in the city, while running experiments at the school's cyclotron in Saxonburg north of Pittsburgh. The school and lab are about thirty miles apart, so we live out here in the suburbs. Our house is midway between school and lab on the route of the small bus Carnegie Tech runs for students and faculty who divide their time, like Tony does, between research at the cyclotron and teaching duties at the campus.

This subdivision is in an abandoned apple orchard in the rolling hills of western Pennsylvania. It seems almost Eden-like after living in the desert and then the flat stretches of fields around Champaign-Urbana. The neighbors are pleasant. There are playmates galore for the children. Tony loves his work. And I am finding time to paint again. After we got settled in, only one more thing remained to be done. We had to find a place of worship.

All of the churches were a fair drive away, so convenience wasn't a factor. But one church was definitely not for us.

I didn't know how the elegantly dressed ladies who called on me that afternoon had found out that we had moved into the neighborhood. They came to the door of our little house as I was trying to get the birthday cake for Meg's party into the oven, take a load of wash from the machine to the dryer, and patch Joey's knee from a tumble he had taken out of one of the old apple trees in the backyard…just your ordinary day in the Herrington household.

One of my visitors was tall and looked like a Valkyrie in her gold straw helmet with a pair of bright pheasant wings sweeping back on either side of its high crown. Her companion wore an enchanting froth of white straw with a concoction of tiny feathered birds nesting in a bouquet of white daisies. It was not their fault that I started to sneeze when I opened the door.

"Hay fever," I apologized. How could I otherwise explain my allergy to church ladies in feathered hats?

One held a small tin of petits fours in her hands. The other, a lovely bouquet of June roses.

"Good afternoon," said Wings. "Welcome to Orchard Hills. Your neighbor, Mrs. Butterfield, across the street has told us that you are new in the neighborhood and that you are a Presbyterian. We're from the Appleton Presbyterian Church Women's Association and we'd like to tell you about our church. May we come in?"

What could I say as I wiped the powdered sugar off my hands onto my chocolate- stained apron but, "please do?"

"Would you care for some tea?"

Where did that come from? It was straight out of *The PK's Manual of Good Manners*. I hoped that they would say, *No, thank you, we can see that you're busy. We'll just leave this literature. Goodbye.*

"Why, thank you," said the Valkyrie. "We'd be delighted," as she took the Tonka toy dump truck off of the couch and sat down. "What a lovely home you have."

Lovely! There were jacks on the floor, a half-dressed Barbie doll on the coffee table, papers from the article Tony's been working on scattered on the floor beside his armchair where he had fallen asleep about 3 a.m. this morning. She wasn't serious! But as she and her friend had come without warning, I just decided that they'd have to take what they got.

I set three of Grandma's Spode teacups and plates and some napkins on the coffee table along with a dish of my "just in case" scotch shortbread on a silver dish. Tea was served.

I caught their reflection in the dining area mirror glancing at each other and nodding in approval.

"We understand that you and your husband are Presbyterians."

"I am. Dr. Herrington is an Episcopalian."

(Okay, I know Tony rarely used the title, but there are times when it seems to fit the occasion.)

"That would not matter at Appleton Presbyterian, my dear. My husband is…was…a Methodist," said Wings.

"You will find our congregation is very open-minded on such things. Our members are both well-educated and cosmopolitan," her friend twittered and smiled a well-educated, cosmopolitan smile.

"Oh, my yes, the very best people go to Appleton. You would fit right in." Why did I feel as if I was being interviewed for a country club?

At this time dear Joey and his sister got into a very loud dispute over a castle they were building in the sandbox in the backyard. For once I blessed their timing and their very healthy lungs. The Bird Ladies set their cups down on the coffee table.

"We'll just leave these brochures for you to look at," said Wings, heading for the door. "Hope to see you Sunday," said Little Birds.

And they beat a hasty retreat.

I gave the children the rest of the shortbread and some chocolate milk.

Then I got out the yellow pages and went from church to church hoping to find a place where we would feel spiritually at home. Somehow, we felt alien at them all. In one, the fact that Tony taught at Carnegie Tech and did research on elementary particles seemed to make him somehow some sort of a heathen to many of the parishioners. We wished we had said that he was in the English Department or something–anything that could not be construed as some covert atom-bomb builder. Why do people think that physicists want to blow up the world?

In another, the sermon was about the *Graven Images Commandment* when we visited there. The minister, who was standing in front of a reasonable copy of daVinci's *Last Supper*, went on and on about modern art as the instrument of the devil and the artists who made it, Beelzebub's servants.

Finally, one Saturday night (actually about 1:00 am Sunday when Tony got back from the lab) we sat at the breakfast table having a cup of hot chocolate and a piece of shortbread, Tony said, "Can we take a break from this church thing? We haven't had time for some just lazy time together all month. Could we just sleep in today and then go for a drive or something?"

And to the muffled sound of my grandfather, and three uncles spinning in their various resting places and my parents' certain disapproval, I said "Yes."

We still haven't found a church for "second best" or even "undeserving" people like us, but we did find a place for Meg in a small nursery school run by Julianne Lewis, a gem of a teacher who runs the school in her home two doors down from us. Joey is green-eyed with jealousy. One day I got a call from Julianne. She said that he had apparently followed his sister to "school" like Mary's little lamb and was having the time of his life. Talk about embarrassed!

I thought he was in the children's room playing while I was stealing a moment to get the laundry into the machine down in the basement.

When I went over to pick him up, Julianne suggested that I stay and have lunch since the morning session was almost done. I loved chatting with Julianne and the children were happy to have extra time to play on the playground equipment she had installed in the backyard for the nursery school.

Julianne was excited that day. Her husband, Captain Hank Lewis, had just gotten his new orders. Soon he would no longer be in charge of the Army troops guarding the Nike defense circle around the Pittsburgh area.

"He's leaving in six weeks to go to Vietnam as a military advisor."

"Is that good?" I asked, ashamed to admit that I was pretty hazy about exactly where Vietnam was.

"Sure it is. He'll be part of the effort to keep the place from falling into the hands of the Communists. That guy, Ho Chi Minh's a real serious Commie, and hand-in-glove with the Chinese. Since the French lost Dien Bien Phu, Vietnam's a plum for the picking, or maybe a domino. Remember Ike's speech about the domino effect? We don't want Indochina to be the first domino."

"I thought you said he was going to Vietnam."

"Same thing. It was Indochina when the French were in power."

I knew from the way she looked at me that this world traveler who had followed her husband to many of his postings around the world knew that I was a geographical dope.

It was true that I had not traveled anywhere out of the United States, but as soon as she said, Indochina, I could place Vietnam. The missionaries who visited my parent's home in Chicago had talked of Indochina as a beautiful place with a gentle population of independent-minded farmers, but I had no idea they might become Communists. Reverend and Mrs. Hoffmeister, who ministered to a Christian congregation in Peking, had been to Indochina years ago and had brought me a pretty woven hat from there. It was shaped like a pyramid and had a fringe of clipped fronds around the edge. It was the best sunhat I have ever worn.

Presbyterian missionaries often stayed in the manse as my parents' guests when they were on furlough from their Asian postings. Usually they were back to raise money for their missions, but they were real family friends as well and often brought me exotic gifts from China. My favorite was a miniature chest of drawers about six inches high, beautifully lacquered in black and painted with flowers and dainty birds. I still have it on my dresser, where it holds some of those old Chinese coins with square holes pierced in them that the Hoffmeisters brought back for me on my tenth birthday.

"Are you going with him?"

"Not this time. The kids and I'll move back to North Carolina to the farm. Mom and Dad can use my help with managing the place now they're getting older, and the kids love their big old farmhouse and the horses and chickens and stuff."

"Yeah, that's probably good," I said, and then threw my arms around my friend. "But I'll miss you."

"Me, too," she said sadly, hugging me back. "The story of my life... leaving friends just when I find them."

"MOM!" shouted her daughter, Angie, "Can Meg and Joey and me have some ice cream?"

"So life goes on," Julianne shrugged and scooped chocolate ice cream into cones while I ran back home for a plate of the just-in-case scotch shortbread.

My heart aches to remember that day, the last happy one I had with my friend. Julianne's last letter said that Hank had been killed in a sniper attack in the jungles of Vietnam. And so she and the children will stay in the big white farmhouse on the red dirt farm just outside of Charlotte where a gold star hangs on the door.

I just can't understand why we go from one war to another. It turns out that rumors of this war started before Tony was even discharged as a veteran of Korea, and I didn't pay attention. And when he first trans-ferred to the U. of I. from Florida, Tony was put up in the housing area at the University of Illinois where the disabled vets from World War II lived while they studied on the G.I. Bill. Now the students he's teaching face, as he did, a draft for this new war as soon as they finish their degrees.

Isn't there any other way?

But Tony's out of this one, thank God. He has completed the years of reserve service he was committed to after his discharge. We pulled from the attic the musty, old, hopelessly worn uniforms he was obliged to keep on hand, tossed them in the trash, and went out to dinner to celebrate.

It seems that we, here in our lovely, tree-shaded homes, with our healthy, well-fed children, are apart from the world outside. Oh, every day we hear the sonic booms of the jets from a nearby airbase as they break the sound barrier in the skies above us. Vietnam is no longer a place you have to look up on a map. It's in the paper every day and parents with draft- age sons are desperate for any strategy that will keep them out of the growing conflict there.

Some are even choosing to go to Canada rather than get drafted.

Oh, we knew real fear when we stocked our basement with food and water in '62 when we were sure that the Russians would attack us with missiles from Cuba. We would look at the children at dinner and wonder if we would be able to keep them safe should the worst happen.

Then last week I heard my next-door neighbor, Lucille, pounding on the door. "Anna! Anna!" she called.

I ran to the door thinking that Lisl, her beloved and very pregnant dachshund bitch, had gone into labor.

"They've shot him. He's been shot and he's not going to live. It's awful. Turn on the radio," Lucy was hysterical.

"Shot who?"

"Him! The President! Kennedy! He's been shot! Oh, my God!"

Then yesterday Tony and I were watching a television report of Lee Harvey Oswald, the man they've arrested as the man who shot the president, as they tried to move him to another jail. To our horror, we watched another assassination. A man named Jack Ruby shot Oswald point blank as we watched. It was horrible.

Today was the funeral of the president in whom we had such high hopes…the guy we all thought would be one of the lucky ones, one of the great ones, one who would show us what we could and should do for our country. And we were left with the image of a little boy on his third birthday, saluting the casket of his slain father as it rumbled past on a caisson.

"It was the Cuba connection," they said.

"A grand conspiracy by someone in the government," was a speculation. "Communists! They're everywhere!"

Rumors are flying, but perhaps the only man who did know the answer is dead, too, and the rumors may remain just that forever.

WHO'S THE STUDENT NOW?
January 1965

I only got a grade of B and Tony is trying to look serious as he says, "Now, Mrs. Herrington, if I am going to support your continuing education, I shall expect this grade to be raised to an A next term."

"Yes, Master, and I shall expect you not to let the children watch those mindless TV programs they tell me about the days after I've been at class."

"But TV keeps them quiet," said the Master of the House. "Do you know what it's like to have a six-year-old and an almost five-year-old running around while you're trying to work?"

I sat on his lap and pushed a lock of hair out of his eyes.

"No, I have no idea how hard it is to work with a six-year-old and an almost five-year-old running around. Why don't you tell me about it? And by the way, you need a haircut."

"Don't think that changing the subject is going to work," he said. But as usual, it did.

I was disappointed in that grade myself. It had been hard to get back in the swing of art studies after so many years away. But I had decided that since I could take classes at the very fine Art Department at Carnegie Tech as Tony's dependent, it was too good an opportunity to miss. So, I drove to the campus to speak with an advisor about getting a second bachelor's degree as an art major. But the advisor, Professor Randall, asked if I wanted to teach art or be a studio artist.

"If you aren't intending to teach, I would suggest that you explore where your weaknesses and strengths are and take courses that will speak to them. Why not start with a drawing class to get back into the swing of things. I'll accept the drawing classes you took as an undergraduate in Champaign so you can start at a more interesting advanced level."

"That would be great," I said. "I was not sure what credits would transfer."

Professor Randall laughed. "I'm an Illini myself. Is Jack Howard still teaching sculpture…" and so the talk turned to who was who and where among the University of Illinois faculty.

It was a fifteen-mile drive to the campus and my classes started at 7 p.m. By then I had already put in a twelve-hour day. Tony agreed to feed the kids the supper I laid out for them and put them to bed on the three nights I had class. It was a hectic schedule for both of us. Now, after that first quarter, we have found a lovely lady who was delighted to come on class nights to get Tony and the children's dinner and tuck the kids into bed. Bedtime stories for Meg and Joey are no longer haphazard TV, but the telling of Mrs. O'Connell's huge repertoire of Irish folktales.

The children have developed a slight Irish brogue from imitating their adored, real-life Mary Poppins.

That quarter I got an "A".

It was kind of funny being a student after all those years. I was, of course, the oldest person in the class, including the recent MFA from the School of the Art Institute in Chicago who taught the class. But I'm kind of small and have a long ponytail, so no one really noticed me much.

My disguise worked so well that I found myself in a rather awkward position one evening. The girl sitting at the easel next to me was one of the long blonde hair, great figure, sexy types and was far more interested in her boyfriend than she was in the model in the stand. Why Mr. Pecarelli didn't ask the young man to leave and stop disturbing the class I wasn't sure. The boyfriend, as blond and preppy-handsome as the girl, was complaining loudly about his physics professor who was giving him an F in Physics 101.

"That son-of-a-gun Dr. Lindman is going to flunk me just because I missed some classes this last three weeks. I'll make it up. I've got the stuff snowed. So I missed the last pop quiz. It's just a little quiz. What's the matter with the guy? Doesn't he know it's Spring Carnival this weekend? Some of us had work to do. Jeez! My dad's going to kill me and it's, all Lindman's fault."

"Oh Wilson," the girl sympathized. "That's awful! Will you lose your student deferment if you flunk out? What will you do?"

"Nah, I'll transfer to another school like I did when I got kicked out of Yale. It'll be my third one. I gotta' find a place where I can get myself into med school. Can't let the Langford family down, can I? Come on. Let's split and get a Coke."

It was so lamebrained and sad I didn't know what to do. When Stan and Mary Lindman had been over for dinner last week, Stan had talked about how he was going to have to flunk a boy and it really upset him. Stan is a terribly conscientious teacher and felt personally responsible if one of his students wasn't "getting it." Could this dopey brat standing next to me be Stan's "failure"?

"Maybe I'll give him a make-up quiz. If he passes that, I might be able to raise his grade to a D. After all, he did have to go home to see his dad who had pneumonia," he'd said.

"Kind of a nuisance having to make up a second quiz," Tony said. "But if his dad was sick, I suppose the kid deserves a break."

Then at the end of the quarter, Stan and Mary asked us over to celebrate the beginning of the summer holidays. Just as Mary put a bubbling casserole of her famous lasagna on the table, the phone rang.

"I'll get it, honey. You go ahead and serve."

He was gone so long that we went ahead and started to eat. Stan finally came back and sat down heavily. Mary looked at his sad face.

"Stan! What's the matter? Is someone sick or something?"

"That was the father of the boy I had to flunk. You remember – the one who had to go home when his dad was sick. But he just didn't apply himself after he got back. I spent lots of time with him, but his mind was on everything else but physics. The father said it was my fault that the kid failed."

I'm paying your school lots of money to see that my son gets taught properly. Since you can't do your job, I'll have to complain to the Dean. Wilson is going to be a doctor like me and he can't get into medical school without a good grade in physics. Your ineptitude will ruin a potentially fine career.

"He went on and on like that. Maybe he's right," said Stan. "It's my responsibility to teach and I failed. I'm going to offer to tutor him this summer and maybe he'll pass next quarter."

"But Stan, you promised we'd take the whole summer off. We haven't been on vacation since the week after you finished graduate school. What about our trip to Canada with Anna and Tony?"

I interrupted Mary.

"Stan, what does this kid look like?"

"About six-foot, sandy hair, probably too handsome for his own good, has a kind of Ivy- League look about him"

"Name?"

"Wilson Langford. Why?"

I told him why.

After I finished my story, Wilson Langford III was finally going to have to find another tutor, and the Herringtons and the Lindmans spent the rest of the evening on plans for the camping trip to Nova Scotia our two families had been looking forward to all year long.

Of course, Dr. Langford II pulled some strings and got his son into another, less demanding school. But if Wilson does get to become a physician, I sure feel sorry for his patients.

SHALL WE OVERCOME?
February 1966

It was two years ago that I got the call. "Anna?"

The voice on the phone didn't sound right. Mom usually said "Hi, dear. It's Mom."

"Mom? What's wrong.?"

There was a silence on the other end of the line. "Mom? What's wrong?" I repeated.

"Joe's in jail. He was arrested in Hattiesburg."

"What? Why? Where?"

"Hattiesburg, in Mississippi. He went down there with some other ministers to march about getting Negroes registered to vote… we don't know what they'll do to him…it's awful…your dad's having a fit because he doesn't know what he can do to help… Joe didn't tell him he was going…it's like a bolt from the blue…what will happen to him…what will we do if they won't let him out of jail…is Tony there…maybe he can figure something out."

Mom was babbling and I couldn't get a word in until she finally ran down.

"Mom, try to calm down. Tony's at the lab. I'll call him and see if there's anybody there who has got some experience with this kind of thing. I know that a couple of the guys were in sit-ins at Berkeley and got arrested there. Maybe they can tell us what to do.

"I'm sure he'll be alright. It's probably not a serious charge and they're just trying to scare the protesters."

In point of fact, I was less confident about that than I let on. From what little I knew of the South's response to the civil rights movement, some of the guys down there had been pretty nasty. It seemed that in the so-called Bible Belt, *love thy neighbor as thyself* had gotten *only if he's white* tacked on to it. There had been plenty of evidence that a radical group of people there could be violent. As far back as 1961, I'd heard about some members of an integrated group called The Congress of Racial Equality being badly beaten when they tried to test the new regulations of the Interstate Commerce Commission by riding a bus from Washington, DC into the region.

But, like many others, I hadn't paid that much attention to the civil rights movement. Tony was still in graduate school and I had two young children to keep out of his hair while he studied. There was the disruption of moving to a new city and a new life. And it all seemed so far away. Now it was right here in my living room as I heard my mother weeping over the phone.

When Tony was working on his degree in Champaign-Urbana, we took care of Chung- He, a Korean friend's baby, while his parents attended a family wedding in Seoul. I took him and our children to the park, never thinking that this was an unusual thing to do. When our friends came back from their trip, they asked if we'd had any trouble with the little fellow.

"Not a bit," I told his mother. "He is a perfect darling. Meg and Joey had a ball with him." And that was the truth. The children had adopted him as their baby and asked over and over if he *really* had to go back home when Hyun-Su and Soo Jin came home.

But gradually it came out in the conversation that Chung-He's parents had been worried that someone would have made some troubling remark about us having a Korean baby.

"Why on earth would they do that?"

"He's dark skinned and has our eyes."

"But he's adorable. Why would that matter?"

"Because his skin is not white and that makes all the difference in the world."

I had tried to understand what Hyun-Su meant ever since. Now today, my brother was in jail because he truly believed that the color of one's skin did not change one's right to vote in American elections for the leaders of our country. I found out later that they had called him a "white nigger" when they took him off to jail. He had put his own freedom on the line to challenge injustice. I felt ashamed.

Where was I when that teacher couldn't eat in the dining room of the Edgewater Beach Hotel? Where was I when, on the day Joey was born, I was asked to give up my private hospital room to a Negro Air Force Colonel's wife so that none of the other new mothers would have to share a room with a black woman? I would have been perfectly happy to share a room with her. Why didn't they just ask me if I would?

Because I didn't want to think about it... didn't want to get *involved*... didn't want to understand that I was my sister's keeper. I was actually so dumb, that I didn't understand what a Negro friend in college meant when she said that the reason we could be good friends was that I treated her like I treated everyone else. Why was that special to her?

When Tony got home, he found me on the phone with Jess. "I'm sure he'll be alright.

The question is, are you alright? Is there anything we can do?

"Okay. I'll try to keep Mom and Dad calm. They're pretty upset. But please keep in touch and let us know if there's anything else you need."

Jess had just filled in the details of the affair for us. Joe and the three other clergymen, a Catholic priest and two other Protestants, one of whom was a Negro, had marched in a voter registration protest in Hattiesburg, and had been thrown in the Hattiesburg jail for violating new, more restrictive rules put in place after some weeks of picketing at the courthouse. One of the policemen in charge of "controlling" their supposedly unruly mob, had claimed that someone in their group had "bellied him" by bumping into his copious beer gut. The four clergymen were charged and found guilty of "disturbing the peace" and thrown in jail. Even there, segregation held sway. The Negro minister was incarcerated in a cell of his own.

At the end of the week, their trial took place and they were banished from Mississippi for life. They got in their car and drove immediately out of the state.

We could not have known then that a major tragedy would happen to three other civil rights protesters after their release from a Mississippi jail less than six months later. James Chaney, a Negro man from Mississippi, and Michael Schwerner and Andrew Goodman from New York had been arrested for speeding when they arrived in Philadelphia, Mississippi to look in to the burning of a Negro church there. The men were thrown into the Neshoba County Jail. After their release on June 21, they went missing until their bodies were recovered from an earthen dam near the town in August. I can only imagine the anguish that their families went through.

But Joe arrived home safely and resumed his place in the pulpit of his New Hampshire congregation. Dad was sure that my brother's career would be ruined by his impetuous trip to Mississippi. He never understood that it was his own example of tolerance that had taught his children that all children were God's children. I don't know if he ever took the pride in his son's dedication to that ideal. He should have! As for mother, she, like Mary, the mother of Jesus, did as the Bible says and *took all these things and pondered them in her heart*. I still don't know exactly how she feels about the whole affair.

But the experience only hardened Joe's resolve to become involved in the rights of the Negro community. Soon, he left his pastorate in the East and traveled south to teach philosophy and religion at a venerable Negro college in Charlotte, North Carolina. The fight for civil rights goes on. Who knows when the battle will be won, if ever.

But Dad never saw the outcome of his son's determination to right an injustice.

On January 2 of this year, Joe and Jess were leaving to return home after a holiday visit with our folks. They were on their way back to New Hampshire to spend their last days in the manse there. They would be leaving the church where Joe had served as pastor for nine years and move to Charlotte, North Carolina where Joe would start his life as a professor, teaching philosophy and religion.

Dad had not been feeling well. He insisted that it was just a touch of flu and that Joe and Jess should go ahead and catch their train east. But almost as soon as they left, he complained of severe chest pains and allowed Mom to call for medical help. When the medics took a look at him, they took Mom aside and suggested that she try to reach Joey before he got out of town. In a wonderful display of human compassion, the railroad reached him at the first station out of the city so Joey and Jess returned for one more brief moment with Dad before he died.

Thank goodness, they were there. Mom told me afterwards how much she needed them beside her as she watched, dismayed and helpless, as her partner of four decades slipped away from her.

Tony and I got the news by phone from Joey just at dinnertime in Pennsylvania. We had a guest for dinner whose own father had passed recently of a sudden heart attack and he knew the shock we were going through. What a gentleman he was, quietly consoling us and then slipping away dinnerless to let us make the plans for me to return to Chicago.

Dear Mrs. O'Connor, came to our aid so that I could leave Tony and the children and fly home. They would follow by car for the funeral.

Once again, I realized the value of Bird Ladies to the fabric of the church. They immediately set to planning the reception after the service, sent innumerable dishes of food and touching offers of support and affection to Mom.

The funeral was a revelation to Joey and me. We had not understood the esteem in which Dad had been held. The local rabbi, the Roman Catholic priest from the church a few blocks away, the Episcopal priest, and, of course, many of his Presbyterian colleagues came to the services. I saw Zack and Miss Marigold McDaniel come in together. Officer O'Shaunessy directed the traffic. It seemed everyone was there. Each of the mourners had a story of how he had been their rock in time of need, officiated at their marriages and baptized their children.

Even my "big sister" from my freshman year at college, Ruth Mayfield, now Mrs. Frank O'Malley, came. I had not known that she had often traveled from her home in Evanston, where Frank was teaching at Northwestern, to hear Dad preach at Sunday services. I was very touched.

Then all too soon, we all had to return home to our families and responsibilities. Mom encouraged us to go, insisting that she would be fine because her sister Grace was staying with her. I was a little dubious about that, remembering the episode of the wedding hat years ago. But they seemed to manage the huge job of getting Mom ready to move from the apartment where she had lived for twenty-seven years.

The problem was that Mom's home did not belong to her, but to the church. She was given six weeks to organize the memorabilia of all those years of living that had collected in the twelve rooms and storage spaces of the apartment. I cannot imagine how she and Grace did it. Aunt Lillian, who knew antiques and their value, supervised that part of the job. Joey and I came back to help by telling Mom what we wanted to keep and getting the things out of her way.

In six weeks, the apartment was empty and ready for Dad's successor, and Mom had ensconced herself in a one-bedroom apartment near the church and her friends there.

This strong, efficient, little woman was now on her own for the first time in over forty years. And when we first visited her in her efficient, modern rooms, she finally let me in on her dark secret. Much as she missed Dad, she was delighted to get out of those huge, now lonely rooms where she had been constantly "on call" for more than a quarter of a century.

"See," she said proudly, showing us the tiny kitchen hidden behind a folding, shuttered screen, "it's all mine and I can paint it purple with pink polka dots if I want."

Of course, she never wanted to. She only wanted to know that she could.

SPRECHEN SIE DEUTSCH?
September 1967

Everyone has, in their past, moments when they should have listened to their parents and didn't. I have more than I can recount in this book, but the one I'm kicking myself about right now happened when I was seven years old. My father, who was fluent in German, announced that he was going to teach me to speak and write that language as his mother, who had been a German war bride from the First World War, had taught him. He and Granny Mac spoke German when she visited us from Scotland. Grandma Lowrie, who had helped raise me, loved it when Granny Mac came. I remembered the two old ladies sitting in Grandma's room chatting away over endless cups of tea, occasionally chuckling at the differences in the Bavarian dialect of Grandma Lowrie and the clear, precise sounds of Granny Mac's northern speech.

But there was a hitch in my father's plan. We were at war and everything Japanese or German or Italian was in bad repute. The propaganda machinery was working very well. German opera, Japanese toys, Italian food all had a hard struggle to survive the onslaught. Revenge was the order of the day and a child of seven was not about to want to learn the language of the enemy.

So, when my husband came home from the lab one day and said, "How would you like to go to Germany for a year? Hartmut called this afternoon and said that his group at the German research facility in Hamburg would like me to come and work there for a year. There's Fulbright money involved, and there's a good chance that I can get a Fulbright fellowship to go over there with you and the kids. What an experience for Meg and Joey it would be! They're just the right age to learn a foreign language. What better way than to learn it where it's spoken?" I could almost hear my father's ghost laugh. "I told you so. Meg's the same age you were when I wanted you to learn German."

But the prospect was exciting. I had never been to Europe. I couldn't speak German, but I knew how it should sound, so how hard would it be to pick it up once I got there? Everyone says that most Germans have studied English, so I should be able to get along. Besides, it would be a chance to learn more about the culture that had helped shape my family, and, through them, formed me. It did sound like an exciting thing to do but for one thing. I was afraid of flying. The idea of sitting in a metal box that surely did not belong in the clouds scared the daylights out of me.

Tony saw something was bothering me and insisted I tell him what it was. He, who flew as casually as if he were driving a car, could have laughed at such foolishness, but as usual, he had a solution to my problem.

"We can go by ship."

Now that was worth the trip. I love to be on the water and am rarely seasick. The kids would have a treat. And Tony really needed a break from the pressures of the lab. There had been a rumor that the Carnegie machine was to be shut down by the Department of Energy, so who knew if he would even have a job here by the time we got back.

Once Tony got an enthusiastic okay from me, and a rather dubious one from the children, things moved very quickly. The funding for the trip was assured by the Fulbright Committee and our plans gathered momentum fast.

Tony, to whom my Mom was as dear as his own, had the bright idea of inviting her to come along. We called her, thinking that she would jump at the chance, but the idea of such a long trip overwhelmed her. Her recent widowhood had been enough change to cope with. She thanked us, but said no thanks.

Then there was the dog. Our current pet was an engaging Welsh terrier named Bronwyn, who would not be welcome in onsite housing at the laboratory. But Mrs. O'Connor, who was sad to think that "her" children would be leaving for a year, came up with the solution. She and her husband had a sort of mini-farm just outside the suburb where we lived. Bronwyn would be living like an only child of doting parents.

One day, Tony came home with flyers showing pictures of the ocean liner on which we were to travel. At last the children really got excited about the trip. Since Fulbrighters are required to travel on carriers of the host country, the *SS Bremen*, run by the German shipping company *Norddeutscher Lloyd,* was a perfect choice. She had been a luxury liner before the war, then a troop ship. Now, handsomely refitted, she was a luxury liner again and she was beautiful.

As soon as the school year was over, we rented the house to a couple from England who were working for a year at the lab. Bronwyn went to make a name for herself at the O'Connor farm as an expert rat catcher. One of Tony's graduate students bought our Buick, and we drove off in a rented Oldsmobile for New York City to meet our ship.

245

Friends from New Jersey came in to town to see us off, which put the crowning touch on our departure. The wharf was chaos. Great nets were swung from the dock over the opening of the ship's hold and we could see our trunks in one of them. Suddenly there was a shout, and the crane slowly set its net back on the ground. Two very embarrassed parents sheepishly claimed a small boy about Joey's age as he climbed out of the net. Despite the danger and the foolishness of the boy's trick, Joey was delighted with it. He was even happier to discover that the boy and his family were traveling on the same deck quite near us. But knowing Joey, I wasn't that enthusiastic to have Mickey quite so close at hand. Who knows what those two could get up to once they put their heads together.

The departure was a festive one. Bob and Judy brought a bottle of champagne and some snacks, which we make short work of in our small stateroom. Another gift was a book called *The Phantom Tollbooth* for the children, which we read and reread on the trip over and many times after. Then it was time for our friends to go unless they wanted to go all the way to Dover with us. "All visitors must depart. The gangplank is about to be drawn in. All ashore that's going ashore," the ship's loudspeaker warned in both English and German.

We followed our friends up three flights of stairs to the deck to watch them going down to the wharf. Then we stood at the rail waving as, with much fuss and bother, we were pushed away from land. And Bob and Judy became tiny specks on the wharf as we set out down the Hudson River.

From our vantage point, the little tugs accomplishing the job looked like a pack of snub- nosed Pekingese worrying a Great Dane. But soon we were heading for our adventure. We moved majestically down the shipping channel, waving farewell to the Statue of Liberty as we passed. I was Emily Kimbrough and one of those characters in an old *film noire* rolled into one. It all felt like a dream, especially when the couple next to us on the rail pointed out a coterie of dolphins who were cavorting in our bow wave as we sailed into the open sea.

Sure, flying to Europe is very exciting, but sailing on a ship like the *SS Bremen* was the best rest I had ever had as a wife and mother. All our meals were planned, served graciously by someone else and the dirty dished spirited away to be returned, sparkling clean for the next meal. There was a play school for the children, which they loved. The weather was sunny and calm, and I could actually read a book or just do nothing if I chose.

Tony, on the other hand, gets fidgety if he can't do physics, so I found him another physicist to talk to. Gunter was sitting on the deck chair next to mine one afternoon and I happened to glance over at the book he was reading. I could see those arcane scratchings I knew so well from proofreading Tony's thesis. The Austrian admitted that he was reading a physics text and that he was a professor of the subject in Vienna. When I got Tony and Gunter together later that afternoon, the two men greeted each other like two castaways united at last on a desert island.

The only questionable motif in this idyllic picture was Mickey, the boy from the loading net. The child was way too smart and imaginative for his own good and that of our Joey. Some misguided soul had given Mickey a very realistic wind-up mouse that skittered across decks in a very satisfactory, lifelike way. Mickey and Joey would hide behind a lifeboat or in a corner and launch the mouse between ladies' legs or right in front of the burly German seamen who worked on the ship. One day one of these fellows decided that they had enough.

I looked up from my book to see one boy in each huge paw of the sailor, his fist clutching each boy by the back of his shirt and giving them a good shaking. The German was speaking in a strange, Dutch-sounding dialect.

"What did he say?" I asked the woman on the deck chair next to mine. "I can't understand him."

She laughed and said, "That's because he's speaking Plattdeutsch. It's an old dialect spoken in parts of Hamburg. He's annoyed with the boys who have that foolish mouse that has been driving the sailors crazy. The sailor told them, "If I see that damned mouse again on my watch, I'll throw it overboard and you after it. Understand?"

"Thank you," I said, and, since the sailor looked quite capable of doing just that, I commandeered the mouse and hid it deep in my luggage.

Mickey was a very literal child. I had been the same in my childhood and I developed a soft spot in my heart for him. Rascal that he was, he took everything quite at face value. For example, when the loudspeaker called us to go to our assigned lifeboats to prepare to abandon ship in case of an accident or fire, Mickey didn't listen to the *in case of* part and took the precaution of putting a note in a Coke bottle which read, "Help! The Bremen is sinking!" and threw it overboard.

I think he was a little disappointed that it was only a lifeboat drill. But when he found out, he knew what to do. He got another coke bottle and wrote another note. "Never mind. It was just a drill," and tossed it overboard to go with the other.

We bade farewell to Mickey at Dover where he was met by his English grandparents.

Nice looking folks. I hoped they knew what they were in for.

Then we sailed from the storied white cliffs and went on our way through a narrow North Sea channel to where we were to land at Bremerhaven at the mouth of the Weser River estuary.

That afternoon, while looking out at the sea, I noticed that we were sailing very close to a string of buoys. I almost wish I hadn't asked Tony why the shipping channel was so narrow in such a large body of water.

"The North Sea's been mined for so many wars, they can keep only the channel we're in cleared. Some of the sailors told me that there are mines still in these waters from the Franco- Prussian War, to say nothing of mines from every conflict afterwards."

It was my first experience of being close to the dangers of real war. There were many more to come.

But in the excitement of landing, arranging for our luggage to be sent on the train to Hamburg with us, and getting something to eat, I forgot about the mines. It was impossible, however, to forget the voyage. After eight days aboard ship, one's inner ear has to rebalance itself. Lunch that day was weird, to say the least. Though I knew that I was sitting still on dry land, my *schnitzel* was rocking as if I were in an ocean storm. It was more disturbing than actually being on board, and it took a while before things on my plates stopped moving and stood still like proper plates should.

There was not much time to worry, however, as our train was about to depart for the Hauptbahnhof in Hamburg and we had to gather our hand luggage and get two tired and excited children to the train.

My brother Joe is a model train buff and had running models of German trains, but this was real life and the feeling of being in a film instead of reality came back. We had a compartment to ourselves and Meg and Joey were glued to the window staring out at what looked like illustrations in one of their storybooks. The train ran parallel to a country road where a little girl in a blue dirndl was driving a flock of robust white geese before her with a long stick. Bringing up the rear was a large dog who looked, from a distance, like Red Riding Hood's wolf but shepherded the flock into proper German order. There were cottages thatched in straw, with flowers bright in their trim little gardens. Old men gathered in front of half-timbered inns enjoying the afternoon sun with their pipes and huge steins of beer.

But the most exciting thing for Meg and Joey was when we passed a chimney sweep, his top hat jaunty on his head, his thin form bristling with the brushes of his trade wrapped around his body, pedaling along the road on his bicycle. Meg and Joey knew then, for sure, that they were not in Pennsylvania any more.

Hartmut, bless his heart, was there to greet us at the Hamburg train station. He saw to the delivery of our luggage to our new home at the lab housing, then took us home for a dinner which by now sat fairly solidly on the table though it still had the slight movement of a gently rocking sea. Finally, we got back into his car to drive to the high-rise apartment building where we would live for the next year.

WHAT DID YOU DO IN THE WAR?
January 1968

It was December 31, 1946 that President Harry Truman declared officially that World War II had ended. But it takes more than the stroke of a pen to end a war. The memories of the conflict that consumed much of Tony's and my childhood were still everywhere in Germany.

I watched old people, who looked startlingly like some of my family, stop dead in the streets when the weekly emergency sirens went off. They would look up at the sky as if the British bombers who turned Hamburg streets into rivers of molten asphalt in a firestorm of destruction were about to appear again. Meg's third-grade teacher showed her the little doll the woman had saved from those times when she and her family huddled in basements as they heard the terrifying booms of the firebombs night after night.

We saw some of this when we walked along the docks, on which Hamburg's ancient reputation as a prosperous Hanseatic port had developed. The facilities were mainly for cargo too valuable to be subjected to a voyage through the turbulent waters of the Kattegat and the Skagerrak. They had evolved into twentieth-century affairs bustling with trade. Yet there were still some docks showing signs of damage from World War II.

My favorite city was Lübeck. Marienkirche, a fine Gothic church in Lübeck, was first built in 1250 and completed a hundred years later. We were lucky enough, one day, to visit the church when the current organist was practicing. Perhaps we stood in the same spot where J. S. Bach had stood as a young man when he came to Lübeck to hear the great organ fill the church with the same chorale by Buxtehude as it had done over two hundred years before when played by the composer himself. Yet on the floor near us in the south tower of the church lay two bells that fell to the floor during an Allied air raid in 1942. They rested where they had fallen, half buried in dirt by the impact of their descent, sad reminders of a bitter war that almost destroyed the building that held so much history.

I never thought that I would serve dinner to someone who had been a prisoner of war of the United States. Yet, when we complimented a guest on his grasp of English cooking terms one night at table, he smiled and said that he had learned it when he was a prisoner of war at a POW camp in Missouri. I said, "I hope we treated you well."

"Very well indeed. One of the men who was captured with me was a chef at the officers' mess in Germany. When he showed the colonel in charge of the prison camp his credentials as a chef, he was put in charge of the officers' mess at the camp. So, he took several of us and made us into *sous chefs*. I've never eaten that well again, except, of course, until tonight," he added gallantly.

Everyone had some story to tell, and I was eager to hear what they had to say. But for the fact that one German grandmother had fallen in love with a Scottish soldier so long ago and the other's father had brought his family to Illinois to homestead, I might have been one of the Germans we entertained regularly, and in whose homes we often visited.

So, I wanted to know what they had gone through. How, for example, had a people who had produced Bach, Mozart and Handel; Goethe, Schopenhauer and Rilke; Riemenschneider, Dürer, and Barlach have allowed themselves to fall under the sway of a dictator as vicious, as venal as Adolph Hitler? Where were these good people when their country was becoming the rogue nation that it had been in that devastating war? Why was he able to subjugate his country and bring it to such a place that the only answer was the destruction of much of the great heritage of a once fine state?

I do not pretend to be an historian. Good heavens! I can hardly remember the dates of my families' birthdays. The only history I can remember and relate with any assurance is art history, and, while I can recall faces and paintings and so on, I have trouble remembering someone's name at a cocktail party two minutes after I've met them.

No. It's more a matter of this "good girl" training that's been hammered into my brain. The Germans appear to me to be very good people. I feel as comfortable with them as I did with my grandmothers. And yet they let an unprepossessing house painter lead them into creating Buchenwald and Dachau, death camps for innocent men and women and children who should have been saved from him. Why didn't they speak up? Why didn't they stop this mad man?

More puzzling still, were the military tombs in the somberly beautiful cemeteries we visited. Here we saw the graves of many of the soldiers killed in the conflict. But for the difference in the language they were written in, the epitaphs were the same. The dead were young men mourned by their loved ones who prayed for their souls and decried their untimely loss. Their *Gott* was the same God of my fathers. Yet the cause for which they had died was diametrically opposed to our Johnnies who never came marching home. There but for the grace of God or *Gott* could have gone my brother and cousins. If the prayers of that German mother had been answered, an American mother's prayer would have become for the soul of a lost son.

Why do we continue to beat our ploughshares into swords? Why don't we all speak out against…?

But then I remembered that I didn't speak out when Negroes were being hung in the South and their homes and churches burned. I didn't speak up when we fell into war in Korea and Vietnam. I even helped build missiles designed to kill and didn't think about it at all. It all came down to that. No one wants wars and no one seems to care about stopping them until it's too late. And who can stop them then?

But, as much as this question occupied my thoughts, what with the antiwar protests in Europe and America, there were many days when being in Germany were sheer delight. We had an international community in the Wolnetron, a five-story high-rise apartment set on a broad lawn just inside the gate to the accelerator at the German High Energy facility. Several families in the building also had children and the playground was often full of chatter in several languages. Meg and Joey became fluent in German in less than two months. It was a case of there not being an option. Either they spoke German or they were outsiders, and they were far too sociable to accept that.

Not only did they speak German, they spoke it in with a Hamburg accent. We of course, would not have known the difference until our Austrian neighbor knocked on our door one day. He had a big grin on his face when I opened the door.

"I had to tell you," he laughed. "Did you know your Joey speaks more like a native than I do? I just heard this kid in the playground and was wondering how a local kid got in the gates to play there. It was Joey." Soon Meg and Joey were mortified when Tony and I spoke German in front of their new friends.

LOST IN TRANSLATION
August 1968

I am of the opinion that German has more grammatical and social pitfalls than any other language. Just when you think you've gotten it right, some German will point out that it is *das* instead of *der*, or that if you use the *sie* form of address instead of the *du* form or visa-versa in error, you are insulting someone. Tony had only become familiar with the *sie* or formal form of address when he took the language in graduate school. When he used it with me instead of the more informal *du* form, everyone thought that we might not be getting along very well.

On our weekend outings to the countryside, the children would suggest that we keep our mouths closed and they would order the rooms. The concierge of whatever inn we were attempting to book lodgings would peer over his high desk to see the source of that very good Hamburg German.

I didn't have time for formal lessons like some of the other wives in the building. I was making a serious attempt to get back to my art when the children were in school. With that, the house, the children and the guests Tony brought home for lunch or dinner, I was either shopping, cooking, doing laundry or bandaging scrapped knees. Many of the Germans I had contact with wanted far more to practice their English with me than to let me practice my German on them.

The only person who absolutely refused to speak English in the building was our cleaning lady, Frau Schmidt. We were her guests in her country, and she expected the courtesy of being addressed in her own language in her own land. Like several Germans we met, Frau Schmidt had escaped the Russian occupation of the East Zone. I believe that she had been a teacher there as she spoke what I was told was excellent German.

We soon became good friends and I looked forward to my twice-a-week German "lesson." What German I have been able to glean this past year is largely due to her persistence in my learning it.

But I was confronted with many more differences than language. There was food, for instance.

The children often brought their friends up to the apartment to play. The lab was a closed site with guards and at first the parents were afraid that their children would get in trouble with the authorities for coming in. But Meg and Joey were pets of the guards, and so Rainer, and Dietrich and Gerda were often in the playground or in the apartment.

So, on Joey's birthday in February, I decided to give a birthday party for some of the local children. German flour for baking is not ground in the same way ours is, so it gives cakes a different texture. As a treat for the children, I had Mother send over a box of chocolate cake mix, which I made into a two-layer cake with chocolate filling and decorated icing.

Then, in the American tradition, I bought some ice cream. The refrigerator in the apartment has a freezer about the size of a small shoebox. Ice cream is sold in small, very expensive packages to fit these very small refrigerators and is considered a major treat. So, when the children saw how many of the little frozen bricks of ice cream were jammed into the freezer, they were awestruck with delight.

The cake, so carefully imported, baked, and decorated, was a flop! It was too high and didn't have the right texture and the children told me in no uncertain terms that it was NOT a *torte*. But the ice cream...as soon as I brought that out, all chatter stopped and the children spooned up every bite, the cost of which had been far more than several liters of excellent Rhine wine.

The two other things that took some teaching before the children would eat them were popcorn and peanut butter and jelly sandwiches. Peanut butter was a hard sell because it was unknown to the children. We got it from the commissary down at the consulate. But after one taste of *erdnusscreme* and *marmelade* on bread, that was all they wanted for lunch at our house.

Why they took so long to cotton to popcorn was another story. One of the mothers explained it to me as she was having her first delighted experience with American-style popcorn. During the Marshall Plan, a shipping clerk had gotten an order to ship *korn* to Hamburg. The American clerk, assuming the Germans knew what to do with it, sent some surplus popcorn over. Food was still in short supply then and the Germans thought that it was a breakfast cereal and so they boiled it and served it with milk and sugar. No wonder the children didn't consider the offer of *puff maize* a treat until they had tasted freshly popped corn, salted and drizzled with butter.

But probably the most unusual pitfall was hidden until I fell into it at the shopping center.

I thought that the English spoke the same language that I did.

257

In the year that we lived in Hamburg, I had the opportunity to see many art treasures of Germany. From the days that I had, as a child, watched the old, expatriate woodcarver work on the carvings which were to replace those lost in a fire at my father's church, I had loved that art form. And now it appeared everywhere we went.

There was one of those engaging, chubby angels called a putto on one of the altarpieces I had sketched hastily before we moved on to other sights. Back at my little corner of the basement at the lab apartment building where I had been given a studio, I had decided to make a more lasting plaster sculpture of the piece. But I had no plaster of Paris with which to make it.

The hardware store at the shopping mall seemed to have everything I might need and the clerk was willing to put up with my bad German. I got the wire for an armature for the little piece and then I asked him for *fünf Pfund Pflaster*. He laughed and said, "You must go across the way to the *Apotheke*."

"I need at least five pounds of *pflaster*, so why did I need to go to the drug store?" I repeated the request.

The clerk asked, *Warum?*

Ich bin eine Bildhauerin, and I need the five pounds of pflaster for an art project, I answered, mixing German and English in my frustration.

"Then you must go to the *Apotheke*."

We were obviously not communicating, so I got out my handy *Langenscheidt Universal- Wörterbücher*, looked up the English word *plaster* and showed it to him. He nodded and sent me to the drugstore again.

By this time, a fairly large crowd had gathered and everyone was telling me in German and English, or a mixture of both, that I MUST go to the drugstore for what I wanted.

Finally, a savior elbowed his way to my side and said in that precise way well-educated Germans speak English, "I think I know what your problem is. You are, I think, an American and that *Langenscheidts* you're using is an English/German dictionary."

"Of course."

He laughed. "But you need an American-English/German dictionary. You see, a *plaster*, often called, in British-English, a sticking plaster, is what you might call a Band-Aid. The word you want is *Gips*, which is the German word for that white powder that hardens when mixed with water. You have been asking for five pounds of Band-Aids.

"There are many instances of such in that little book," he continued, pointing at the traitorous little book in my hand, "*lift* for elevator, *lorry* for truck, *trainers* for gym shoes, and on and on. The best way for you to really understand some of these is just to watch TV commercials and get yourself a copy of a picture dictionary in German."

Then I remembered that another couple who were Fulbrighters in Heidelberg had, like us, sent their children to the local German schools. They thought that if the children took English, they would enjoy finding out how their German friends were learning the language. However, Brenda and Rick were horrified at the teacher's mispronunciations and gently tried to correct them. Soon the teacher called their embarrassed parents in for a conference. "I am trying," she said coldly, "to teach my children to speak English like British ladies and gentlemen. You may keep the children in the class if they promise to speak only German there. I don't wish to have the children picking up an American accent."

There are so many memories of our time in Hamburg, that they alone could fill this book. We have returned to the USA and a new life, but the friendships we made in Germany will, I'm sure, last a lifetime.

AUF WIEDERSEHEN
September 1968

Our memorable stay in Germany ended with an equally memorable sail home. I loved being on the *SS Bremen* again, even though a North Atlantic gale hit a day or so into the trip. That was an experience that I now look back on with more aplomb than I felt at the time. But one day when the sea had calmed, the captain announced that a large pod of whales had been sighted off the starboard bow and he politely hoped that no one would mind if we went over to take a look.

Soon about a dozen gray giants were swimming gracefully on either side of the ship, breeching and blowing as if they were showing off just for us. What was a bit of *mal de mare* to see that? Not for the first time was I glad my fear of flying had caused us to take the ship.

We are also looking forward to returning once more to Illinois where one of the most exciting events in Tony's field of physics is taking place. He will be among those physicists, engineers, designers, contractors, and office staff who are charged with building the world's largest particle accelerator, a national laboratory that will become man's peephole into the deepest secrets of the universe. That sounds pretty awesome when it's written down on paper, and it is. And he is really excited to be part of it.

When it had become apparent that we would not be returning to the now-closed cyclotron at Carnegie Tech, Tony wrote his thesis advisor, Professor Jacob Silverman, to inquire about working at the new machine. The answer came back in the form of an offer to return to Illinois, and get to work as soon as possible.

Probably the best thing about the change for me was that I would once more be in touch with two cherished people, Rachel and Jacob Silverman, who were my mentors in that arcane art called "being a physics wife." To have Tony working with Jake, as he preferred to be called, and have Rachel nearby again; to have the experience of creating a significant part of equipment to probe the mysteries held in the tiniest particles of our universe was almost too good to be true. So, we are both glad to be back.

But on that first day, after the *SS Bremen's* little tugs had worried her into her berth at New York harbor, we almost wanted to get back on board and sail back to Hamburg.

It was August 29. Settled in our hotel room in Newark, New Jersey, where we had gone to wait the arrival of our Volkswagen at that New Jersey port, we turned on the television. There, in graphic black and white, we witnessed the turmoil in our country about which we had only read during our stay abroad.

The Democratic Convention was being held in Chicago that year amid major unrest over the war in Vietnam. There on the television, the first thing we saw on our return was the Chicago police brutally beating anti-war protesters in Grant Park. What had happened to our country while we were happily driving in the German countryside?

Of course, things had often been tense in Europe as well. There were many protests against the war in Vietnam and the students were as vocal there as here. America was held in very low esteem. We saw graffiti on walls where President Johnson's name was spelled with the *S* in the form of a swastika. The student movement in Hamburg University, both strong and vocal, had been disruptive. The administrative board of the university once held an important meeting at the closed site of the laboratory in Blankensee, rather than risk student disruption at the downtown campus. Amerika Haus, an American political and cultural center downtown, was surrounded with American soldiers armed with drawn bayonets. The day after Tony and I got back from a Fulbright trip to Berlin, a prominent student rebel there named Rudy Deutsche was shot, causing great tension in that city. Colleagues coming back from French holidays told of difficulty changing francs into dollars and advised us to get francs in Germany before vacationing in France. But none of this had prepared us for what we saw that day here in America. It looked like a bloodbath to our shocked eyes, a most unwelcome sight to greet us upon our return.

But we were eager to find our faithful green Volkswagen, which, apparently because we had delivered our car to the docks in time as instructed, ended up in the back of a queue for boarding on the *SS Bremen* and was shipped on a following freighter.

Early the next morning, Tony left me with the children in the Newark train station where our luggage had been stored and went to the docks to pick up the *Käfer*, our VW "bug" that had carried us through so many memorable times.

"I shouldn't be long. I'll be first in line at this hour," Tony said and went out to get a cab to the docks.

But he was wrong. By eight o'clock in the evening, after having read *The Phantom Tollbooth* several times, bought the children far more junk food than they were allowed, refereed endless games of tic-tac-toe, and swallowed my unrest, I called the police.

"I don't want to bother you, but my husband went to the docks to pick up our car almost twelve hours ago and he's not back. My children and I are in the Newark train station, so no one would know we're here. Could you find out if anyone named Anthony Herrington has had an accident and is unable to call me?"

"You're in the train station?"

"Yes."

"Then stay where you are. Don't leave the station. That neighborhood's not safe to walk around in at night. We'll send someone over."

Soon, two burly members of Newark's finest appeared at the soda fountain where the children, now apprehensive, too, were uncharacteristically quiet.

"Any reason to suspect suicide or foul play?"

"Not suicide. He's pretty careful in neighborhoods he doesn't know, but I am worried something could have happened to him."

"A mistress?"

"A what?"

"Could he have a mistress he's run off with?"

Perhaps it was the tension, but I got the giggles. "He doesn't have time," I laughed. "He's a physicist."

The avuncular cop, who I'm sure thought I was hysterical, put a calming hand on my arm and said solemnly, "Now honey, the wife's always the last to know."

Just then, I saw Tony over the cop's shoulder. He broke into a run when he saw me surrounded by the men in blue.

"Anna. What's wrong? Are you…where are Meg and Joey…Why?"

When he was assured that we were okay and it was he who had caused the fuss, Tony explained why a couple of hours had turned into twelve. It was drugs. A large Mercedes touring car with diplomatic plates and a shipping record showing that the vehicle had made twelve trips across the water in ten months aroused the authorities. They decided to take a look at the car.

It was unfortunate that the Mercedes was just in front of our *Käfer* in line, because it was packed with heroin. The steering wheel was hollowed out and filled with it. Rocker panels, spare tire, seat cushions, anything that had or could be made to have a cavity in which to stuff the drug had been filled with the white powder. All of the activity of returning the other cars to their owners ceased. No one was allowed to get out of the waiting line to call their families. Some enterprising youths bought sandwiches at a nearby deli and resold them to the hungry folks waiting to pick up their cars. It was, in fact, a mess.

But now we have our car, and we're ready to take on a new life in our own car. We thanked my men-in-blue politely and went out the station to our faithful *Käfer* and drove to the first decent motel we could find. Tony ordered room service for us all, while Meg and Joey watched a cartoon on the TV, and we watched them to make sure that they didn't turn the dial and get exposed to more of the beatings in the streets of Chicago. But I must admit to teasing Tony about that mistress story the cops had… the wife being the last to know and all.

The next stop was to Washington, DC and a short visit with Dad and Mom Herrington.

Dad is working for the National Science Foundation there now and loves it. The children were excited to see their grandparents again and vice versa but, of necessity, we had to save showing the children the sights in their nation's capital. Our next adventure was waiting in Illinois, and we had to stop in Pennsylvania to pick up Bronwyn and close affairs there. We had sold our house there by mail and telegraph while we were in Hamburg and needed to tie up some loose ends about getting the furniture sent on to storage while we looked for a house in Illinois.

Now I am sitting at my typewriter here in our new home in a suburb far west of Chicago.

Bronwyn is cheerfully chewing on a rawhide toy, Meg and Joey are off to school, and I'm looking at clutter wondering if we will ever get settled again, and if the children will adapt as easily to being back in Illinois as they did to being in Germany.

That does sound like a foolish worry. But friends have told us that their children had trouble with "re-entry." They said that the excitement of the new place and of being "special" sometimes carries children along. They have to concentrate so hard on learning the new language and so on that they don't have time to think of much else.

I know that even though they have had almost two weeks of hearing only English spoken, they still talk between themselves in German. And Joey, who talks a lot in his sleep, is still speaking the language when he does.

But here, no one will know that they are still thinking in German. Even the little German that I acquired there pops up in descriptions, shopping lists and the like. This is not an affectation but, like my dinner plate's restlessness after I get on dry land after eight days on the *SS Bremen*, it is just a fact of switching the brain from one language to another.

It's not just the language that slips into our American life. The manners themselves can show up at strange moments.

Herr Doctor Professor Dietrich Schmidt, a distinguished physicist from Darmstadt and I were having breakfast while he was staying overnight in our house in Wheaton during a visit to give a seminar in the makeshift meeting room in the temporary auditorium building at the new laboratory.

Tony had overslept, having been very late at a planning meeting, and

Professor Schmidt was wondering when they should be leaving to drive out to the lab so he could set up the slides for the seminar he was giving.

"Tony," I called up the stairs. "When is Dr. Schmidt supposed to be over at the lab?" I was startled to hear Dr. Schmidt's hearty, deep-bass laughter.

"My dear Frau Herrington. We are sitting here in our dressing gowns eating your delicious eggs and ham. I think it is time for us to use the *du* form. So, I am Dietrich and may I call you Anna?"

"Of course, Dietrich," I laughed as we linked elbows on our pact.

SAVING RAYMOND
October 1969

The front door opened and let in that wonderful crisp autumn air that, even though we no longer lived in that abandoned orchard in Pennsylvania, always made me think of ripening apples. Two boyish voices were shouting at each other and I was shocked. They were calling each other racial epithets and howling with laughter. Such language was strictly forbidden in our house and Joey knew it.

I marched out from the kitchen where I was finishing up the sandwiches for lunch so that Meg and Joey could get back to school on time. We lived at the farthest edge of the perimeter beyond which children were allowed to stay in the school for lunch and by the time they walked home and back, there wasn't that much time to eat.

"Nigger!"

"Who you calling a nigger, you dumb honkey!"

Joey and an African-American boy I had never seen before were wrestling on the living room rug, while Meg looked on with an older woman's contempt for such childish behavior.

What was so crazy about the whole scene was that the African-American boy was calling Joey a "nigger" while Joey was calling his friend a "dumb honkey." For some reason, they found this so funny that they were almost limp with laughter.

When Joey caught sight of me, he stood up and pulled his new friend to his feet. "Hi Mom, this is Raymond."

"It's nice to meet you, Raymond. Are you on your way home to lunch?"

The other boy tucked his shirt into his faded jeans and shook my hand in a serious way.

Joey answered for him. "Can he stay and eat with us? His sister's not home today."

"Of course. Now run and get yourselves cleaned up."

"Yes, ma'am," said Raymond, and Joey punched him affectionately in the arm. "Yes, ma'am," Joey echoed.

The boys elbowed their way into the little bathroom by the kitchen, did a fair job of cleaning up, and soon were wolfing down peanut butter and jelly sandwiches, applesauce, and milk while I made more so that Meg would have something to eat.

That night at dinner I asked Joey about Raymond.

"He lives over on Roosevelt in those apartments. His mom and dad are dead. His brother and sister take care of him, but they aren't ever home 'cause they have to work, so he just walks around at lunch. I don't think he even eats lunch much. Can I bring him here again?"

I was delighted to say yes. Joey had been feeling very much a misfit since we came here to the suburb where many of the employees of the new laboratory had found housing. I hadn't had much time to get everything he needed before school started, so he still sometimes wore his German cap or socks. In addition, he would still use the German syntax with his English, and not even his teacher understood why he might say seven and twenty instead of twenty-seven.

Some of the children were quite cruel, as children can be, and they would take his German hat and throw it into a tree, or call him a Nazi because they had heard that he had lived in Germany. The children I could understand. They had no idea at seven or eight what that name meant, but the teacher's attitude I found unforgivable.

Instead of using the experience as a chance to broaden her class's understanding of the world, she made Joey feel foolish.

"It's a shame," she told me in one conference, "that Joey didn't have American new math because the Germans really don't teach math as well as we do."

"I'm rather surprised that you say that, since his father and I found the German math text both clever and a good tool. Joey did very well in math there."

"You have got to tell Joey to pay better attention to his assignments," she told me on the phone several days later. "He was told yesterday to write a short story about a house we had read about in his reader. And he wrote a story about a dwarf."

"Did you ever call the house a mansion?"

"Yes, we were reading *The Secret Garden* and I mentioned that the child lived in a mansion."

I burst out laughing. "Then that's the problem. The word *männchen,* meaning 'a little man or dwarf', sounds very like 'mansion' in English."

It went so far as to have Joey's counselor tell us that our son had been culturally deprived because he had gone to German schools, learned the language, and traveled through much of the country.

I began to suspect that Joey was too smart for his own good and had used the German/English pun on purpose. There is a deep streak of rascal in our son. I can't imagine where it came from.

So it was natural that Joey and this orphan child, who found it hilarious to call his buddy by a hurtful name to remove its sting, would become friends. And that Joey, whose grandfather died when he was only four, had inherited my father's love of bringing his friends home to eat. Raymond didn't miss a lunch from then on. Even when Joey was down with a cold or off to visit his grandmother in Chicago, Raymond would show up promptly at noon at the back door to the kitchen. On school holidays, we'd share sandwiches and, when the weather was bad and Joey wasn't there, he'd keep me company while I baked or ironed the laundry.

Then last month, Raymond's normally cheery, "Hi, Mrs. H." was muted and his eyes looked so sad, I thought that he was sick.

I put my arm around his shoulder. "Are you okay?"

"I guess so." He answered and then, to my surprise, he threw his arms around me. "We're moving away. My brother's moving down south where Mom and Dad were from."

Then he brightened up.

"We'll have our own house, just like this. And maybe a dog like Bronwyn or something. Miz Sweet Alice said so. She's Mom's sister and she misses us 'cause she's real old."

"That sounds wonderful for you, Raymond. We'll miss you though. Will you write when you get there?"

"I sure will," he said, as Joey called from the garage where he had been feeding his pet snake, Slinky.

"Hey, Raymond, you going to come and watch Slinky eat his mouse or what?" Raymond grabbed the last half-sandwich off the plate and slammed out the back door. "I'm comin'," he said, through a mouthful of peanut butter and jelly.

Now Raymond has been gone a month.

He did write to give us an address in Chicago, and the news that the house didn't ever happen.

The letter read:

Dear Joey and Meg and Mrs. and Mr. Herrington,

We are back from Mississippi because my aunt, Miz Sweet Alice, she died and her house got taken by the sheriff 'cause she didn't have no money for him for taxes. My brother, he got a bad back and can't work, so we had to come back to Chicago. He got a short temper with his back hurting and all. I gotta watch my step or he gets out that old belt and I get whomped more than before. My sister, she's working at McDonald's, so we eat okay, and I'm in school but it's real big, and I don't like it like I liked where I went with Joey and Meg. But my sister says when my brother gets his back healed maybe we'll come back.

Please write. It's sort of lonely here.

Your friend, Raymond

That part about the belt shocked me. I had often seen welts on the boy's arms and once, when the boys got drenched in a rainstorm and he had to put on one of Joey's shirts, I had noticed welts on his back as well. He always had some reason for them, and I hadn't paid attention to what was surely happening to the boy. But lately, I have been reading a series about child abuse in the *Chicago Tribune* and had come to realize that Raymond probably had been beaten. I had never met his brother or sister, if that was indeed their relationship. They never seemed to care how much time he spent with us.

I should have questioned him more, or looked into his circumstances more carefully. It was the teacher in the Marine Room all over again. I had looked the other way. When I talked to Tony about it though, he was hesitant to intrude.

"Raymond hasn't complained, has he?" he asked. "If we go poking around into his family affairs, his brother might not let him come here anymore, and I suspect that we're the best shot at his having a good meal. You see how he's filled out since you started feeding him."

But now I had this letter and an address. I had answered it as soon as it arrived, telling Raymond how sorry we were about his plans falling apart. Then I began to wonder how we could help the boy. We called the Department of Children and Family Services in Chicago to see what we should do, and I had an appointment with them this morning. It was not very encouraging, but at least someone besides us had his address and knew about Raymond's situation.

So I was feeling pretty good on the train coming home. We were side-tracked waiting for an incoming train to pass when, from the train window, I noticed the boy with the book bag. He looked so like Raymond I was startled – tall and gangly, glasses askew on his nose, the big hands that foretold the big man to come.

He was walking quickly down a path bordering the tracks, obviously coming from the schoolyard nearby. The gang of boys following him had the look of young thugs, with their matching jackets and fancy new gym shoes. They appeared to be heckling the boy ahead who made the mistake of breaking into a run.

"Don't!" I called.

"Is something the matter, Ma'am?"

The conductor was a burly black man I had traveled with often and who seemed to consider his riders family who needed looking after.

"There," I pointed at the scene out the window. They're beating him up." The gang had pulled the boy's book bag from his shoulder and were ripping and throwing books to the wind.

Then they pushed him down, took off his glasses, crushed them underfoot and, just as our train started to move slowly over the switches, we saw them throw the glasses over the chain link fence along the tracks.

I bowed my head and took Raymond's letter from my purse.

"He looked so much like him," I said, showing the letter to the conductor. He read it and gave it back.

"So many Raymonds," he sighed.

"Well, I'm going to try to save this one."

"Good luck," he said, and went to open the doors for the next stop.

For the rest of the trip home, I daydreamed about the wonderful things we could do for Raymond, about new glasses, about protecting him from abuse, perhaps even making him a member of our family. I was all optimism as I walked to the front door from the garage.

On the mat inside the door, the mail lay where it had been pushed through the letter slot.

On top of the heap was a familiar envelope addressed in my own handwriting.

It was stamped in red: *Moved. Left no forwarding address.*

AFTERWORDS 1970

The house on Gregory Street in Urbana seemed smaller than we remembered it when we brought the children back to see where their lives had begun. But the elm, born not long before the children, was a real tree now, spreading its shade on the patch of front lawn. Two spruce trees, planted at the birth of each child, had grown tall and straight. Caroline's, one set of branches taller, was just her height. Steve measured close to his, planted twenty months later.

Satisfied that their trees and their roots remained safe in Illinois soil, they piled into the car with us. "Let's eat!" Steve said. And we set off for the Student Union cafeteria for hot dogs and potato salad, our standard treat before Dad's Fulbright grant had taken us all across the Atlantic to Hamburg.

Later, another trip took us again past the little house. It was deserted in a street fallen on hard times. Hanging from one rusty hinge, the screen door skewed permanently open. The elm, a requirement of the GI loan that built the house and home to a succession of wary cats escaping our cheeky dachshund, had succumbed to Dutch elm disease. The children were crestfallen.

"Are you sure this is the place?" asked Steve.

"Our trees!" said the Caroline. "Let's look in the backyard."

Together they rushed through the broken gate to the backyard to where the spruce trees had stood. Two weathered stumps remained, half-covered by dandelions and chickweed. Their Christmas-tree perfection had probably been the downfall of the spruce. At least we hoped that each had ended life decked in lights and tinsel.

I saw the loss in my children's faces and remembered when I, too, tried to go back to where I began. The rambling white clapboard house with its lovely patch of spring violets had the world's best Bartlett pear tree growing next to grandma's bedroom window, and my brother and I had climbed out that window onto the porch roof to deprive the squirrels of its golden fruit. But tree, violets and house had been replaced by a parking lot.

Now from my bedroom window in another town, I watch moonlight turn the leaves of our ancient oaks to silver. Some of these old giants were seedlings the year our nation was born. They have seen it rip apart and heal again, survive depressions, go to wars, find peace and prosper. Houses with such history should be protected landmarks.

But how long will these living treasures be cherished? Will they be here to shade coming generations who, if they have been sacrificed to parking lots, will have only faded photographs like those by which my children's children will know the spruce and grandma's pear tree?

Will the tiny acorn sprouts I am encouraging through their baby years have the chance to become such majestic landmarks? They are safe with me. But in a moment, as oak trees measure time, their fate will pass to other hands. They will still be infants and vulnerable as children are.

Before I go to sleep, I ask whatever God took his eye off of those vanished trees to pay attention this time and protect his tree children, as I pray he will protect my human ones.

Outside, moon-silvered leaves rustle in the night wind as it curls around the house. I feel the sound of those whispering giants adding their prayers to mine.

The End

WITH THESE WORDS, the Presbyterian Princess abdicated. In *Presbyterian Princess*, Anna tells her story successively in the voice of the child, the teenager, the college student, and the young wife, which serve to give an authentic sense of the times in which they took place. Nancy Carrigan wrote *Presbyterian Princess* in memoir form for good reason. It is a thinly veiled story of her life with characters and situations altered into fiction. The little girl, Anna, is expected to do everything correctly, never to put on airs, be sweet to all seven hundred parishioners and be dressed nicely, but for practicality, not show. The unheard voices of "they", that mysterious set of eyes and ears and mouths waiting to catch her in some impropriety, rarely leaves her subconscious. Nancy – Anna – began to draw and then write as soon as her mother gave her paper and pencil to keep her quiet during church.

Here, Nancy has dropped her veil. Her true self and family stand revealed. Nancy's poetry is emerging, driven by her artistic temperament. She is no longer worried about how the ladies of the church may be offended by her views when she says, "...whatever God took his eyes off of those vanished trees..." Roughly half her life, Nancy lived as the Presbyterian Princess or in the shadow of that life. While the Princess was always an independent sort who thought for herself, she became an artist, a poet/writer, a leader, and a mother and wife. With Dick, she authored two novels of science-fiction published in *Analog Magazine*, produced an illustrated children's book, and a body of poetry that has garnered an extensive list of prizes and publications. She edited a trade publication, *The Water Well Journal*, books and pamphlets for the School of Agriculture at the University of Illinois, and a college alumni magazine. Her name changed, in part, when she became a wife, but also for a second reason – the intrusion of Nancy Kerrigan, the figure skater, into her persona. Nancy Kerrigan was a silver medalist Olympic skater. To Nancy Kerrigan's misfortune, she was knee-capped by the friends and relations of her competitor, Tonya Harding. Nancy Kerrigan herself also made the mistake of dissing Mickey Mouse on an open microphone in a parade at Disney World. In a further twist, many years later, Nancy Kerrigan's brother killed her father. As a result, Nancy Carrigan was constantly losing her laundry and various other parts of her life into the *K* part of any alphabetical list. During this period, Nancy began using "Nancy Jean Carrigan" regularly. Still in all, the Nancy Kerrigan odyssey really cemented Nancy Carrigan's spoken name into anyone's memory that met her.

Nancy's art was more significant to her life than her poetry and writing. In the words of the *Chicago Tribune* she was described as, "…sampling many media in serving her muse, Ms. Carrigan is a well-known visual artist who has shown her work in both New England and California, as well as in her hometown of Chicago." In the 1980s, Nancy became interested in dance. To better execute her sculptures, she took dance lessons. Ultimately, she won a prize at a dancing poetry festival that resulted in a dance produced at the San Francisco Legion of Honor Museum and an invitation to come to China as a guest of the government. Disney even commissioned a sculpture from her for the ESPN Zone in Chicago.

Along the way, Nancy decided that her early life in the church might make a sprightly, light-hearted story of the life of a minister's child. What she didn't appreciate was the marketing of writing. True, she had sold two novels, but *Presbyterian Princess* was a new challenge. In both art and poetry, Nancy followed her bliss. Approaches to doing art and writing differ. Art can be a solitary activity with success predicated on exhibiting and sales. Written work, on the other hand, is often extensively workshopped. It also relies on finding agents. *Presbyterian Princess* was extensively workshopped by Nancy. Different agents had different perspectives. First- and third- person versions were tried. A critic could argue that the story became overworked. Still, Nancy was able to voice the story so that it starts from the perspective and language of a child and gradually moves to the Princess as an adult. Finally, she settled on this version. We have used it with only very small editorial changes.

When Dick first heard the concept for *Presbyterian Princess*, it sounded good – a privileged but plucky girl growing up in a castle of a church. Dick seconded the idea. Two problems developed. The first was, "what would the ladies of the church think?" Like a general who knows too many secrets, there were some stories Nancy just could not tell. As a result, names were changed to protect the innocent and not so innocent. With one major exception, the problem with telling tales that can't be told has been solved. Perhaps if there is a next generation biographer, she will find a way to tell that part of Nancy's history. The second problem was that the central story was a little thin. It lengthened out into Nancy's married years, and ultimately broadened into some of the areas where Nancy had become deeply disillusioned with politics and religion. Originally, Dick had been concerned by this turn. It changed a merry story about a happy young girl into a more serious one. At first Dick (Tony) was concerned that the target audience for the "fun" life of a minister's kid was at war with the audience that might appreciate something about religious frustration.

This view was a mistake on Dick's part. People who knew Nancy know that she often had important points to make, but these were sometimes lost in her unfailing desire to please. Nancy's relationship with religion and the church was complicated. Growing up with a Presbyterian minister father, a minister brother who left the church during the civil rights struggle, a changing world view of women's rights, and even a midlife association with a number of Big Bang cosmologists, had left her with her own strong perspective. In her artwork, this can be particularly seen in her series patterned on Dürer's famed *Adam and Eve,* and her cosmological paintings *Star Madonna* and *The Astrophysicist and the Ant.*

There is little in *Presbyterian Princess* about Nancy's mature life. She was an enthusiastic mother and very excited when her granddaughter Brooke appeared. Her art and poetry speak for themselves. Partly as a result of the art, she took up dance and became deeply involved with several Chicago-area dance companies. Along the way, Nancy and Dick bought a small condo in Aspen. That led to another whole set of writers, artists, dancers, scientists, and even skiers. All of these activities were laced with amusing and some not-so-amusing stories.

Nancy was also deeply involved in helping to establish the cultural and social life of Fermilab from the earliest days. For a time, she led the Fermilab cultural series. When the first Soviets came to Fermilab, we each had Soviet families assigned to us. One, the leader of the group, Anatole Kuznetsov and his wife Elena were assigned to Nancy and Dick. Dick was away the day they arrived, and Nancy ended up at their apartment. Nancy, the hereditary teetotaler, found herself in a series of vodka toasts. Finally, after trying valiantly, she told Anatole that she couldn't drink anymore because she had to drive home. Anatole replied, "That's the trouble with America. Too many cars!"

It would be a mistake to think that Nancy lived a simple straightforward life. Her interaction with civil rights turmoil and the Cold War give some perspective on this. In *Shall We Overcome,* Anna asks, "Where was I when that teacher couldn't eat in the dining room of the Edgewater Beach Hotel?" In *What Did You Do in the War,* she asks, "…I didn't speak up when we fell into war in Korea and Vietnam…" These words echo Pastor Martin Niemöller's famous lines, "First they came for the socialists, and I did not speak out, … Then they came for me and there was no one to speak."

Nancy's father was a conservative Presbyterian minister, but her brother Ralph reflected a newer brand of Christian activism. Ralph transferred from Princeton Theological Seminary to Union at Columbia to study under the influence of Paul Tillich and Reinhold Niebuhr. Niebuhr had graduated from Elmhurst College just a few years before Nancy's father arrived there.

Niebuhr brought Paul Tillich to Union when the Nazis dismissed Tillich from his professorship in Germany. Tillich and Niebuhr had a strong influence on Protestant thought in America, including Barack Obama. Ultimately, Tillich's ties led back to Karl Barth in Switzerland and the Confessing Church in Germany, where the theologian Dietrich Bonhoeffer was executed by hanging in 1945 as the Nazi regime collapsed. Years later in Pittsburgh, we had a neighborhood acquaintance from the Pittsburgh Theological Seminary where Barth's son Markus was a professor. Barth's son was a student in a class Dick was teaching at Carnegie Mellon.

Directly or indirectly, Nancy knew several other people who had put their lives on the line for their beliefs. As portrayed in *Shall We Overcome,* Anna's brother, Joe (Nancy's brother Ralph), was incarcerated in Mississippi. Only a few months later in much the same circumstances, James Chaney, Andrew Goodman, and Michael Schwerner were murdered.

The father of a young German colleague of ours, Hartmut Sadrozinski, was executed for his involvement in the July 20, 1944 plot to assassinate Hitler. In 1968, when Nancy and Dick lived in Germany, we visited a relative of Hartmut's in Kassel and went to see the Documenta art show. The relative's house was attached to a factory that made surveying instruments. The US bombed the factory during World War II. The roof fell in on a lovely oriental rug. Our host served our children tea and crumpets on that rug. They made a fine mess. The lady said, "don't worry, when we were bombed, we just took the rug outside and shook it out in the yard!"

In the spring of 1968, while we were in Hamburg, Nancy and Dick went to Berlin for a large Fulbright meeting in what turned out to be a very tense Cold War confrontation. Plucky as always, Nancy soldiered through. A day or so later, Rudi "the Red" Dutschke, a famous and controversial socialist, was shot and nearly killed on the Berlin streets where we had just been engulfed in the crowds of protesters.

The point here is, while Nancy led a largely peaceful life in her own 'Garden of Eden', she was also a part of tumultuous times. Carrigan's art was forged by the garden, but also the jungle beyond.

Throughout her life, Nancy enjoyed robust good health. Then a dark cloud passed over her life and she was taken from us. The family was able to put together a wonderful memorial service with the fine cooperation of Immanuel Presbyterian, a long block or two from home in Warrenville. The service reflected her upbringing but was respectful of her perspective. After the memorial service, people walked over to her home to see Nancy's art once more. The church was filled with friends from the arts, Fermilab, and the neighborhood. The family spoke and her cousin, Lois McMullen, an Episcopalian priest, helped with the service. The service closed with "Joyful, Joyful, We Adore Thee", Henry Van Dyke's hymn based on the mighty Freidrich Schiller poem "Ode to Joy" that Beethoven used in the final movement of his Ninth Symphony. Dick has been particularly struck by the passage

Whoever has found a beloved wife, let him join our songs of praise!

The strains of "Ode to Joy" have followed Dick since then; at the Aspen Music Festival after the memorial with Eric Owen as the first voice, and in September at a fantastic performance with Owen again and the Chicago Symphony. Indeed, the hymn and the Ninth Symphony have formed an arch over our lives, from Nancy's church in Chicago, to the Berlin Wall in the Cold War.

Dick Carrigan

Caroline Carrigan

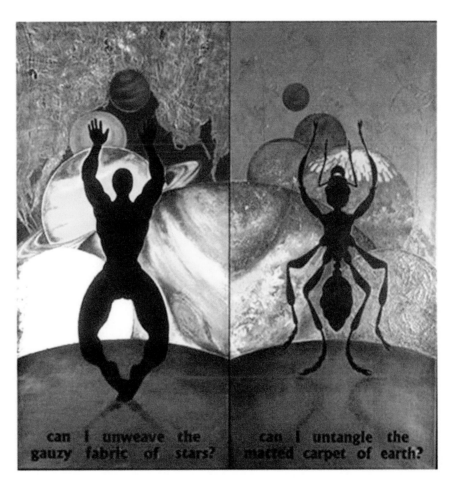

Astronomer and the Ant.

Nancy Jean Carrigan's evolving cosmology.

The Astrophysicist

How can I unweave the gauzy fabric of
the stars

when each parting strand reveals a
farther curtain

hiding another

and another

and another?

I focus on the place where the mysteries
began

but my ever-more sophisticated eyes
only reveal

what I cannot see. So the answers still lie
wrapped

in the gauzy fabric of the stars

where each parting strand reveals a
farther curtain

hiding another

and another

and another.

The Ant

How can I untangle this matted carpet
of earth

when behind each shadowed clot or
stem lies another growth

hiding another

and another and another?

My antennae seek that place where the
mysteries began

but my slender legs grow tired and I
must find food.

So the answers still lie hidden

in this tangled carpet of earth where the
bright side

of each passing clot and stem

reveals a shadowed other

and another

and another.

The Eagle's Child

The Eagle's Child

On seeing Internet pictures
taken by the Hubble telescope
of the birth of a star in the Eagle Nebula

I saw, with my astonished eyes
a story told in ancient light—-
celestial birth in distant skies
like our own Sun-star took its flight.
A nameless star which formed and grew
in dull galactic primal dust
sought freedom from the womb as new
young stars and poems always must.
Has it, like Sun, a circling globe
with sea-fish, birds, and clever ape
who's built a magic eye to probe
the skies and let her mind escape
its bounds to ponder ancient light
and move her poet's pen to write?

The Other

Your skin is Grecian olive. Your skin is
dark as night.

Your hair's a braid of silken black. Your
hair is waves of light.

Your eyes are slanted Asian. Your eyes
are Nordic blue.

Your face is hid in Muslim veils. Your
mother made you Jew.

Are you *The Other* – not like me?

Your heart delights in friendship. You
shrink from words of hate.

Your hands are skilled at many chores.
You're more than child or mate.

You're source of life's beginning. You're
comfort when it's dying. You long to see
men live in peace. You hear the good
earth crying.

You are *A Mother* – just like me.